FIRE IN THE CANYON

FIRE IN THE CANYON

A NOVEL

DANIEL GUMBINER

ASTRA HOUSE ⋀ NEW YORK

Astra House
A Division of Astra Publishing House
astrahouse.com
Printed in the United States of America

Library of Congress Cataloging-in-Publication Data

Names: Gumbiner, Daniel, author.
Title: Fire in the canyon : a novel / Daniel Gumbiner.
Description: First edition. | New York : Astra House, [2023] | Summary:
"Since his release from prison, where he served a two-year sentence for
growing cannabis, Benjamin Hecht has grown increasingly reclusive.
He keeps busy cultivating a dozen acres of grapes outside the town of
Natoma, California, but he interacts with almost no one, except for his
wife, Ada, and almost never leaves his farm. Most notably, his
relationship with his son, Yoel, whose trust he betrayed years ago, has
continued to degrade. When Yoel comes up from Los Angeles for a visit in
early June, a wildfire sweeps through the region, forcing the Hecht
family to flee to the coast, and setting in motion a chain of events
that will transform them all"—Provided by publisher.
Identifiers: LCCN 2023013928 | ISBN 9781662602429 (hardback) |
ISBN 9781662602412 (ebook)
Subjects: LCGFT: Domestic fiction. | Novels.
Classification: LCC PS3607.U5458 F57 2023 | DDC 813/.6—dc23/eng/20230421
LC record available at https://lccn.loc.gov/2023013928

First edition
10 9 8 7 6 5 4 3 2 1

Design by Richard Oriolo
The text is set in ACaslon Pro Regular.
The titles are set in Trade Gothic LT Std.

For John Mulroy and Claire Boyle

"No matter how we have assaulted and abused it, the land sooner or later imposes itself on us, makes us behave, sets the rules for our existence. . . ."
—WALLACE STEGNER

FIRE IN THE CANYON

1

T HAT FALL, across the Gold Country, it rained steadily, and the people of that hilly land, who lived up and down the spine of the state, looked forward to a season of balanced precipitation. The land, it seemed to them, existed in a state of fragile equilibrium. If there was too much rain, the grasses grew tall, and in the summer when they dried out, they provided extra fuel and triggered large fires. If it rained too little, there was drought, and the land was both thirsty and more prone to ignitions. It had always been like this in the Gold Country, as long as the oldest of them could remember, but it seemed the margins for error had grown thinner. Anyone who was watching could see this.

So it was particularly concerning when, early that winter, the rains came to an abrupt halt. There were weeks of cold, weeks of wind, weeks of thin overcast cloud cover, but there was never any rain. The wildflowers crisped up along the side of the road and the hills turned brown and the air smelled of dry sage and it was, all of a sudden, the opposite of what many had expected. Had the land ever looked so parched? Had the reservoirs ever run lower? The water districts held meetings, reallocated resources, preached austerity. The fire safety committees updated evacuation plans, scheduled projects of vegetation management. And as May rolled around, and the prospect of any further, significant precipitation came to an end, a waiting game began. Their hand had been dealt. No new cards would be played. The odds were what they were and nothing could be done to change this.

Up on his farm, near the town of Natoma, Benjamin Hecht could not help but feel concerned. Every year, the conditions seemed to be getting worse, the season lasting longer. And yet, worrying about the prospect of a fire helped nothing. So whenever a rush of fear arose, Ben distracted himself with the work of his farm. This was not difficult to do. Over the years, he had amassed a wide variety of projects, which required near constant tending. At present, he had ten new chickens, two dachshunds, honeybees, a small flock of sheep, one guard dog, ducks, geese, several CBD plants, one acre of Primitivo, two of Grenache, two of Barbera, three of Gamay, and three of Syrah. And he had recently acquired, via the guy who ran the concession stand at the Speedway and also bred poultry, two baby emus.

At sixty-five, he was still decently strong, and able to handle the work of the farm. He had a big white bristle of a mustache and, in the last decade, he had developed a slight and inevitable paunch. His wife, Ada, liked to call him "David Crosby without the voice." The two of them had one child, Yoel, who lived in Los Angeles, and worked in TV development. Yoel was close with Ada, but he no longer spoke to Ben. For years, Ben had tortured himself over the collapse of their relationship, but these days, he had more or less made peace with it. Yoel had his life and Ben had his. That was just the way it was.

In general, Ben felt happy with his lot. Would he have liked more money? Of course. He missed taking Ada out to dinner in town. He would still be taking her out, these days, if she hadn't told him they needed to cut down on their expenses. He had a hard time reining in that kind of thing. He got swept up in the emotion of something and forgot about the bigger picture. But he was working on it. Things had been extra tight recently, and they had to find ways to enjoy themselves on a budget.

Ben was particularly looking forward to their annual solstice party. This was a Hechtian tradition, which they had been hosting at their house for nearly two decades now. In June, after Ada sent out an email invitation, the first RSVPs started to trickle in. It was an odd but familiar mix: the Sacramento cousins from Ada's side, Ada's old college boyfriend turned family friend and his wife, the Chons, and their neighbors from down the road, the Girouds, who sometimes brought their daughter, and their daughter's boyfriend, Nick, who had a stone fruit allergy you had to look out for.

The day before the party, Ben woke up around sunrise. He had written the Girouds to double-check, and they had clarified that neither their daughter nor Nick would be joining them. This cleared the way for him to make a peach pie. He also wanted to make a couple of apple pies. Today, he would just deal with the crusts, leave the baking for tomorrow. He put on his old green suspenders and work pants and walked into the kitchen. Once he made coffee and set about gathering his ingredients, he realized they were out of butter. He would need to go to the store. He poured his coffee into a thermos, laced up his boots, and went outside.

The day was already warming up, the sky swirled with a few unambitious clouds. As he walked down the stone pathway to his car, he heard, in the distance, the squawk of one of his chickens. It occurred to him that he should let out the birds before he left. He made his way past the chapel, where they kept the oak barrels of house wine that still needed to be bottled, past the vegetable garden, and down to the coop. It was located on the edge of the property, next to the forest, and it housed their new chickens, as well as their ducks and geese. He'd built the structure almost a decade ago, with his brother, who now lived out on the coast, in Talinas. This was the summer after Ben had been released from Lompoc prison camp. An eighteen-month sentence for growing medical cannabis—one of a few local growers the sheriff had pursued, with the help of the federal government. And it was the same summer, not months after returning home, that he'd started a small, clandestine grow out in the forest. A terrible idea.

Several yards away from the coop, he poured out feed into a few tin troughs. Then he walked back down to the coop, unhitched the door, and released the flock. The birds flipped and flopped and flew toward their food, kicking up dust and dry pine needles in their wake. To the right of their troughs were two blue plastic kiddie pools. He filled them both with water from the hose. Once they had finished eating, the ducks and geese began to hop in, one by one, to take their morning bath. There was some kind of hierarchy in terms of who got to take their bath first. If a willful duck tried to jump the line, they were nipped in the butt, usually by this one brown-feathered goose. He was the smallest goose and evidently had a complex about it. Ben sipped his coffee and watched the animals bathe for a moment before continuing on down the hill, toward the emu pen.

The emus lived nearby the beehives, in a large fenced-in enclosure. They were about three months old, but already nearly three feet tall. As adults, they could grow to be as tall as six feet. When he had first acquired them, he'd tried to put them with the other birds, but this had not gone well. A skirmish ensued and a small white duck had almost been stomped to death. So now he kept the emus down here. They were lanky, mostly docile creatures, with wrinkled, leathery talons and shaggy gray feathers. As he approached, they grew excited and began sprinting back and forth across the enclosure. They loved to sprint—mostly, Ben felt, to show off how fast they could go. They were a bit vain in this way.

He poured out their feed and watched their heads bob as they ate. When they were finished, he brought the hose over and sprayed it into the pen. The emus began running back and forth across the pen, leaping through the water like kids playing in lawn sprinklers. This was their preferred method of bathing. As he watered the emus, he thought about how he needed to rejigger the irrigation in the Primitivo blocks and add guano to the CBD in the greenhouse and fix the strap hinge on the door to the sheep pen. He turned off the hose and was about to head up to the greenhouse, when he remembered that the reason he had come outside in the first place was to drive into town for butter. This was the problem with a farm.

.   .   .

HE MADE HIS way back up the hill, past the chickens, who were now pecking around at the brown grass, past the vegetable garden and the chapel, and over to his yellow Toyota truck. Inside the truck it smelled like weed and mountain soil. He started the engine, turned on the air, and tuned the radio to the classical station. From the glove compartment, he pulled out a container of Swedish tobacco. He opened it and placed one of the minty packets between his cheek and his gum. As he backed up across the gravel driveway, he felt the tobacco kick in and, combined with the two cups of coffee, this produced a low-level euphoria.

It was about a fifteen-minute drive into town, on Mountainview Road, through the black oak and blue oak and manzanita, over one-lane bridges and cool mountain streams. Winding down the hill, he occasionally caught a glimpse of the high peaks in the distance, their granite spires and smooth domes. He turned left onto 51, drove past the feed store and the massage and wellness clinic and the old hotel that claimed to have once hosted Mark Twain. Then it was left on Smith Flat Road, past the new brewery and the taqueria, and right onto Center Street.

Natoma was a Gold Rush town, founded by nineteenth-century miners, who built Victorian homes along Redbud Creek. Today, its residents were a mix of ranchers, artists, old prospectors, hippies, digital nomads, and retirees. Center Street, the town's main drag, had more or less been preserved in its historic configuration, and featured a number of businesses, including a crystals shop, several bars, a steakhouse, a used bookstore, a sixty-seat movie theater, and a popular cheese store run by a Basque man named Ander. There was also the food co-op, which was where Ben was heading now. It was located in a shopping center just off Center Street, next to the discount liquor store.

When he arrived, the parking lot was jammed. Inside he grabbed a package of butter and then made his way over to the cashiers. Given how many people were at the store, the lines weren't too bad. The worst one was for under fifteen items. People always got fooled by the under fifteen items line, thought ten people there would go faster than two people with full carts. This was usually, in Ben's opinion, a miscalculation. He went to one of the shorter lines for people with any number of items.

As he got closer to the front, he realized it was Rudy's line. Rudy was a very talkative man who had moved here in the late seventies to prospect and who, over the years, had worked stints at most of the businesses in town. He lived down by the canal with his wife and was always complaining about how there wasn't enough parking in town anymore. Last fall he had petitioned the city council to build a parking garage. He was a decent guy, but Ben always found himself caught in conversation with him for longer than was comfortable and he wasn't in the mood. He looked over at the other registers to see if he could slip away unnoticed, but their lines had grown long.

"Lot of people in here," Ben said, when he made it to the front.

"Lot of people," Rudy said. "My shift's over soon, thankfully. My daughter and her kids are coming up from Sac this afternoon."

"Oh, that's nice," Ben said.

"You know, I liked your wife's new book."

"You read it? That's great."

"Yeah, I liked it, but I didn't get why she included that scene at the journalist's friend's house. Like, what was the point of that? It was such a long scene. And nothing happened."

Ben took out his credit card, tapped it on the machine.

"Well, sometimes," he said, "the scenes where nothing is happening have the most stuff in them."

He had no idea what he was talking about, was just trying to hurry along the interaction. Rudy ignored his meaningless comment.

"Other than that one part, though," he said, "I thought it was interesting. Really made me feel like I was in Nevada. I used to live in Fallon for a while. I was in Tonopah too. They have a clown motel there. Anyway, you already know that. It's in the book. I'm just saying, she got that part of it right, the feel of the place."

Rudy reached back and snatched the receipt.

"You know," he said, handing the receipt to Ben, "they're turning off the power tonight."

"They are? Is that why there are so many people here?"

"Yeah, probably. Got everything you need?"

"I think so."

"Because we're closed tomorrow. Tomorrow's Sunday."

"Right," Ben said. "I'm OK, thanks."

"Well, let your wife know I liked the book. Tell her I'll read the next one too."

Ben walked outside, set his groceries down next to the truck, and took out his phone. He hadn't turned it on yet. He tried to keep it off while he slept because he didn't want to get cancer and then sometimes, when he woke up, he forgot to turn it on. There was the notification. The utility company would be cutting power to their area starting around three o'clock. The outage would last for at least a day, possibly longer. It was the second time the utility had threatened to cut power that summer and it wasn't even July yet. Everything would be OK for the party, though. Ben had a generator at the house and plenty of fuel. He started the car and the classical radio station came back on.

"Up next," the DJ said, "some memorable music inspired by insects."

THE DACHSHUNDS, now awake, greeted him at the door. Harriet and George. They were both eight years old and had come from the same litter. During the day, they wandered the farm without supervision, more or less staying out of trouble, but on occasion, shredding his copy of the *Mountain Gazette* and scattering its remnants across the front yard. Though Ben had brought them home, they had bonded with Ada and were basically her dogs now, sleeping by her side of the bed every night, and only rising when she did.

Ben dropped the butter in the kitchen and walked back outside to say hi to Ada. Years ago, he had converted a section of the barn into her office and, most mornings, this was where she could be found. The barn was on the north edge of the property, next to the toolshed. He knocked on the side door and entered. Ada's office was filled with books, old magazines, empty bottles of kombucha. Her desk was positioned in front of a large, clear window, which looked out on their backyard, on the old elm tree and just beyond that, the pool. Ben could see yellow jackets hovering above the pool now, flying in circles, periodically swooping down to the surface for a luke-warm sip. He put his arms around his wife, kissed her on the crown of her head.

"Good morning, darling," he said.

She turned around to face him. Her gray hair was pulled up in a bun and she wore a necklace of small shells, which she'd made ages ago, while on a writing retreat in Mexico.

"Good morning," she said. "You need help with anything?"

"I'm just doing desserts right now," he said. "And then I'm going to go clean the yard."

"Is it OK if I keep working for a bit," Ada continued, "or do you need help?"

"I should be OK."

"I'll be done in a minute."

"No, keep working," he said. "It's fine."

Ada was nearing the end of a new novel, and when she was like that, she needed to write every day. It was an issue of continuity, she said, of staying in key. She was hoping to have a draft ready for her agent soon. She still wrote everything by hand, which seemed crazy to Ben, but she said it helped her tap into a slower, more considered type of thinking. Plus, when-ever she was on her computer, she just ended up getting lost on social media or reading some dumb article, probably on the subject of the Enneagram. They'd recently found out about the Enneagram and they were both obsessed with it.

Ada usually worked her way through several notebooks over the course of writing a book. Sometimes, when she grew tired of writing at the house, she'd load the notebooks in her red backpack, take a ride into town, and write at a café. She'd been terrifically productive with this routine and didn't seem to be slowing down any time soon. This was good, because these days, they were largely reliant on the money from her writing and her speaking engagements. Ben also sold his grapes to two wineries, but those profits were insubstantial compared to what Ada earned.

A few years ago, after Ben lost his entire crop to powdery mildew, they'd needed to take out a loan on the farm. They were still paying it off, but it had momentarily solved their cash flow problem. At the time, taking so much money out of their property had worried them, but now the end of the situation was in sight. Once Ada finished and sold this next book, they'd likely be able to pay off the whole thing and be done with it.

"Did you hear they're cutting the power today?" he said.

"I know, I saw. I called everyone to tell them they should come anyway. Carole just texted to see if she can invite Bernie."

"That's fine, I think we'll have enough food with her bringing chicken and the Chons bringing burgers."

"Carole's bringing potato salad."

"No, she's bringing chicken. Your cousin is bringing potato salad."

"Oh, you're right," Ada said. "Ugh, my memory."

She covered her eyes with her palms.

"Doesn't help that Yoel woke me up last night with five texts in a row."

"What was he texting you about?"

"He's coming to the party."

For a moment, he stopped breathing. He coughed a bit, cleared his throat.

"The party tomorrow?" he said.

"Yes, I texted you about it this morning."

"I didn't see it. I didn't even know you invited him."

"I invite him every year," Ada said, "but he never comes."

Ben couldn't remember the last time Yoel visited the farm—it was at least two years ago. Ada sometimes went down to visit him in LA, but Ben was no longer invited on those trips.

"He didn't say anything else?" Ben asked. "Is Sally coming?"

This was Yoel's fiancée, who he lived with in LA, and who also worked in TV development, at a different company.

"No Sally," Ada said. "He just told me that he's coming for the party. Oh, and he also mentioned he had a lunch planned with Oliver."

"From high school? I thought he lives on the East Coast."

"He's back visiting his parents for the weekend."

"Oh, right," Ben said. "And when does Yoel get in?"

"Tonight. He's flying into Bidwell and renting a car from there."

"OK," Ben said.

"OK?" she asked.

He just looked at her.

"Think about it like an opportunity," she said.

"Sure."

His mind went to the container of Swedish tobacco in his truck. He was trying to limit himself to one packet per day but maybe he would break that rule today.

"I think it's a great opportunity," Ada said.

"I'll go deal with these crusts," he told her.

THAT EVENING, Ben sat in the kitchen, drinking a glass of house wine and waiting for Yoel to arrive. He could feel the shadow of it all approaching. For the past few years, Ben had done his best to put Yoel out of his mind. It seemed like that was what had been asked of him. In fact, Yoel had literally asked this of him: sent him a letter, told him he didn't want Ben to contact him anymore. The rage he'd felt then, the sorrow. Ben had made mistakes, of course, but he'd apologized. What more could he do?

In Ben's opinion, Yoel expected a kind of purity from him. But he was impure. He had always been impure. If Yoel had his way, Ben would simply be a different person. Someone with pedigree and a stable, white-collar career. Instead, he was an embarrassing old hippie. A self-righteous hippie. That was the word Yoel always used: "self-righteous."

Ben knew very little about his son's life these days, except for the fact that his career had stagnated. The production company he worked for kept promising to promote him but they never did. Ben learned these kinds of things from Ada. He had always been surprised that Yoel had decided to stick with his current career. Not that there was anything wrong with television production. People needed their television produced. It was more that Ben thought that Yoel was capable of something bigger. What about this job held Yoel in its sway, Ben wasn't sure.

Ada joined Ben at the kitchen counter, made herself a cup of tea. She had changed into a T-shirt and sweatpants, and her cheeks had been scrubbed red by the gritty nighttime face wash she used. Ben watched her as she sipped her tea and sorted through their mail. Grocery store coupons, a letter from her alma mater, plus their utility bill. She opened the bill and grimaced.

"We need to use the AC less," she said.

Not that they were using the AC much at all. They turned it off as much as they could bear, but they'd been under a heat advisory for the past week, and there was only so much a person could take. Ada walked over to the thermostat, checked to see that it was off, and then came back to the counter. Ben was staring down at his tin of tobacco, rotating it back and forth with one hand, like a combination lock. Ada watched him for a moment.

"Remember," she said, looking over at him. "It's an opportunity."

They had discussed this again at dinner. She wasn't exactly sure why Yoel was coming but he was coming. And wasn't that great? Ben felt a touch of hope when she said this, but it soon faded. Why would this time be different? Would it not go the way it always did? A couple days of walking on eggshells, and then some dumb blowout argument. He thought they had figured this out. They kept their space from each other. That was how this worked best for both of them.

Outside a strong, dry wind blew down the mountains and out into the valley. It was so loud that he almost couldn't hear the sound of the car as it made its way up the gravel drive.

"There he is," Ben said.

They opened the front door and walked outside. The light on the porch was low. He glanced over at his wife. A vein in her temple was throbbing gently. They stood there for a moment, waiting. Some sort of green beetle buzzed toward the light, then landed on Ben's arm. He squashed it and it smelled like grass.

"Yoel?" Ben called out.

No response. Then the slam of a door, and a figure walking toward them, emerging out of the darkness. He was wearing a backpack and he had a gym bag over his shoulder.

"Hi," he said. He sounded tired.

THE FOLLOWING MORNING, light leaking through a slit in the white blinds. He rolled over and turned on his phone. After a few beats, it came to life, and an alert popped up: the red flag warning was extended for another three days. High temperatures and heavy wind were expected. There was also a message from Yoel, sent to both him and Ada.

"Went into town for coffee," it said. "If you want me to pick anything up while I'm here, just let me know."

It was a surprisingly warm gesture. His arrival last night, while brief, had also been warm. Maybe *warm* was too strong of a word but it wasn't tense in any way. They'd hung out in the kitchen for a few minutes, talked about his flight, the car he'd rented. Ada had asked questions about Sally and Yoel had given a few sleepy answers. Ben left the interaction wondering if maybe Ada had been right. If maybe this could all go well.

In the kitchen, he set the kettle to boil for coffee and turned on the classical radio station, at a low volume so as not to wake Ada. Then he set about gathering his ingredients for the pie fillings. In the fridge, he found a big bag of ripe apricots. He washed one off and took a bite. It was delicious, far better than the out-of-season apples he'd picked up at the co-op. He could make two apricot tarts, then, instead of the apple pies, plus the peach pie.

He began dicing and chopping the fruit for the pies. As he worked, he thought of the doughnut peach tree that was in front of their house in North Oakland, back when he was working as an antiques salesman. It was a beautiful, vigorous thing, which every summer burst forth with a crop of flat, fuzz-less peaches. By fall, only the ones at the very top of the tree remained unpicked. They would fall to the grasses below, and neighborhood raccoons would come feast on them at night.

Yoel had spent the first few years of his life at that house, before they moved up to the farm. Those had been such sweet years. Ada had written about them in her first novel. There was a character loosely based on young Yoel. He had the best lines in the book. Ada was able to capture the way he learned language so well. He had a limited vocabulary at the time so he would need to get creative to describe things. Once for example, he had looked at an avocado pit, called it a "hole." They knew exactly what he meant.

Ben had read and reread that first book while he was in Lompoc so many times that he almost felt as if he'd written it. In the back of the book, he'd kept a photo of the three of them standing in front of their Oakland house. He was pretty sure he still had that same copy of the book along with the photo. If he did, they were in a box on the other side of the barn, the side Ada didn't use. That was where he kept his antiques and other miscellany. The space was mostly full these days, and he needed to go through it all and clear some things out. That would be a good project for the quiet winter months. Then he'd at least be able to consider picking something up at the estate sales he went to.

He still went to estate sales around the county, though these days, he rarely bought anything sizable, given their storage constraints, and Ada's rightful insistence that they already had far too many antiques. So he just went to look, he told himself—to see if there was anything he just couldn't live without. If he got something, it was usually a book or some kind of old print. Years ago, when Yoel was a kid, he would bring home all sorts of stuff. He used to like to pick up creepy porcelain dolls, the kind that were at every old lady estate sale in America for some unknown reason, and hide them around the house for Ada and Yoel to find. This had been a long-running tradition between the three of them, which admittedly, he may have found funnier than they did.

After the pies were in the oven and the kitchen cleaned, he remembered that he still needed to go up to the sheep pen to replace the strap hinge. It was totally rusted, about to snap off. He could probably do that before the pies had to be pulled. He gave the counter one more wipe, and then looked up to find Yoel standing in front of him.

"Smells good in here," he said.

Ben took in his appearance. Yoel was twenty-eight now, but he looked younger than that. He had his mother's thick eyebrows, Ben's bumpy nose, and the rarest of things for a young Jewish man: blue eyes. That came from Ada's mother's side. Today, he was dressed in a polo shirt and chinos, and he was carrying an iced coffee.

"Can I help with anything?" he blinked a few times. He always blinked when he was nervous.

"Well, um," Ben said. "I was going to go fix this hinge on the sheep pen."

"Do you want a hand?"

"Sure," Ben said. "Yeah, actually that would be great."

Outside a light breeze was blowing, bringing with it smells of melon and dry strawberries. They made their way down to the toolshed. The structure was originally built as a barn, but they had always used it as a toolshed. In recent years, it had also become something of a storage shed, after the large barn reached capacity. There was an old sofa in here now, a broken wine cooler, water jugs, a life vest, two space heaters, a Victorian roll-top desk he was maybe going to refinish and sell, big dog crates he'd used to transport their birds, and the beekeeping suit he'd bought at a flea market in town.

He loved beekeeping, had become obsessed with it when Yoel was in middle school. The week he'd gotten his first hives delivered, years ago, had been sort of chaotic, and he'd needed to beg off on chaperoning Yoel's class field trip to San Francisco. But Yoel hadn't seemed to care. When he'd come home, and seen all the hives buzzing with activity, he'd been thrilled. Ben had bought him his own small suit so the two of them could work with the bees together. It was probably in here somewhere too, Ben wasn't sure where.

Amid all the detritus in the toolshed, Ben eventually found the hinge they needed. It might not have seemed like it, but everything was somewhere. He threw the hinge into the plastic tool bucket, along with a cordless drill and several different kinds of screws.

"I just finished deep cleaning the place," Ben said to Yoel as he stepped back outside.

Yoel looked confused.

"A joke," Ben clarified. "Just joking."

"Ah," Yoel said.

They walked silently up to the sheep pen, which was situated on a hill to the east of the house, next to a section of the terraced Barbera lot. The sheep were currently foraging the hillside around the pen, fenced in by his movable electric perimeter. Now that bud break had passed, it was unlikely he'd release them into the vineyard again. Once they had finished working through the remaining grasses up here on the hill, he'd guide them down to the irrigated pasture, just behind the chapel, where they'd spend the rest of the summer.

Ben had eight ewes, all of whom were watched over by their guard dog, Eddie, a Great Pyrenees who they'd bought from a breeder in Gold Creek. Years ago, some people in this area would set out livestock carcasses laced with poison to kill coyotes and bears and mountain lions. These days, most people simply had guard dogs. Eddie was one hundred pounds, a good dog who always stuck close to his sheep. He was nice enough to humans but for the most part he preferred sheep, as a guard dog should.

When they entered the paddock, Eddie was lying down underneath a mossy oak, watching them. The sheep also looked over at Ben, determined that he had no food, and wandered away to munch on milk thistle. In the spring, Ben had, for the first time, attempted to shear them himself. Normally, he outsourced this task to a man named Cullen, the son of an old Cornish miner, who sheared almost all the sheep in Rose County. But last year Ben had been feeling adventurous and he thought he'd do it himself. The sheep came out looking quite patchy, and ever since then, it seemed they had a lower opinion of him.

Ben walked over to the pen, unscrewed the broken hinge and tossed it into the tool bucket. Then he lifted the gate and held it in place while Yoel drilled pilot holes.

"Those are three inch?" Ben grunted, straining to keep the gate steady.

"Three inch, yeah," Yoel said. "But this is going to be lower down because I can't drill in the same spot."

"That's fine."

Yoel pulled out a few screws, began fastening them, the drill making its squirming mechanical noise. Seeing Yoel out here like this reminded him of high school Yoel. The two of them used to work together on the farm all the time in those days. It was hard to believe, given how much Yoel disliked the farm now. Whenever he came up, he would complain about how isolated it was, how it smelled, how the internet went in and out.

"How is work going?" Ben asked.

"Eh," he said. "It's fine. It's a job."

It saddened him to hear his son describe his work with such lifelessness. But he resisted the urge to make any kind of suggestion. That never went well.

"How are things up here?" Yoel asked.

"Things up here," Ben repeated. "Things are good. Money a little tight," he admitted. "But things are good."

Yoel nodded.

"You just wanted to come by for the party?" Ben asked. The phrasing of the question was obviously bizarre, but he didn't know how else to ask it.

"Yeah," Yoel said.

"OK, cool. Glad you'll be here for it."

"Me too."

Yoel fastened the final screw and the two men stepped back to appraise their work. It wasn't perfectly flush but it would do the trick. Yoel turned and gazed around the farm, taking in the vineyard, the hill where they used to grow irises. Yoel had managed that project while Ben was in jail. It was his senior year. A hard year, there was no getting around it. Ben's image splashed on the front page of the paper, everyone in Yoel's school talking about it. But they had been on the same team then.

Ben took the metal chain and wrapped it around the fence pole and the door. As he was doing this, he heard Yoel murmur behind him.

"Look," he said. Ben turned and saw five chipmunks, standing all in a line on their hind legs. They looked like a flock of seagulls on a beach, staring out at the waves. One by one, they dropped down to all fours and scampered off toward the forest.

"Weird," Yoel said.

AT THE PARTY Ben drank wine and milled about from person to person. Most of these folks were closer with Ada than him, but he liked all of them. His closest friend, Wick, had unfortunately not been able to make it this year, because of work. Ada's cousin Allan also had to bail at the last minute. Ben was actually relieved about this, because last year, Ben had promised him a jar of honey in exchange for a few albums from the record store in Sacramento where he worked. Allan had sent him the records, but Ben had accidentally given his last jar of honey to someone else, and he was still out. So he would live to see another day on that one.

Ada had positioned herself in front of the bar and was pouring drinks for everyone. He could tell she was a bit tipsy because her voice had gotten quite loud. Across the room from her, he could hear her explaining what a tallit was to Peter and Carole Giroud.

"I always forget the prayer you need to do before putting it on," she said. "Every Rosh Hashanah I have to look up the prayer on YouTube."

Yoel, for the most part, seemed to be enjoying himself too. Ben watched him tell Myron Chon about the new TV show he had worked on, which starred Chastien Rogers. Yoel's company worked mainly with mysteries and true crime, developing ideas with writers and selling them to networks. Ben wandered over to them during that conversation. The truth was, he really wanted to hear more about Yoel's life and his work. But once Ben arrived, Yoel slipped off to get some food.

Sometime around eight, Ben began setting up the dessert table. He'd made fresh whipped cream to go with the tarts and pies, and there were also some brownies that Carole Giroud had brought.

"OK, everyone," he called. The whole party turned to face him. "We've got some brownies here from Carole. Plus I baked these two apricot tarts and the peach pie."

Then he leaned over, cut himself a slice of everything.

"Come get in here," he called to everyone else.

When he picked up his fork and turned around, he saw Yoel staring at him.

"Where did those apricots come from?" he asked, his voice serious.

The din of the party had not yet resumed and everyone was watching Ben and Yoel. Ben was confused. At first he thought this was maybe some kind of joke.

"The fridge," he said. "We had a big bag of them."

"Oh my god," Yoel said. He had started to blink rapidly. "Did you use all of them?"

"Yeah, I don't get it—"

"Those were for Oliver," Yoel said, interrupting him. "They were from my yard back home. He really likes apricots and I promised I'd bring a bag up for him."

The party was really listening now. Ben saw Ada watching him, an expression of concern on her face. He caught Carole's eyes too, who was wincing, biting into a piece of bruschetta.

"Well," Ben said, "maybe we can bring him one of the tarts." He looked around at everyone in the room. "No one eat that tart," he said, smiling.

"He's vegan," Yoel muttered.

Ben thought for a moment.

"Maybe we could just scrape some of the fruit out?" he ventured.

But Yoel was not listening anymore. He had turned and strode out of the room. Ben heard the front door open and slam.

"Excuse me," he said to no one in particular. He rushed past Myron, who was stroking his goaty beard, and headed after Yoel.

It was dusk now, and the nighthawks were out. They flew across the front yard in their odd, jerking manner, hunting for insects. Looking over to his left, Ben saw that Yoel was out on the street, walking up Mountainview.

"Hey," he called. "Hang on."

He reached him when he was about fifty yards up the hill, next to one of their neighbors' mailboxes. Father and son stared at each other for a brief moment. Ben took in Yoel's eyes. In the low light they appeared dark blue, like water just before freezing.

"Do you ever think about asking before you do things?" Yoel said.

"C'mon," Ben said, "it's not that big of a deal."

"It's always about you and your projects. Whatever shit you're consumed by in that moment."

"It was an honest mistake," Ben said. "I was trying to do something nice for everyone. Forgive me for trying to do something."

"All you have to do is say I'm sorry."

"I didn't do anything wrong," Ben said. "You always want me to apologize for things when I haven't done anything wrong."

"That's the problem," Yoel said. "You never think you're wrong."

"I do think I'm wrong. I'm wrong all the time."

"See, even right now you are insisting you're right about being wrong."

"I don't know what to tell you Yoel," he said. "It's too much with all the criticisms."

"You think I want to criticize? I don't want to criticize. You are just so . . ."

He trailed off.

"Look, I'm sorry," Ben said, "but it's always such a hair trigger with you."

"That is such a shitty apology," Yoel said. "That's your apology? You're unbelievable."

Yoel inhaled through his nose, fuming. The two of them fell silent for a moment. The evening air was quiet, like always. The only sound around them was the chirping of the nighthawks, the occasional booming noise that accompanied their dives. Ben stared at his son.

"Why are you even here?" he said. "If I'm such a dick, why are you here?"

Yoel looked off to his right, at their neighbor's yard. Rusty farm equipment, an oil drum with scraps of wood inside it. Muted color leaking across the landscape: browns and greens and blues.

"Sally and I broke up," he said, still not looking at him. "I've been talking to Oliver about it on the phone a lot. I thought it might be nice to come meet him here."

Yoel closed his eyes and squeezed the bridge of his nose, like he was staving off an immense headache.

"I'm sorry to hear that," Ben said.

"And I guess I thought," Yoel said, still squeezing his nose, "that it might feel good to come home too."

He looked up at Ben and smiled, started to laugh. A tear rolled down his cheek, into the corner of his smile.

"I guess that's what I thought," he said, shrugging.

Then he turned around and continued walking up the hill, into the fading light of the day.

THAT NIGHT, after the guests had departed and everything had been cleaned up, Ben lay in bed with his lamp on, trying to read the library book he'd checked out about the geology of California. Ada was next to him, reading a new novel about a vampiric cult, which had received several big awards. She sat upright, like she always did, turning a page now and again with one fine-boned hand. A little while ago, they had heard the front door open and close so they knew Yoel was back and in his room. Ada had tried knocking on his door soon after, but he'd told her he didn't want to talk. So now they were lying in bed, both attempting to read, but mostly unable to focus. Ada set her book down on the bedside table and looked over at him.

"I'm sorry, I just can't believe they're separating," she said.

"I know."

"He didn't say anything else about it?"

"No."

"Why do men always stop after gathering the barest possible amount of information?"

"He walked away from me, I told you."

Ben set his own book on his chest, looked up at the ceiling light above them. It was one of these new cloth-like fixtures, a white, pouchy thing that sort of resembled an IV bag.

"Do you think it was terrible of me to use the apricots?" he asked.

"It wasn't the smartest thing you've done," she said.

"He just expects me to be perfect."

"Ben, he's going through a major life change right now. You've got to cut him some slack."

He took off his glasses and rubbed his eyes.

"I'm going to go try to talk to him again," she said.

She stood up, put on her house slippers, and left the room. He sat there waiting for her to return but she didn't come back.

Yoel must have let her in. He tried to go back to reading but he was still having trouble focusing. Ten minutes passed, then twenty, then thirty. They were really talking for a long time in there. He figured he might as well go to bed. He walked into the bathroom, poured himself a glass of water, and then turned off the lights.

Lying there in bed, he tried to settle his mind, but sleep wouldn't come. He kept thinking about what it used to be like with Yoel, about the ease they'd had with each other. They were like twins, Ada would say, and it was true. He thought about the day he was born, the feeling of holding him close to his skin, the weird smudge above his right eyebrow, that sense of responsibility and love, like a song inside him.

He had been a good father. He had prided himself on it. Whenever Yoel needed anything, whenever he'd been lost, he'd come to Ben. Even when he trespassed, when he'd made mistakes, he'd still come to Ben. The time he threw a party while Ben and Ada were in Portland for one of Ada's book events and some weirdo stole their whole VHS collection. The time he drove people in his car before he had a license and got pulled over by the sheriff. He could fess up to Ben, he could be honest with him, because Ben was always there to help him.

An image came back to him: the two of them backpacking the east side of Big Sur, with Yoel's childhood dog, Martin. They hadn't gone backpacking that many times together. This trip had been Yoel's idea, when he was a freshman in high school and just getting into that sort of thing. On the second day, they wandered up a hill for a day hike and lost the trail. Ben stared out at the surrounding clumps of manzanita and it all looked the same. Martin, who was off leash, started trotting away through the bushes. Ben didn't want to chase after him, afraid of becoming even more disoriented. But Yoel followed Martin, who was, it turned out, leading them right back to the trail, like a dog from a Hallmark movie. When Yoel got to him, he was standing right there on the path they'd taken up the mountain. They sang his praises all the way down the hill, gave him a hunk of salami when they got back to camp. He was a good dog. Thinking about him now, Ben felt acid rising in his throat. What happened to Martin, he didn't deserve it.

THE WIND WOKE him in the night. A battering storm, the house flexing under its assault. He listened to the noise for several minutes and then got out of bed and walked into the living room. Through the window, in the low moonlight, he could see the big elm tree shuddering, pine needles and leaves and other detritus whipping past it. The night was dark and cool and starless. He opened the sliding door and stepped out onto the patio. He turned his hands over, felt for rain. Nothing.

He went back inside, returned to bed, but he couldn't fall back asleep. He kept rearranging the way he was lying on his pillow. The roof groaned, sounded like it was about to be peeled open like a can. The gusts had to be fifty miles per hour, at least. He put his earbuds in, lay awake listening to a playlist of Beethoven string quartets. He dozed off for a bit but the wind woke him once more. He decided he would get up. It was 6 A.M.

In the dark kitchen he made coffee and flipped through the previous day's *Mountain Gazette*. A local off-roading competition was expanding in size. A man had written a letter to the editor about how he had fallen off his roof. And the board of supervisors was hosting another public debate about what to do with the eighteen-mile stretch of defunct railroad track that ran through the county. Should it be turned into hiking trails or revived as a tourist excursion train?

When he was done with his coffee, he tossed the paper in the recycling, and headed out to feed and release the animals. The wind had lessened slightly, but not by much. As he made his way across the farm, he thought he smelled a hint of smoke. Over by the coop, he paused and looked around. It was still dark and difficult to see. He sniffed a few times, and yes, that was definitely smoke. Subtle and pleasant, like a distant beach bonfire. He took out his phone and checked the county wildfire website.

"There are currently no fires impacting Rose County," it said.

When he came back down the hill, the first light of day had begun to emerge. He went inside, poured himself another cup of coffee, and walked out to the porch to scan the horizon. The plume of smoke was unmistakable. It was far off to the left of the house, across the canyon. He grabbed his binoculars from the kitchen and tried to identify the fire's exact location. If you looked out in the direction of Lucia's Rock, and then looked beyond that, you could see it. As best he could tell, it was slightly east of Ponderosa, at least five miles from Natoma. There was almost nothing up in that area, no farms or vineyards or developments of any kind. He took out his phone and checked the county wildfire website again.

"There are currently no fires impacting Rose County," it still said.

Standing there on the porch, binoculars in hand, he called 911.

"911, what is your emergency?"

"I want to report a fire."

"OK, is it in the Ponderosa area?"

"Yeah, that's it."

"We're getting a lot of calls about that. Where are you?"

"I'm a couple miles up the hill from Natoma."

"East of Natoma?"

"Yeah, but west of Sherwood Road."

"OK, so it's east of Ponderosa so it's miles from you."

"So the fire hasn't entered the canyon?"

"No, the fire is east of Ponderosa. At this point you are not in danger and do not need to evacuate, but stay close to your phone."

"Thank you."

He hurried back inside the house and rustled Ada awake.

"We have to get ready to go," he said.

2

I **N RECENT YEARS**, during the months of the fire season, the residents of Natoma had grown accustomed to seeing smoke. The smoke came from fires burning in other parts of the state, or sometimes nearby, in the mountains, and it settled over the town for varying lengths of time. When the smoke was there, many in Natoma turned to a free app, which, through a network of sensors, provided real-time data on the quality of the air. Seemingly overnight, they had all become amateur air pollution analysts. Some adjusted their app for different settings but most agreed that the US EPA PM 2.5 AQI setting was the most reliable. When the readings on the app were particularly bad, they stayed inside or, if they had to go outside, they wore an N95 mask.

Depending on the day, and the intensity of the smoke, various forms of disruption occurred: you couldn't go for a run or host a birthday barbecue, or your kid's summer camp was canceled. Sometimes the smoke was visible, sometimes not. Sometimes it was thick and blue and other times it was like a white fog. There had been a few times, over the last couple of years, when the smoke turned the sky red. It turned this color, they were told, because of the way the smoke particles scattered the sun's light.

The first time the sky changed color, the people of Natoma walked out onto their porches and stared at the horizon. Shopkeepers stood in their doorways, pointing. Kids biking through town, wearing N95 masks, pulled over on the side of the road. One of the Reen brothers, no one could remember which one, wandered down Center Street humming, "red sky in the morning, sailor take warning." The sky stayed red all day and then, the next day, a less shocking white haze took its place. The people of the town muttered to each other at their dinner tables. They told their kids not to forget their masks when they left the house. No one needed to tell them it was a bad sign.

As someone who worked outside all the time, Ben tried to track the smoke as much as possible. In the mornings during fire season, when he could remember to do so, he pulled up the app and checked the numbers, because the particles that lodged in your lungs—and allegedly, stayed there for the rest of your life, causing all sorts of health problems—were not visible to the human eye. But he almost never stayed inside. Even if the readings were bad, he put on a mask and went about his business on the farm. As long as he took off his clothes when he came back inside, washed them, and jumped right in the shower, it was safe. At least, this was what his doctor had told him.

And so Ben was quite familiar with the smoke, had been working in it now for years, observing how it changed over the course of a day, a season. But the smoke the morning after the party was unlike anything he had seen. It was thick and deeply black, like the smoke from an oil fire. In the minutes since he had come inside to rouse Ada, it had already grown much worse. When he opened his app, the readings in the region were registering in the 400s and 500s. An AQI of over 150 was considered unhealthy for the general population.

They worked quickly, and by the time the official evacuation order came for Natoma and its surrounding areas, they had all the animals packed into two horse trailers. They'd talked about this plan scores of times, so it felt surreal to actually be doing it. First, they'd loaded their personal possessions, then proceeded to gather the animals. The emus, ducks, geese, and chickens were placed in crates, crammed in with the sheep and Eddie. Two mini Noah's Arks. Ben would tow one with their yellow Toyota truck. Ada would tow the other with the newer Ford. And Yoel would follow behind them, in the blue sedan he'd rented.

They headed for Ben's brother's place, in Talinas. Normally the drive would have taken around two hours but the highway out of town was jammed. The sky was greenish brown from the smoke, the color of mold. As he sat in traffic, he called anyone he could think of to make sure they got the news: the guests who'd come to the party, his friend Wick, a few of their neighbors. He spoke to them all through his N95, his voice slightly muffled. He hadn't remembered to grab an N95 on his way out but fortunately there'd been one in the glove compartment.

During the trip, he found himself thinking about the fire in Pine Ridge last year. Pine Ridge was a foothills town north of them, more conservative than Natoma, and primarily populated by seniors. The fire there had been a catastrophic event, an urban conflagration that was later likened, by one fire chief, to the Bombing of Hamburg. It was started by a worn C-hook on a transmission line, and fed by sixty-mile-per-hour winds.

With over eighty casualties, it became the deadliest wildfire in the history of the state. In the days after the fire, horrendous stories began to emerge. Old women trapped in basements, dying of smoke inhalation as they called 911 for help. A family staying afloat all night in a freezing irrigation pond by clinging to a raft of logs. A group of friends burned alive in their car as they tried to flee. Those who survived found themselves instantly homeless. Many stayed in hotels paid for by their insurance or in friends' homes, or they ended up at the mega supermarket parking lot in nearby Bidwell, which had become a temporary evacuation outpost. Most of the Pine Ridge refugees ended up permanently relocating to Bidwell, but others moved to different towns in the foothills, including Natoma. He thought of those people with a sinking stomach, imagined them becoming refugees for a second time.

After more than three decades living in the foothills, Ben had grown accustomed to the presence of fire. There were the bouts of smoke and, periodically, there was a fire to the east of them, usually deep in the forest. It was not uncommon to hear a Cal Fire helicopter overhead as he worked in the vineyard, flying toward one of those fires. An evacuation of Natoma, however? That was unusual. The last time Natoma proper had really been threatened was 1998. This was in part due to the town's location, on the western side of a long, arcing canyon, which had been carved centuries ago by a glacier, and through which ran the Harde River. Fire almost never entered the canyon, and in their lifetime, it had never crossed it. Most fires started in the wilderness east of the town and moved north or south. The '98 fire did enter the canyon, and seemed headed for Natoma, but it hit a rocky area and the winds switched, pushing it back into previously burned black. Cal Fire had eventually gotten the upper hand and been able to contain the blaze. The Hechts had been out of town that summer, but they'd heard about everything from their friends and neighbors.

This fire had not entered the canyon, based on the conversations he was having. It had started in Bennett Gulch—and, for this reason, been named the Bennett fire—and was striping a clean route along the northeast edge of the canyon, close to his property. On the phone, one of Ben's neighbors, Carlo Belloti, told him he'd watched the fire crest the hill and cross through the Studebaker Preserve. It didn't seem like it was heading directly for their houses, but it certainly didn't seem like it was heading away from them either. Carlo had to hang up before he could say any more.

Ben didn't make any more calls after that, instead driving in silence, his whole body tensed. Eventually, improbably, it felt to Ben, he arrived in Talinas, passing the hill with the cross on it and the sign that read CROSSONAHILL.NET. He had visited Talinas hundreds of times in his life. It was a town he felt he sort of belonged to, though he had never lived there. Turning down Main Street, he drove by the Station House Diner and the bookstore and the bakery. He rolled down his windows and the air smelled like ocean, like wet shells and salt.

Ben's older brother, Andrew, and his wife, Jenny, had arranged for them to board their animals with a friend of Jenny's family, Al Garther, who lived on a ranch in the hills above town. Ben and Ada headed over to Al's to drop off the animals, while Yoel drove directly to the house. When they made it to the ranch, Ada got out of her truck and walked over to Ben. She was wearing strappy sandals, sweatpants, and a concert T-shirt that she often slept in.

"Can you tell me why I only brought sandals?" she said. "I really wish I had brought some shoes that weren't sandals."

Al Garther wasn't around but his ranch manager, Diego, was waiting for them when they arrived. He was a tremendously tall man, who wore a leather tool belt and a hat that said GARY'S OYSTERS. He assured them that they could care for the animals as long as they needed. Ben tried to give him the feed that he'd brought, but Diego refused.

"No, no we'll take care of them for you," he said. "Don't worry about that."

He was floored by the kindness of this man, taking on all this extra work, and for nothing. He thought back to when he first arrived at Lompoc, when he was new, "a fish," and everyone brought him gifts: socks, sweatpants, toilet paper, pens. He had been surprised and heartened by this generosity. And he was heartened now too. He wanted to convey the depth of his gratitude, but he was so strung out, so exhausted from the stress of the evacuation, he couldn't find the words.

"Thank you," was all he said. "Thank you so much."

"It's really no trouble," Diego told him.

The poultry and sheep were all tagged so they threw them in with Al's other animals. Diego said it would be fine for Eddie to stay with the sheep too, that it would be good to have another guard dog around. The emus, however, would need their own setup. Diego put them in an old, unused sheep pen, which had been made from cow panels and T-posts. After the unloading was finished, Diego said he had to go refill the flytraps in the olive orchard. He shook their hands, hopped on an ATV, and drove off. Ada and Ben walked back up the hill from the sheep pen to their vehicles, which were parked by the main farmhouse. The wind was hard and cold and Ben's hip was hurting.

"We need to do something really nice for them," he said. "Bake some pies or something. Actually, I don't know if I can do any more baking. I think I've had enough pie baking."

"We'll figure something out," Ada said.

"Or maybe we could just buy a pie? No, buying a pie seems like such a lame move. I'd buy them something else before I bought them a pie."

They were back at the vehicles now. He massaged the joint of his hip.

"Honey," Ada said. "I need you to relax."

"I'm just really grateful they're helping us."

"I know. I am too, but we can figure this out later, OK?"

"OK."

"OK, good."

"Maybe my brother will have a good idea."

"Maybe," she said.

ANDREW AND JENNY lived just outside of town, in a small cottage surrounded by cypress trees. Andrew worked remotely, for a conservation nonprofit in San Francisco. Jenny was in her midfifties, about five years younger than Andrew. She had been born in Malaysia, to British parents, and then moved to Talinas as a child. For years she had been a bartender, but now worked caring for a retired woman in Five Brooks. She and Andrew had two daughters, Rebecca and Noa, who were about the same age as Yoel. Rebecca lived on the East Coast and worked at a law firm that represented unions. Noa had just finished grad school at Davis and had moved to Oakland. In high school, she had been a serious basketball player, and Jenny and Andrew still kept a basketball hoop next to the driveway for when she came home and wanted to shoot around. As Ben arrived at the house, he came incredibly close to toppling this basketball hoop with the trailer, but Ada, who had parked farther down the street, ran over shouting for him to stop.

"Just slow down," she said, after he had pulled back out and was preparing to try again. "There's no rush."

Once he had successfully parked, he sat there for a moment, closed his eyes, and took a few deep breaths. His mind still felt like it was on roller skates. He looked over at Andrew's house.

A few years ago, Andrew had tried to broker a peace between him and Yoel. They'd met here, at Andrew's, and gone camping for a night at Bootjack Lake. Andrew had mediated a conversation, a fairly direct one, about what had gone wrong in Yoel and Ben's relationship. And things did get better for a while after that. When Yoel went back to Los Angeles, he began texting updates to both Ben and Ada, instead of only Ada. He and Ben even talked on the phone once. Previously, when Yoel called the house and Ben answered, he would immediately ask for Ada.

But then things deteriorated again, when Ben and Ada went to visit him in Los Angeles. This was a few months after their camping trip, sometime that fall. The plan was to visit Yoel and spend some time with Sally, who Yoel had just started dating. The first night they were there, everything had been great, but on the second night, Ben went out for drinks with an old college friend, Derek, and then brought him to dinner with Yoel, Sally, and Ada. Ben was having such a nice time with Derek and he'd just thought: the more the merrier. But Yoel was furious that Ben did this, especially when the whole point of the dinner was for Ben to get to know Sally. It didn't help that Ben and Derek were also thirty minutes late. After that, Yoel had sent Ben the letter asking him not to contact him.

These memories briefly cycled by while he gathered himself. Ada stood there waiting for him. When he got out, she took his hand, and the two of them walked up the brick path, past the young avocado tree Andrew had just planted, and knocked on the front door. Jenny answered and embraced them.

"Oh my god, you guys. How are you doing?" she said.

"We'll be OK," Ada said. "We're safe."

"That's the most important thing," she said.

"Thank you so much for taking us in," Ben said. "And for arranging to keep the animals with Al."

"Of course," she said. "Come in, come in."

She led them into the living room where Yoel and Andrew were sitting on the couch together. Andrew got up and hugged Ben. He was wearing a blue moleskin shirt and he had grown out his hair and his beard, both of which were now entirely gray. Younger brothers weren't supposed to go gray.

"It's so good to see you guys," Jenny continued. "I can't remember the last time I saw Yoel. He was just telling us about his project with Chastien Rogers."

Ben nodded. Yoel looked up at him and the two of them shared a momentary glance, before Yoel looked away.

"It's very exciting," Ada said.

"We haven't gotten to your new book yet," Jenny said, "but it's on my bedside table."

"Oh, there's no rush."

"Have you heard any more news?"

"It's burning twelve hundred acres now," Ben said, "according to the radio."

"It's actually twenty-two hundred," Yoel said. "I just saw a post—" He stopped himself, pulled out his phone. "Anyway, yeah, it's a lot."

"You guys must be exhausted," Jenny said. "What can we do? Can I draw you a bath?"

"I'm OK," Ben said. "Ada, do you want to take a bath?"

"I think you should take one, honey," she said. "And lie down for a bit."

"Take a bath, Ben," Andrew said. "Come on."

"OK," he said. "Thank you, everyone, for your interest in my bathing needs. I will take a bath."

Jenny led him upstairs to the bathroom and brought him a fresh towel. After she left, he undressed and turned on the water. He stood naked in front of the mirror as he waited for the tub to fill up. An old man's wide, wet eyes. Blotchy skin with pronounced green veins. Arms still strong from farmwork, but immediately useless, if and when his back decided to seize up, which was about once a month, one of his more regular maladies. There were also the worsening cataracts, the enlarged prostate and its accompanying nighttime urinations, the hypertension, osteoarthritis in the left hip, rotator cuff trouble in the right shoulder, and the constant low-level burn of his hereditary acid reflux.

He knew old age was upon him. This was something he was accustomed to thinking about. But living without the farm? That he had not considered. It had been everything to him, every day, for so long. They'd built most of the structures on the property in the late nineties, when the income was really flowing in. Three hundred thousand dollars a year in cash, no taxes. In the winters they traveled all over the world, but mostly to Belize, where they had bought a small shack on the water. During harvest, friends came from all over to trim and smoke weed and take saunas and drink their homemade wine out of old apple juice jugs. He'd helped build or design almost everything on the property, planted the vineyards, the fruit trees, the gardens. Half a life of work.

He turned off the faucet and eased himself into the scalding water. He had some idea of what was in his insurance policy, but not much. He had always been bad with fine print. His mind glazed over when it came to legal documents. It had been years since he'd reviewed or thought about their policy. He was afraid to admit this to Yoel who would, surely, take him to task for it. He knew, generally speaking, that they were slightly underinsured, but he couldn't remember the details. He would look into it tomorrow.

On the far wall, above the sink, he watched the shadow of a cypress branch bobbing in the wind. Some distant neighbor had fired up a lawnmower. Ben listened to the drone of the motor, its periodic revving and relaxing. The bathwater no longer felt too hot. He leaned his head back and looked at the ceiling. Then he slid down in the tub until his chest was submerged, his neck, his entire head.

. . .

AT FIRST, Ben expected Yoel to leave, take the car to SFO and fly home from there. But apparently he'd told Ada he was going to keep his flight out of Natoma the following week. Ben suspected it was because he wanted to stay close to Ada to provide her with support. During those first few days of waiting, they spent a lot of time together, going for hikes in the surrounding area, taking trips into town. Ben and Yoel, meanwhile, were conspicuously avoiding each other. His brother had obviously noticed.

Most of the time, Ben wasn't sure what to do with himself. He went over to check on the animals once, followed the news constantly. Wick sent him a video of a DC-10 dropping fire retardant over the rim of the canyon. The fire was 15 percent contained, 40 percent contained, 80 percent contained. Cal Fire held press conferences, led by their incident commander. They described the geography of the fire, where the crews were currently fighting it, and what air attacks were underway. The fire had missed Natoma, they knew this now, but several structures in the area had burned, and there were two reported injuries, both to firefighters.

"This was a dangerous fire," their state senator said on television, "but it could have gotten a lot worse. We owe our thanks to the first responders."

Still, Mountainview Road remained closed, and they had not been cleared to return to their home. Ben tried not to engage in future-tripping. He had looked up the fire insurance and learned that it was, more or less, what he'd expected it to be. But he simply didn't know what had happened to the property. He started taking long walks through the neighborhood alone. He knew he was traversing the edge of a deep sadness, but nothing was officially sad yet.

One day, Andrew suggested the two of them go for a sail on the bay. He'd recently acquired a twenty-four-foot fiberglass sloop for free from a woman who had, for many years, used the boat only as a painting studio, but had grown tired of paying slip fees. Neither of the brothers had sailed as children, but they'd gotten into it in their twenties when they'd accompanied their friend Larry and his older cousin on a passage from San Francisco to Zihuatanejo.

It was a calm morning, a hint of moisture in the air, but still no rain. They packed a canvas bag with sandwiches and headed down to the docks. The boat, Ben noticed upon arrival, was not in great shape. Algae and other green organisms were growing on its hull, at the waterline. The brightwork looked not very bright at all. He hobbled aboard and stepped down into the galley. Inside he found a couple empty bottles of wine, a paperback swollen with moisture, an open box of stale pretzels.

"Don't forget your pretzels down here," Ben said.

Andrew laughed. "He's always got jokes," he said, uncleating a dock line. "If you had a boat it would be ten times worse."

They motored out toward Horse Island hoping to find wind, but there wasn't any so they just kept motoring. They passed empty beaches and little coves, houses that appeared to have been built out of driftwood. The boat nodded capably through the swells, a mackerel sky above, two cormorants trailing behind them.

"Did you have to put much work into this when you got it?" he asked.

"The carburetor on the outboard needed to be rebuilt," Andrew said. "But everything else, the whole rig, it was all good to go."

"What about the slip fee?"

"Not so bad."

They puttered along the shoreline, waved to an oysterwoman who was making her rounds. At a certain point, Andrew turned to starboard and ducked into a small inlet. The water was calm here, greenish yellow. Just underneath its surface, belts of dark red kelp swayed, thin but tough, like strips of fruit leather. Over on the shore, tiny waves broke against a beach of pebbly sand. Andrew dropped anchor and pulled out their sandwiches.

"It's been nice seeing you guys," his brother said, handing him his sandwich. "I know the circumstances are bad."

"It has been nice," he said. "We should come down here more."

"Definitely, we want to come up your way too."

Andrew paused for a beat and then said: "Been meaning to tell you, we love that wine you guys sent this year. It didn't have that . . . What's it called?"

"Mousy flavor."

"Yeah, you guys got rid of that. That was good. You could sell that stuff."

"I don't know about that."

Andrew took a bite of his sandwich and leaned back against the built-in compass in the cockpit.

"You don't have any plants up there right now, do you?"

"What? Oh, no, I'm just doing a few CBD plants."

"Only the CBD? Like, if people were wandering around, they're not going to stumble on something."

"Andrew, there's no point in me growing anymore," he said. "You can't make money on it. The market is oversupplied."

"I'm just checking."

"And if I was going to do it, I'd get a license from the CDFA."

"Right."

"I'm just doing the grapes and a little CBD."

"Is the CBD under the limit?"

"It's all under the limit. Everything's under the limit."

"OK," he said.

"Did Yoel request this line of questioning?"

Andrew leaned over to grab a chip. Ben could see the sweat-drenched curls on his neck.

"He brought it up the other day, yeah," Andrew said.

"I knew it."

"He just said something in passing. I think he was worried. What's going on with you guys? It seems worse than usual."

"I don't know. It's always something with him. He blows things out of proportion."

Ben turned away from his brother. Andrew had always had a good relationship with Yoel. Ben had been jealous of it at times—the fun uncle role, much easier to play.

"Ben, I'm going to be honest with you," Andrew said, "because I'm your brother and someone needs to do it. I still don't think you understand how hard it was for him those eighteen months you were away."

Ben felt a crack inside him opening, the memories threatening to flood through it. The cool gaze of the judge, his eyes the color of oyster meat. Ben standing before him, the court packed with his supporters. The judge admitting that he was a good citizen, but then saying, "I gotta obey the law—how do I get around that?" And Yoel sitting there, gentle and down-trodden, his shoulders hunched.

"You missed everything then," Andrew continued. "His college trips, his graduation, everything. And then he had to be the kid whose dad got locked up. His whole senior year he walked around with that. Other kids giving him shit. It was a lot."

"Yeah."

"I know it was hard for you too. I'm just saying. He was only a kid."

"I hear you," Ben said.

"He's staying cause he wants to make it right. He could've just gone home."

Andrew let the comment hang there for a moment.

"The apricot thing was dumb," he continued. "I agree with you. Probably, with some distance, Yoel would agree with you too, but it's deeper than that. You know this."

The wind was picking up, a breeze darkening the water by the mouth of the bay. Ben thought about chasing Yoel down on Mountainview. He thought about the look on his son's face, the image of him walking up the road. He looked back at his brother.

"I hear what you're saying," he said.

BACK AT THE HOUSE, they found Yoel in the living room with Ada. They had been outside eating lunch, they explained, but the wind had changed direction, and the air had grown smoky. Another wildfire was burning up by Willits, Yoel said, and the air was expected to get worse in the coming days. He had taken a video call that morning with two TV directors from San Francisco. Apparently the smoke was bad over there too.

"It's probably the wind we had yesterday," Yoel said. "Kept things a little clearer."

"How was the meeting?" Andrew asked.

"Oh, good," Yoel said. "Interesting guys. One of them had a friend who was in the fires last year, up in the wine country."

He turned to Ben. "He was telling me about this blog where this lady keeps track of all her rebuild costs," he said. "Not that we're rebuilding, hopefully, but he was just saying it's like a good, honest log of everything. Maybe it would be useful for neighbors or something, you know?"

"That does sound helpful," Ben said.

Yoel seemed to be evaluating the tone of the statement so Ben elaborated:

"I'd love to check it out."

"I'll send you the link," his son said.

"Thanks."

THAT EVENING, before dinner, he looked over the bookshelf for something to read. Ada was in the bathroom, taking a shower. He hadn't brought his book with him, hadn't had time. Neither had Ada. Most of the books on the shelf were novels, but there were a number about filmmaking too. Years ago, Andrew had gotten into documentary film and was actually planning on making a documentary about Ben's case, but it never happened. Andrew had taken a new job, and no longer had time to work on it.

Ben passed over the filmmaking books and found a small book about rattan furniture, which he'd gifted to Andrew years ago. An inscription on the first page: "If you would just take my brilliant interior design recommendations your place would look a lot better. Love, Ben." What an asshole. He had been a rattan evangelist for a while. This was when he was working at the antiques shop in North Oakland. Flipping through the book, memories of that old shop came back to him. The smell of varnish and dust. His former boss, Soraya, a somewhat reclusive yet brilliant woman. She loved rattan too, was an expert in restoring it. She could also do cane, rush, Danish cord, you name it.

Soraya's shop was where he'd met Ada. She just strode in one day, with her friend Anita, who she'd come west with. Two Jewish girls from the Bronx, living in a blue Victorian in Ivy Hill. He was familiar with the neighborhood, he told them, used to go to the movies at a theater near there. For some reason, his voice got choked up in that moment, the dryness of the air or something. Most people would have probably just ignored it, but Ada didn't.

"Are you crying?" she asked.

"No," he said, laughing. "No, sorry."

He was smitten with her right then: her unflinching attention to the world, her fearlessness. The black jeans and curly hair and that smile helped too—an irresistible combination. A few weeks later, the two young women were evicted from their Victorian, he couldn't remember exactly why. The landlord wanted to raise the rent or something. Ben invited them to stay in the extra room in his house while they looked for a new place. After a couple of weeks of searching, Anita did end up finding somewhere else to live, but Ada never left.

He leafed through the book and then looked over to his right. Ada's backpack of writing notebooks was sitting there on the floor. That was what he'd really like to read, Ada's new manuscript. She was his favorite writer. Everyone probably said that about their writer spouses but for him it was true. In her work he saw a mirror of his own thinking, a reflection of things about the world which he knew to be true, but which he would have never been able to express so clearly himself.

All of her work had some autobiographical element, though her later work had become increasingly less autobiographical. In the later books, she would usually take some seed from real life and then expand it into a fully-fledged novel. From their experiences in Belize, she had written a historical novel about British Honduras, and the war for independence there. She had also written a wilderness survival novel, based on an account of a young girl who had gotten lost in the woods in Dover, and lived for over two weeks off berries and roots. Her most famous novel, though, and the novel that had won her wide acclaim, was a quiet book about a woman teaching herself to paint frescoes. She'd been inspired to write it after visiting a series of frescoes in North Carolina. The book was a finalist for a major award and became a best seller.

In the years after publishing that book, Ada's career really began to take off. He had felt so proud of her. She had worked long and hard for her success, had fought the whole way. It was also, at the same time, a huge financial boon for them. In years prior, Ben had carried most of the weight with his cannabis revenue, but they had saved very little from that period. Ada received her first big deal—after the success of the fresco novel—around the time those funds were running low. And she had continued to receive healthy advances since then.

He never knew what she was writing about. She didn't like to talk about it while she was working, said it was like letting the air out of a balloon. But it was always so exciting to see what she had done when she was finished. It was like unwrapping an incredibly ornate and expensive gift. He wondered what this new book would be about. She'd just told him the other night that she was getting stressed out about it, that she'd fallen out of rhythm with the chaos of the evacuation. He told her not to worry, that once they got back to the house, she'd find her groove again.

As he was sitting there, thinking about all of this, he received a call from Carlo Belloti. He told Ben that Mountainview was open and people were heading back to their properties. He said that he had driven past their house that afternoon and, from the road, it appeared to be OK. Untouched. Ben thanked him profusely for this news. Carlo offered to go over tomorrow to take a closer look, but Ben told him he didn't need to. They would head up themselves first thing in the morning. And then he thanked him four more times.

Ada emerged from the shower, wrapped in a towel.

"You should really do that," she said as she dried her hair with another towel. "It feels great."

"Carlo just called. The roads are open. He said it looks like it missed us."

"Oh my god, Ben."

He got out of bed and embraced her. Her body was warm from the shower. She pressed her face into his neck and he could feel the wetness of her tears. He was crying himself.

"I didn't think . . ." she said.

"Me too."

"We'll go tomorrow?"

"We'll get the animals in the morning and then go."

She pulled back, smiled, and then sniffed.

"We still need to get them a gift," she said, wiping a tear from her cheek.

"We'll pick up a few things in town tomorrow. And we can send them some wine too, and some CBD."

"I can't believe it."

He stood there, waiting for Ada to get dressed. Baggy jeans, yellow wool top, tiny hoop earrings. He thought about everything he was going to get started on in the vineyards when they returned. There would be at least one more mildew spray and fruit dropping and then his annual defense campaign against the birds and squirrels. It was possible there was going to be an issue with smoke taint. But he could test for that. He'd cross that bridge when he came to it. The important thing was that the farm was still there. The important thing was the house was untouched. He was cracking his knuckles. He was stretching out his hip. They were going home.

3

B **EN'S OLD YELLOW** Toyota had, at one time, been well known throughout Natoma. It was short and box-shaped, and jacked up very slightly, so that it looked a bit leggy, like a deer or a tall dog. He had purchased the vehicle about a decade ago, from Jimmy Reen, one of the five Reen brothers, all of whom worked at the scrapyard and had somehow, over time, developed their own peculiar family accent, which sounded sort of Portuguese. Jimmy Reen had bought the truck a few years earlier from Mary Lopez, the former Natoma mayor, who was often seen driving the truck down Center Street during her 2004 reelection campaign. This was what had constituted its momentary brush with fame.

At the time Ben acquired the truck, it was still fairly new, though it had been dented in places, the side door damaged. Jimmy Reen had blamed this on the mayor, said she was an incautious driver. Internally, everything seemed to be in working condition, though the price was low enough to cause concern. And Ben was right to have been concerned. In the first year after he bought the truck, he had to replace the spark plugs, the air conditioning, the muffler, and most expensively, the head gasket. For a moment, he considered parting with the thing—and in fact, got very close to selling it to a young woman, who was opening a nursery and was going to use it to transport plants—but ultimately, he decided to keep it.

Ben wouldn't have called it a lemon exactly, but he wouldn't say it was reliable either. It broke down occasionally and sometimes overheated when towing a heavy load. As a result, on the ride back up to Natoma, Ben planned to take a couple of breaks to give the old machine a chance to cool down. When he stopped for the first time, in Sacramento, he took one breath, and then rummaged in the glove compartment for his N95. A stinging, dirty smell hung in the air. There were two fires burning south of them, by Fresno. All told, there were nearly a dozen active fires across the state. The fire that had passed through Natoma was still burning as well, though it was almost entirely contained. The number of structures lost had been confirmed at seven. No homes had burned.

As they merged onto 99, they dropped into a decimated landscape, gray fields and hillsides stretching out into the distance. There were signs warning of various road closures. The smoke seemed to be growing denser. It filtered the light, gave everything a weary, dreamlike quality. At one point, a Cal Fire truck passed them on their right, covered in pink fire retardant. Ben tried to tune his radio to the local classical station but found that it was out. Instead he heard the muffled signal of some distant country song. He turned off the radio and drove the rest of the way in silence, the yellow Toyota chugging up the incline.

They exited at Smith Flat Road, passed the taqueria and the new brewery, which had a sign in its window: THANK YOU FIREFIGHTERS. He felt himself tearing up. He felt a headache coming on. He turned right onto 51 and, as he approached Mountainview, he could see the remnants of a roadblock. A man in some kind of protective suit was standing there. He stopped Ben and asked for proof of residence. Ben showed him his driver's license, explained that the two vehicles behind him were his wife and his son.

"And you all have masks?" he said.

"Yes."

"OK, head on through."

Not every hill was burnt but many of them were. Blackened trees lined the road, spires of obsidian. He passed a burned pickup truck, fallen powerlines, a neighbor in his front yard, felling a charred young pine with a chainsaw. When he drove over the streams, they seemed cloudier than usual, the water light brown like rum.

He pulled into the driveway and saw the house, but the sight of it didn't bring him much relief. He was, in some way, still processing what he had just seen. He didn't feel grateful for his luck, only afraid. They looked around at everything: the chapel seemed fine, and there was the orange tractor, also unharmed. On the front patio, there was still laundry hanging out to dry. They hadn't bothered to grab it in their rush to leave. It was all wrinkled and crispy now, covered in soot and ash.

They left the animals in the trailers and walked toward the house. Yoel had his phone out and was filming. They were all still wearing masks. Inside, the smell of trapped smoke was overwhelming, even through his mask. It mixed with the odor of spoiled food: everything that had been left in the refrigerator and freezer had gone bad. Ada began opening windows to air out the smell, but this only let in more smoke.

"We should probably turn on the generator and use the air purifier," she said.

They had bought the air purifier during last year's fire season, when Ada had started having trouble breathing. Ada pulled it out of the closet and Ben went around to the side of the house to turn on the generator. When he came back in, Ada was sweeping up ash on the floor. The air quality sensor on the purifier was red. He told Ada he was going to inspect the rest of the property before unloading the animals. Yoel said he'd come with him.

They stepped out the screen door and onto the back patio. The yard over by the chapel, which was mostly just a patch of calla lilies, was green and alive. The hillside above, however, was entirely blackened. Smoke leaked from the stump of a nearby manzanita. Much of the hill up this way had been a manzanita thicket, a home for mountain quail. They began to walk up the slope, through the burnt grass and trees. At a certain point, Yoel noticed several flares. Firefighters had been here.

"They must have burnt all this to protect the house," he said.

They turned left, walked toward the sheep pen, through the terraced rows of Barbera. The vines did not appear to be burned but that did not mean the grapes were untainted. He would need to send off samples to a lab to find out. It was good, at least, that the fruit was underdeveloped. Ripe fruit in August would have been at much greater risk of smoke taint. He knelt down to examine one of the Barbera clusters. Its tiny hard berries were dusted with ash. The leaves nearby were also lightly dusted, specks of white against the deep green, like a splatter of paint. Overhead, he could hear the hum of a helicopter. He looked up to see it passing over them, its red drop bucket hanging down at an angle, bent by the wind. It was probably heading to the reservoir to pick up more water.

When they arrived at the sheep pen, they found it intact. This was not surprising: it was on a mostly bald hill, adjacent to the Barbera, and encircled by defensible space. They paused for a moment here and looked around at the surrounding country. Yoel pointed out that, in the distance, you could more or less make out the path of the fire. It had come from the hills above them and broke around the outside of their house, burning through the woods on the north and west side of the property. After sweeping across Mountainview, it appeared to have continued in a southwesterly direction, down through the forest, and toward Bennett Road. Off to his right, Ben saw that the fire had come close to his neighbor's property to the north, but had never reached it. The prevailing winds from the mountains had kept it moving downhill. He looked out at his neighbor's walnut grove, at the cattle fence separating their properties, and then back across the burn scar. His gaze settled on the edge of his Primitivo block, where the barn and toolshed should have been. The structures were no longer there.

They hurried down the hill, past the coop and the chapel and the vegetable garden. Ben was having a hard time breathing, was huffing through the mask. When they made it to the spot where the structures had once been, they stood there for a moment, marveling at the comprehensiveness of the destruction. Both buildings were entirely flattened. The metal roofing, warped and twisted, lay on top of the debris. Sections of it were blue from how hot it had gotten. Nearby the Primitivo vines were damaged, their leaves visibly singed.

He walked over to the remnants of the barn, scanned it for metal objects. The wood he had no hope for but perhaps some of the metal objects had come through? Some of his older mirrors maybe, or some of the hand tools or the cookware? Oh shit, his fucking letters were in there. And what about Ada's office? All her books? He needed to get gloves and a shovel and come back down here. He circled the ruins for a while, in a haze, trying not to think about what was gone now. There was no reason to think about it. It was gone. At a certain point he stopped and looked over at his son.

"Two out of seven right here," he said.

"Let's get you into the shade," Yoel said.

Ben nodded. Then he pulled his mask off, put his hands on his knees, and vomited into the black dirt.

THAT EVENING THEY made dinner with cans from the pantry. Yoel pulled out a jug of the farm blend from under the sink and poured himself and Ada a glass. Ben didn't have one. He wanted to go easy on his stomach, stick to water. He'd brought a pack of water bottles from the chapel for everyone. They weren't sure if the well water was contaminated. The gas lines, at least, seemed to be functional. Ada had tested them. And the odor of spoiled food had mostly dissipated. The smell of smoke was still there but at least the kitchen no longer reeked of rancid meat. Ben and Yoel had moved the refrigerator outside earlier that afternoon. He would bleach the whole thing tomorrow.

As they ate, Yoel told them that the evacuation center at the Espino Boy Scout Cabin had been closed. He had been watching a live stream of the news on his phone. He said fire personnel were still extinguishing hot spots along Bennett Road. Ada offered to call their insurance agent in the morning. She also told them that the county fair, which was supposed to open on July 4, had been postponed. She seemed in decent spirits, despite having lost her office. She'd grabbed all of the important stuff, she said, the research materials she would need moving forward.

When they were finished with their meal, he washed the dishes, dried them, and set them on a counter where they would be hit by the sun in the morning. This was how they had washed dishes in Belize, when their water had not been potable. He should have gone and laid down after that, he felt so awful. His eyes were dry and irritated and his chest was filled with nervy air. But instead he took a notebook, sat down on one of the ashy couches, and began listing objects of value that had been incinerated in the toolshed. He knew they would need this information for the insurance company and he figured he might as well get it down now, so Ada would have it in the morning when she made her call.

But he couldn't focus. He kept getting distracted thinking about all the random things that had been in the barn: their box of Halloween costumes that Ada had handsewn, Yoel's Bar Mitzvah kippahs, those photos of Ben holding Martin as a puppy, the handwritten letters he'd sent to Ada from Lompoc and the letters she'd sent him. These things were of little to no material value, would be meaningless on an insurance claim. In the bedroom, he could hear Ada on the phone, calling neighbors whose homes they'd passed on their way in.

As he was sitting there, Yoel walked into the room with his laptop. He said he had made a hotspot with his phone so they could use the internet tomorrow morning, if they needed to.

"A hot what?"

"It takes my phone's service and makes it so your computer can connect to it."

"Ah OK," he said. "Good, thank you. Did you tell your mom? She wanted to make some posts on her site."

"On Facebook? Yeah, she knows."

"OK, good, good."

"Look," Yoel said, "I mentioned this to Mom but I think I'm going to stay for a bit longer."

"Don't you have to get back to work?"

"It's not a big deal, I can work from here."

"Jerry won't mind?"

"He doesn't have anything in production for the rest of the summer so it'll be easy for me to work remotely."

"So you'd be with us for the rest of the summer?"

Ben was shocked. That was an extremely long visit. Even when Yoel and him had been on better terms, he hadn't wanted to stay on the farm that long.

"Yeah, I mean, if you don't want me up here for that—"

"No, no," Ben said. "I definitely want you to stay."

"I just figured you are both going to have so much extra to do."

Yoel sat down in the armchair across from him. On the table in front of them there was a plastic tub of cashews. Yoel unscrewed the top, popped a few in his mouth.

"Still good?" Ben said.

Yoel nodded.

"I can't believe this happened," he said.

"It doesn't feel real," Ben said. "My mind is . . . my mind . . ."

He gestured toward the notebook in his hand.

"I've been trying to think about what was in the toolshed for fifteen minutes and all I've got down is: 'pruners, loppers.'"

"It's a start."

"I just can't believe it came across the edge of the canyon like that, across Mountainview. A fire coming from Ponderosa? I've just never seen that happen. I've seen a fire come up the ridge, cross Bennett Road and go north toward . . . what's that road?"

"Laurel Valley."

"Yeah, that's what you see, but this . . . I've never seen it go the other way."

"It makes you think about Pine Ridge."

"Of course."

They fell quiet for a moment. He was still trying to wrap his head around it all. Everything he'd just seen, the news that Yoel was staying, the million things he now needed to take care of. In the distance, he could hear the steady rumble of the generator. Another thing for the to-do list, he realized. He would have to get more propane soon. It was amazing how quickly the generator could run through propane. They had it connected to a five-hundred-gallon tank, which Ben always tried to keep full, especially these days. There was a guy from Dover who filled it for them. Ben was making a note about calling him the next morning when they heard a scream from the bedroom.

Ben and Yoel hopped up and ran toward Ada. In the bedroom they found her sitting on the bed with her red backpack. There were books splayed everywhere on top of the comforter.

"I thought I had my notebooks in here," she said, her voice quivering. "But it was only my research books. The whole time I was just carrying around my research books."

She looked up at Yoel and Ben, an expression of terror on her face.

"Where else could they be?" Yoel said.

THEY SEARCHED THE HOUSE, the vehicles, the trailers, every bag they'd brought with them. All night they did this and the whole following day. They called Andrew and asked him to search his entire house too. But nothing turned up. Ada said she knew what had happened. She had been planning to go to the café the following morning so she had loaded her research books into her bag, hung it on the wall of her office, in the barn. The morning of the fire, she'd grabbed it first thing, but for some reason, she'd assumed the notebooks were already in there too. For some reason, on that morning, she thought she'd put the notebooks in there the night before. But now, in her mind, now that she really thought back on it, she remembered that it had only been the research books. The notebooks had been sitting there on her desk. In her office. In the barn.

After a full day of searching, the reality of the situation began to set in. Ben was still holding out hope that they might turn up, but it wasn't looking good. Ada, on the other hand, had grown despondent. He watched her rifle through the house for a fourth time, a fifth time. As the sun was setting she grabbed a pair of work gloves and walked out the front door. He called after her, asking what she was doing, but she didn't respond. Worried, he laced up his boots and followed her outside.

"Ada," he called again, "Ada, where are you going?"

It was cool now, the sun slipping behind the hills like a fresh cantaloupe, the last birds calling out in the still air.

"Ada," he yelled, looking around in the pale light. "Where are you?"

"Over here," he heard a soft voice say.

He walked down the gravel path, over to the area where the barn once stood. Ada was on her hands and knees, sifting through the incinerated wreckage.

"I think I had a paper weight on top of them," she said, eyes on the ground. "I'm remembering that now. I can see it in my mind's eye. A little paper weight on top of the notebooks so the pages didn't blow when I opened the window. I can see it in my—"

"Sweetie," Ben said. "That stuff is toxic. You need more gear to go through that stuff."

"It was a little red paperweight," she said. "Do you remember what I'm talking about?"

He was standing on the edge of the debris, watching her, his hands on his hips.

"I do."

"We got it in Belize. I got it in Belize. At that little artisans market. The one in the mornings, on Thursdays."

"I remember."

"If I could find that maybe I could dig down and maybe there would be something . . . maybe something came through."

She was crying now, tears dripping onto her work gloves, onto the ash and twisted metal. To her right was a cement bench, which had sort of survived. It was all bubbled and buckled.

He couldn't believe this had happened. All the dumb things they had grabbed on their way out. Animal feed. Good god, he had walked around grabbing bags of animal feed, wasted time packing it into the truck, trying to get it all to fit, instead of thinking to make sure Ada had her manuscript. Why had he not double-checked to make sure she had it? He asked her to double-check about her passport, about her toothbrush. Jesus, he could remember that now: they were standing under the eucalyptus trees and he asked her if she had her toothbrush. But not once did he mention the manuscript. The whole thing was too painful to comprehend. He couldn't imagine what it had to feel like for her. He walked over to Ada and put his hand on her shoulder.

"Let's go back inside, honey," he said.

She stopped digging but stayed crouched there on all fours. Her head was hung, tears continuing to drip. Suddenly, she stood up, turned to her right, and kicked over the ruined bench. She stared down at it for a moment, wiped her nose with the side of her forearm. Then she looked out at the vineyard.

"Fuck me!" she screamed, her voice echoing across the hills. And then a bit a quieter: "Oh, fuck me."

THE FOLLOWING MORNING Ada called her agent, Julia, and told her what had happened. At first, Ada said, Julia seemed to be reeling. She said "oh my god" several times, kept asking Ada if she'd truly checked every last inch of the house. Once she gathered her wits about her, she encouraged Ada to try to put down everything she remembered about the book right away, while it was still fresh in her memory. She didn't have to rewrite the whole thing right now, of course, she was dealing with so much.

But at least then she'd have as much information as possible, if she did want to try to retrace her steps. Ada agreed to do this.

They spent the next couple of days cleaning and making phone calls to friends and family, telling them what had happened. Ada did not want people knowing about the lost manuscript so they didn't mention that part. Several neighbors stopped by, including Carlo Belloti and the Chons. *We're so sorry*, they all said, when they saw the barns. *At least the house is OK*. No one else on Mountainview seemed to have lost a structure. Not that there were many structures on Mountainview. It was a sparsely populated area. It had always been sparsely populated. That's why they'd selected it, so many years ago, to farm cannabis.

Carlo, who had stayed for the whole thing, said the encroaching fire had sounded like thousands of ships, like their sails were luffing in the wind, flapping violently. That first night, he had stood on top of his roof for hours, scanning the area for spot fires. If things had gotten bad, he said, he was going to jump into his pool. But the fire had stayed on the other side of Mountainview, the Hechts' side.

"At one point I saw like twenty turkeys on your roof," he said. "I swear to god. I don't know where they came from but I guess they knew it was safer up there."

One morning, Jodie McClellan showed up with a platter of Italian meats and cheeses. She lived off Smith Flat Road, with her husband, Walter, who had worked for the USGS but was now retired. Their youngest son, Anthony, had played little league with Yoel. Apparently, Anthony now lived in San Francisco, where he had founded his own real estate company. Ben learned this when Jodie stopped by. He had been surprised by the visit but Ada wasn't.

"She always over-involves herself in situations like this," Ada said.

"What do you mean?"

"She courts tragedy. I'm not complaining, I'll gladly accept the food, but she comes for the gossip. She did the same thing when you were arrested."

Later that same day, Oliver Brandon stopped by to visit Yoel. Ben hadn't seen him since Yoel was in high school, though he knew the two of them stayed in close touch. He was heading back to the East Coast that night, where he worked as a math teacher. They all sat in the living room and talked about the fire and, to Ben's great relief, no one mentioned a word about apricots. Yoel seemed comfortable around his friend, told the story of their return to the farm. Ben was reminded of what an orator he could be. He captured the emotion of it all so well. Ada was the writer but Yoel had always been great in front of an audience.

The air was still smoky so they didn't go outside, except for necessary things: feeding the animals, letting the dogs out, cleaning the refrigerator. At some point, Ada and Ben debated heading back to Talinas, to escape the smoke, but they decided to stay. Things were not so bad inside, with the air purifier—and what would they do with the animals? Move them all again? It was too much of a hassle.

Up and down Mountainview, workers for the utility company were felling burnt trees that now threatened their power lines. Ben could hear them shouting to one another in Spanish, could hear the sound of their chipper. At the end of the third day, the workers drove off, and power was restored shortly thereafter. Yoel said there were a few rumors circulating online about the origins of the fire. Some suggested the utility company's transmission lines were responsible. Others believed it was a blown tire on a stock trailer. Officially, according to Cal Fire, the cause was still under investigation.

In addition to the devastation of losing Ada's manuscript, they began discovering other items that had been lost in the barns. At unexpected moments, he'd remember some object that had been in there. Those cowboy boots he wore throughout his twenties, his friend Ronnie Mull's painting, which he had been intending to frame. Why hadn't he kept more stuff in the house or the chapel? Why had he jammed everything into the barns?

Apart from Ada's manuscript, he was perhaps most heartbroken by the loss of their letters from Lompoc. While he was in the prison camp, Ben had written to Ada every Saturday. In Lompoc, Saturdays were free. Inmates could play sports, take classes, make phone calls, and buy soft drinks at the commissary. The conditions in the camp were not the same as those one would have found in a standard prison. There was no barbed wire, no guard towers, and little violence. People were assigned to Lompoc usually because they had committed a nonviolent, "white-collar" crime.

For the most part, Ben felt lucky to be in this watered-down version of prison, where during the week, his main job was to rake the leaves of the eucalyptus trees that lined the perimeter of the camp. But the experience was still lonely and he worried about Ada and Yoel. Writing Ada on Saturdays was one of his most treasured practices, a stabilizing anchor. He preferred to write to her in the morning, just after breakfast, when his mind was clearest. And his favorite place to write was the law library. There was usually only one other person there, a criminal defense attorney in jail for bank fraud. He had filed many appeals for his own case, was at work on a new one. He showed it to Ben once: it was extensive, cited hundreds of cases. The lawyer could reference many of its passages from memory. He joked that it was his life's work.

Ada would always write him back promptly. Her letters were long and beautiful, filled with updates about Yoel and the farm. Sometimes Yoel would write too. This was when Yoel was still on his side, sympathetic, before Ben had gotten out and started the second grow. The letters usually arrived on Wednesday or Thursday. When it was time for mail call, Ben would line up at the end of the hallway, next to the supervisor's office, and wait for his name to be called. He would read every letter from Ada many times over. When he went to go write her back, he would bring her letter with him to the library, so he could consult it as he was drafting his response. Once, the criminal defense attorney had seen him reading one of her letters and commented on its length. Ben told him that his wife was a novelist.

"Well, I'm sure this whole situation will make for a good story," he said.

"My brother's actually making a documentary about it," Ben told him. It had been true at the time.

ADA COULDN'T STOP thinking about the lost manuscript. It was haunting her, she told Ben. At all hours, she would take down notes, try to rerecord sentences or scenes or plot threads. She knew she would never be able to recreate the book completely but maybe she could get close to it.

Ben tried to shift her perspective on the situation. He suggested that something new might come out of it, something different but equally beautiful. He told her she would remember what really mattered, but she insisted this wasn't true. Her memory didn't work like that. It was more like a stream, she said: some recollection would come floating past her, and if she didn't reach out and grab it in that moment, she might not ever see it again.

Ada's memory had long been a source of struggle for her. In her thirties, she felt that it would hold her back from becoming a great writer. Novelists had to remember things, to be able to recall vivid details. This was what made for great writing: to have all of your experiences at your command, and to cull from those experiences that which was most extraordinary, most telling and true. Over the years, she had somewhat disabused herself of this complex. She had begun to take careful notes, had devised methodologies and systems that allowed her to capture and retain the information she needed.

But in her mind, it was still, always, her greatest weakness. If she had a better memory, who knew what she could have created? She would never be able to write a memoir, for example. She didn't remember her childhood with enough detail, and during that time in her life, she had taken no notes. When she read Nabokov's memoir, she was filled with admiration and jealousy. Oh, to be able to recall every detail with such specificity. She made peace with not being able to do this, and then she lost her sense of peace about it. That was how it was with the great struggles.

And now, her memory was being called into service in a new and different way: to save her most recent book. She'd been working on it for over four years now, had written hundreds of pages. She never spoke about what she was working on but now that the manuscript was gone, she had started to mention certain things about it to Ben. She said that there were three different narrators. That the first narrator's passages had been easy to resurrect but the other two were proving more difficult. It was, she told him once, late at night, the best thing she had ever written.

In light of her difficulties, Ben tried to shoulder whatever he could around the house. He handled most of the cleaning and cooking, had taken over dealing with the insurance company. He now knew that you had to file the items you lost under one of sixty-five categories. You also had to list the amount you believed each category was worth. "Hardbound Books," for example. That was one of the categories. At first he thought it was going to be difficult, but once he got into the rhythm of the work, it wasn't so bad.

After he filed the lists with the insurance company, the claims adjuster called, said he would be out to visit the property in the next week. On the phone he told Ben they were lucky that their house had wood walls. Unlike drywall, wood did not retain smoke after a fire and wouldn't need to be ripped out and replaced. Ben decided to go tell Ada about this, after he hung up. He thought it was encouraging news and might cheer her up a bit, but she seemed unmoved.

"Can we go for a walk?" she said. "We'll wear masks. I need to get out of this house."

It felt good to move his legs, but being outside made Ben feel almost more trapped than he did inside. With each in-breath, you tasted the smoke. It did not get better, if you were in one area or another, because it was everywhere, always. They headed toward their favorite trailhead, which was just down the road from them, and ran alongside Dorado Creek, a tributary of the Harde. Harriet and George knew where they were going and, despite the smoke and the altered landscape, they seemed eminently comfortable. At one point, George paused and jauntily peed on the trunk of a charred tree that he was accustomed to marking.

As they neared the trailhead, Ben saw a man approaching from below. He was wearing an orange shirt and, at first, Ben thought he might be a worker with the utility company. But as they got closer, it became clear that it was James Thompson. He was also walking his dog, a big chocolate lab. James was a winemaker who consulted for many different wineries in the foothills. He lived on a huge property at the top of Rose Mountain, which he'd bought from Hector, one of Ben's old friends and one of the first cannabis growers in the area. Hector and Ben had been close back in the day but Ben hadn't spoken to him since he'd left Rose County. In the intervening years, James had put in a new sixty-foot dam on the property, which provided him with his own small, private reservoir. Ben saw him from time to time in the neighborhood, and sometimes at growers' meetings. He was a bit haughty but overall Ben found him to be a nice person.

"How are you guys?" James said, as the dogs greeted each other. Ben noticed he was maskless, despite the polluted air.

"I'm still in shock," Ben said. "How are you? Is everything OK up by you?"

"Yeah, didn't touch us, thank god. I saw the whole thing happen. Watched it all from Rose Mountain. Wanted to be here in case I needed to protect the property."

"And things are OK up there?"

"Yeah. You know, we're way up there at the top of the mountain so I watched it come right across the rim of the canyon. I could see everything. I actually watched your barns burn."

"You did?" Ben said. "What did it look like?"

"Um, you know," he said. "Like barns burning."

"Right."

"They're saying it was some guy with a flat tire on his trailer."

"I heard they were still investigating," Ada said.

"Yeah, as they should," James said. "I don't believe the flat tire thing. Up in the hills like that? You know what goes on up there. I bet it was some guy shooting at a transistor with his rifle. Probably some transients."

He pulled his dog toward him. The dog seemed relieved to be separated from Harriet and George, who had been subjecting him to a thorough inspection.

"Well, I should get back for dinner," he said. "Hope everything works out. Feel free to call if you need anything."

They nodded and continued on toward the trailhead, heading into the ravine. Things were not burnt so bad down here by the creek. Yellow pines grew along the rocky banks, with their broad branches and resilient red bark. There were shaggy gray pines here too, their huge cones hanging like brown pineapples. Ben's hip was feeling a bit funny so he stopped under one of the gray pines to stretch it out. Ada stood next to him, looking out at the creek. There was a sandy island at its center, the water breaking around it.

"Was that a little weird?" Ada said.

"What do you mean?"

"The way he talked about watching our barns burn."

"I think he did watch them burn."

"It just seemed like a weird thing to say."

"In what way?"

"Like, he was rubbing it in or something."

"I don't think he was doing that," he said. "I think he's just an awkward guy. I don't think he meant anything by it."

"Something about it felt off."

She waited for a moment, then said: "Ah, whatever. Maybe I'm just all messed up."

He looked down at Ada, standing beneath the pine. He thought again about the evacuation, about failing to double-check with her about the manuscript. His dear Ada, she didn't deserve this.

He wasn't sure what James Thompson's intentions had been but Ada almost always had a good read on others. When her fresco novel was nominated for the award, the judges said it demonstrated "a discerning yet openhearted awareness." It was the same thing he'd noticed when he met her: she was critical, but not in a way that closed her down. She was always on the hunt for stories, always eager to learn. When he first brought her to Rose County, she was immediately enamored by it. They went to the river, scrambled down a ravine choked with granite boulders. Randomly, they met a bighorn biologist that day, who had parked at a turnout behind them. Ada struck up a conversation with the guy, pulled out stories from him that Ben would never have suspected were there.

It was Ada, also, who initially suggested they move up here. Ben didn't need much convincing. He had always wanted to live in the mountains. Even though he'd been raised in Oakland, every summer, his family had camped throughout the Sierras. It was a mythic place to him, a perfect country. And so, together, they began to craft a plan: Ben would grow cannabis and she would write and take on odd jobs. The whole process took some time—they needed to save money and Yoel's birth delayed things—but eventually they bought the farm and moved up to Natoma.

Between the two of them, they had always been able to maintain a sense of levity. It was the trick to their marriage. Years ago, when Ada received word of the nomination for her novel, Ben had been visiting Andrew in Talinas. She'd tried calling him but he was not near his phone at the moment and didn't pick up. So she emailed him, instead. She sent a link to the press release and then wrote, "I fucking rule."

He thought this was the funniest thing and, to celebrate the nomination, he got her a pen engraved with the phrase "I Rule." She still kept it on top of her bedroom dresser. Over the years, in both good moments and bad ones, he would sometimes remind her that she ruled. And this was what he did now, standing on the banks of the creek, gazing down at his wife, luminous in the pine-filtered light.

She looked up at him. Her mouth was covered by the mask, but by the way wrinkles were gathering around her eyes, he could tell she was smiling. She put her arm between the crook in his elbow.

"Oh, Ben," she said. "What a nightmare."

IT RAINED THE next night, quietly, waking no one. In the morning, when Ben went outside with his coffee, the air smelled like a wet campfire. Clouds moved quickly across the sky, wind blew in from the west. A day or two of rain in June or July was not uncommon. Normally, he would not be too excited about it, because it automatically triggered the need to spray for powdery mildew, but today, looking around at the smokeless skies, he was filled with relief.

Ben and Yoel spent the morning feeding and checking in on the animals. Two feral chickens had shown up on the property the other day. They were skinny and could fly well enough to get over the fence that enclosed the coop. They clearly wanted to join the flock but the other chickens were not interested. Whenever one of them tried to go inside the coop, the flock would cluck relentlessly at it and peck it until it left. Still, the feral chickens did not give up. They hung around, kept trying to befriend the other chickens. Ben admired them for this. Yoel did too.

"Those guys are survivors," he said.

After Ben and Yoel had finished with the morning chores, they decided to drive into town for supplies. Yoel worked in the afternoon and evening, but in the morning, he had been helping out Ben with things around the farm. He knew how to do pretty much everything, had worked alongside Ben from the time he could walk all the way into high school. Perhaps it was due to the chaos of his mother losing her manuscript, but in recent days, he had not seemed particularly irritated by Ben's presence. Ben, for his part, had decided to let Yoel take the lead. There were things they needed to talk about, things Ben wanted to say to him, but he didn't want to rush it. He was glad that, so far, it had been easy to work together. There had been no major fights, though there had been some silences.

That morning, for example, as they drove down Mountainview, second cup of coffee in hand, they said little. Now that the smoke had cleared, the fire's impact had become even more evident. Blue oaks, once festooned in green mistletoe, had been charred from crown to trunk. Gone was the toyon and the coffeeberry and the whiteleaf manzanita. Gone the lichen on the slabs of clean mountain slate. Gone the tawny color of the hills and the chamise and the late-blooming lilies. There were no more maidenhair ferns, no more beds of bear clover. Everything had a dreary, exhausted look to it.

In Natoma, however, things seemed more or less normal. Power had been restored there days ago and almost all businesses were open. On Center Street, a man in a bucket hat was standing outside the Cash for Gold store, biting one of his nails. A couple walked hand in hand past the movie theater. And on the pedestrian overpass, a series of tattered banners had been strung up, with anti–fossil fuel slogans. Ben had been seeing more of these recently. One of the banners appeared to have a kind of sign-off. It read: BROUGHT TO YOU BY THE SAN ANDREANS.

They went to the co-op first, and then drove over to the hardware store. Ben wasn't going to replace everything he had lost in the toolshed in one go, but there were some basic things he needed to go about his regular day-to-day work on the farm. He grabbed a circular saw, a posthole digger, a hammer and nails, a drill and screws, wire cutters, and pruners. An older man in a mustache rang him up. The total was going to be eye-popping. As Ben was watching it climb, a younger man emerged from the back and recognized Yoel.

"Holy heck," he said. "Hi!" Then he turned to the man who had been ringing them up: "Ron, do you know who this is?"

Ron looked up at Yoel, took in his face for a moment, shook his head.

"This guy is like a celebrity," the young man said. "He's a Hollywood . . . He hangs out with . . . What is it you do again?"

"I work in development."

"Ah."

Yoel seemed to realize this needed clarification.

"We work with writers to develop scripts and then get them sold," he said.

"I see. Well, cool man. I love those videos you make. I watch every one. Me and my buddy, Paul, we love them. They are so funny. I know you have a lot of followers so you probably don't notice."

Yoel nodded.

"You remember me?" the young man said. "I was two grades below you. But we were in leadership together. You always sat in the back, with the other older kids. I remember when you came up with that idea for the Rubik's Cube Dance, where everyone had to dress as a different color. It didn't really work out but I thought it was a great idea. I always thought you were going to do something cool."

"The issue was they wouldn't let people trade their clothes," Yoel said, "to solve the Rubik's Cube."

"Right, that was the problem. So stupid. It was such a good idea."

"Remind me your name."

"Jeremy. Laramie."

"Jeremy Laramie?"

"Yep."

"Got it. Good to see you."

He was tall and skinny, with a sweep of rye-colored hair that hung down across his forehead. Ben thought back to what Andrew had said on the boat about how Yoel had been forced to weather the stigma of his arrest in high school. But this kid seemed to have only the brightest opinions of Yoel. Ben was relieved to see that.

"You come back to see your folks?" Jeremy asked Yoel.

"Yeah, just came back for the week."

"Holy heck, that was some week."

"Yeah, it was um . . . not what I expected."

"You guys are buying a lot of stuff, huh?"

"We lost our toolshed," Yoel explained.

"Oh shoot," he said. "Oh man. Here I am blabbering away and . . . I'm so sorry."

"It's OK," Ben said.

"I wish I could give you a discount or something but I just started here."

"I can give them a discount," Ron said.

"Oh wow, that's great," Jeremy said. "I'm really glad to be able to offer that to you."

"I'm offering it to them," Ron said.

"I'm really glad we can offer that," Jeremy said. "It is a sincere honor. Ron, what's the code for that so I know for next time?"

"You don't get the code."

"OK, cool, no worries, I'll get that another time," he said. Then he turned back to Yoel: "Anyway, great to see you, dude."

"Yeah, you too," Yoel said.

"Will you be around for a while?"

"Yeah, I'm going to stay a bit longer, help them out."

"Well, maybe I'll leave you my number then. Or I could just DM you. Yeah, I'll leave you my number, cause I don't think you follow me back, but anyway, sometimes I know about, like, a party or something. Not cool parties, not like the parties you probably go to. Obviously, this is Natoma, but since you're here . . ."

"Yeah, sounds good."

Ron finished ringing them up, tacking on a 35 percent discount, a significant break given the size of the purchase. For a moment, Ben considered asking if he could pick up a few more things on the discount, but that seemed over the top. No need to spend too much right now. Better to wait until they got the insurance reimbursement. When Ron handed him the receipt, Ben held it in the air.

"Thank you for this," he said. "It's very generous of you."

"Good luck," Ron said.

"**WHAT ARE THE VIDEOS** you do?" Ben asked Yoel when they were back in the car. In front of them, a woman was trying to stuff a bike into the back of her hybrid SUV.

"It's just me talking into the camera," he said. "It's just dumb stuff. I don't know. Comedy."

"Is it for work?"

"No, it's just my own thing, my own profile."

"I'd like to see them," Ben said.

"Yeah, OK, maybe," he said.

"Does Mom watch them?"

"Sometimes."

"Do you not want me to see them?"

"I don't know. I don't care, I guess."

"You don't have to show me them."

"I just don't think you'll like them."

"Why do you say that?"

"I don't know," Yoel said. Then he cleared his throat, looked straight ahead. "Should we get going?"

THAT NIGHT, with Ada's help, Ben created a profile for himself, and began watching the videos. They were mostly about Yoel's day-to-day life, little dispatches he made while he was at work, or out walking around his neighborhood in Los Angeles. They were witty, confessional, self-possessed—his natural storytelling ability on display. Sometimes he would do bits, different characters, like this one about an irate stage dad whose kids keep getting cast as squirrels. Ben was reminded of the variety show Yoel had put on when he was a little kid. He'd called it "The Johnny Pickerson Show." There was something of that kid in these videos. After Ben finished each one, he sent Yoel a message complimenting him on it and saying what he liked about it. At a certain point, Ada made him put on headphones so she could focus on her book. After about a half hour of watching, Yoel knocked on the door.

"Hey, Dad," he said.

"I'm watching the videos!" he said.

"I know."

"I feel like a celebrity has just walked into my room."

"Just so you know, those messages you're writing, you're posting all of those to your public profile."

"I thought I was sending those to you."

"No, you're reposting all the videos on your profile, with the messages you're writing to me."

"Oh shoot," he said. "I just meant to send it to you."

"I know."

"How do I send them just to you?"

"Here, I'll show you," his son said, sitting down on the foot of the bed. "Give me your phone."

WICK CAME TO INSPECT their well the next day. He had waited out the fire with his friend, Alfonso, who lived on Rose Mountain, and had dug firebreaks around his whole property. Wick ran a pest control business, but he knew about many other things, including wells. Ben had three wells on the property, which drew water from the granite below, ancient snow melt. He led Wick over to the first one, which was next to the coop. Yoel joined them. Wick was wearing a tie-dye T-shirt and his hands were smudged with motor oil. He walked slowly, with a slight limp, the result of a forklift accident he sustained in his forties, while working in a wine cellar.

"Man, it's good to see you guys," Wick said as they walked over to the well. "Yoel, I haven't seen you in forever. I'm glad you're here to help out your old man."

"Yeah," Yoel said. "Crazy times."

"Very crazy," Wick said. "The craziest thing, actually, was that woman at the Save Mart."

"What woman?"

"You didn't hear about this?" Wick said. "A woman down at the Save Mart, she won a million dollars on one of the California Scratchers. Thirty-dollar ticket and won a million dollars. Two days before the fire."

"Where is she now?"

"Shit, I don't know. Probably in Tahiti or something. I saw the whole thing happen. Right at the Save Mart next to my new spot. It just goes to show you that you don't know what the fuck will happen to you. That's the credo I live by. Also, don't sweat the small stuff. That's another one of my credos. There's a lot of misperceptions out there about me, you know what I mean? In large part, I think, because I do pest control. But you can't worry about correcting misconceptions. Misperceptions. It's all about just taking it nice and easy and letting it rip, you know? Your dad knows what I mean."

Ben didn't entirely follow but he nodded. They were at the well now, and Wick had begun to walk around it.

"You want to look for any melted wiring or PVC," he said. "Make sure the bladder hasn't busted here or anything. You get that sample like I told you?"

"Yeah," Ben said.

"Yeah, so you're going to want to drive that into town today, to Premio Supply. They're open. Everything's open in town. It's only Mountainview that got fucked up."

When Wick had finished inspecting all three wells, they walked over to look at the burned outbuildings. The rain had turned the rubble into a gray-black slurry.

"Shit," Wick said. "Yeah, so they just diverted the whole thing around your house, didn't they?"

"That's what it looks like," Ben said.

"But you didn't find any flares over on the other side of the property?"

"Not yet. I think the sheep grazing helped protect us too."

"Damn," Wick said, looking down at the burned structures. "Ada's whole office. Are you going to rebuild?"

"No. At least not now. Maybe if we get some insurance money in, but I don't know when that will be. The guy's coming over tomorrow. We just got power back a couple of days ago."

Wick sighed, rubbed his gray stubble. His fingers were thick and flattened, as though they'd been hammered out.

"I want to help you guys," he said. "What can I do to help?"

"You already helped us, with the wells."

"What about, like, a stress animal? I've got all these dogs at my house."

"That's OK."

"There's nothing you need help with, Dad?" Yoel said.

Ben fanned himself with his shirt.

"Well, after the claims guy comes, I need to clean up all this stuff," he said, gesturing at the debris. "But I need to do a spray in the next few days too."

"Let me clean this up," Wick said. "I'll take some time off to do it."

"Are you sure?"

"Yeah, I can borrow Alfonso's dump truck."

"Do you have protective gear? You know, there's metals and stuff in here."

"Oh, I've got the gear."

"OK, well, that would be great, cause the longer this sits here the more it leaches into the soil."

Wick nodded and then scratched something on the back of his arm.

"Son of a bitch," he said. "The mosquitoes at my new place are fucking crazy."

THEY SET UP a temporary office for Ada in the old computer room. She would go in there in the morning, but then she'd come out a couple hours later and spend the rest of the day in the garden. She had always gardened but over the last couple of weeks, she had expanded the range of her gardening significantly: the driveway was now lined with flowers, as was the fence line near the front gate. Every day she watered and pruned, blew the oak leaves off the stone paths in the yard. This was how Ben knew she'd stopped writing, when he heard her fire up that leaf blower. Multiple times a day she was leaf blowing the yard. It was obviously excessive but, he thought, maybe a part of her process. If she needed to mourn through leaf blowing, so be it.

The day the claims adjuster arrived, Ada was in town picking up more starts for the garden, so Ben greeted him alone.

His name was Ronaldo—"like the soccer player," he told Ben. He walked around the property with a clipboard and his phone, taking pictures and making notes. He had tables that said how much an outbuilding was worth, based on its size. He had the list of their belongings that had burned. Unfortunately, he explained, because their policy could only pay out a certain percentage of money for outbuildings and landscaping, their settlement would be capped at around ten thousand dollars.

"That's it?" Ben said. "But our homeowner's covered six hundred thousand."

"Yes, but your homeowner's was for the house. Those are outbuildings. Your coverage, minus the deductible, for outbuildings is ten thousand."

"But those are old buildings."

"I know," Ronaldo said, "but they're outbuildings."

"With the cost of lumber these days, I mean, we wouldn't get close to rebuilding those for ten thousand."

"I'm afraid this is what the policy affords you," Ronaldo said. "You're welcome to dispute this but I'm telling you, the policy is very clear."

Ben stood there, thinking about what they owed on the loan this year. The insurance money would pay for the replacement of his tools but not much more. He wouldn't even be able to build a smaller shed—at least not this year. He'd have to store most of his stuff in the chapel. Still, it was better to keep producing than abandon the vineyard at this point. The grapes would be their only income for who knew how long—whenever Ada finished with her rewrite.

Ronaldo seemed to be able to tell that Ben was making some calculations in his head. Standing in their kitchen, he sighed and wiped sweat from his brow.

"If anything comes up with the house in the next two years," he said, "you should definitely contact me. You've got two years to file additional claims."

Prior to leaving, Ronaldo gave them advice on how to prevent erosion on the hill above the house. He had a lot of experience seeing that kind of thing, he said. To start, they shouldn't scatter grass or barley seed. Most if not all of the erosion would come after the first rain, so seeds would have no time to germinate and stabilize the soil. Seeding the slope would only lead to high fire risk the following year, when those plants dried out in the summer months. Creating a barrier with hay bales wasn't great either. Silt from the hillside would build up behind the bales and eventually push them downhill and then they'd have wet hay bales in the house on top of the silt too. No, the best thing to do was to use check dams to divert the flow of the debris. You couldn't stop the first flush, Ronaldo said, but you could redirect it away from the house. He recommended that Ben build three of these contraptions on the hillside, each one spaced twenty feet apart. He didn't need to do it right away, but it should be taken care of before the winter rains.

When Ronaldo was finished explaining all of this, Ben walked him back out to the driveway. Now that the smoke had cleared, the weather was pleasant and bright. All around them the summer vines shimmered greenly.

"Your defensible space was good," Ronaldo said, "but don't let up on that."

"I've got the sheep, that helps," Ben said.

"Because it'll be back. We're seeing areas burn and then burn again."

"I know."

"It's kind of like a driverless car. It's just going to eat up whatever is still in its path, and there's still fuel out there. You get an ignition somewhere, it could sweep through again."

Ben nodded.

"I'll be back in touch with that e-filing," Ronaldo said. "You should get the loss of use payment within a week. I'm going to do my best to get everything processed as soon as possible."

He paused and looked out at the vineyard, and beyond that, the gently sloping hills, folding in on one another, the burn scar running downhill, wide and black.

"Good luck up here," he said. "I always wanted to grow grapes myself."

4

BEFORE THE HECHTS bought their farm, it had been owned by a cattle rancher, and before that a Cornish miner, who had worked at the Yellow Daisy Mine and, allegedly, had a gambling problem. Farther back than that, there was no record. The Mountainview area in general, was unexceptional—similar, as far as the townspeople were concerned, to many of the other winding roads in the region. If you were to ask one of them about it, they would probably have nothing to say. Or, if they said anything, it was likely: "Isn't that where Lucia's Rock is?"

Lucia's Rock was round and smooth and owed its name to a young Italian immigrant who used to have a cottage nearby. Legend had it that Lucia made a deal with the devil to preserve her good looks for fifty years. The nature of the deal was such that Lucia had to kill every lover she slept with. Once a year, she would take home a new man, and then kill him by pushing him down a trapdoor and into a basement filled with sharp blades. For decades after her death, the cottage was believed to be haunted. Anyone who moved in there began to suffer from a variety of ill effects: chronic insomnia, sickness, a sense of prevailing restlessness. These days, the house remained unoccupied, though there was a rumor that a large grower from Lodi was considering buying the property, ripping the fields, planting grapes. People in the town shook their heads when they learned this. Only a person from far outside the county would ever consider doing something like that.

But in another sense, the Lodi grower's potential purchase was unsurprising. Good grape-growing acreage in Rose County had become increasingly valuable. The region was "up and coming," so to speak, drawing the attention of tastemakers who otherwise rarely strayed far from the wine country or the Central Coast. Many people had grown grapes in the region during the Gold Rush, but they had almost entirely gone out of business in the twentieth century, due to phylloxera or prohibition or lack of demand. Most of the vines on these properties were removed to make room for peaches or walnuts or grazing land, but some were simply abandoned. With the surge of interest in the region, growers were reviving these abandoned vineyards and planting new ones.

When Ben and Ada first bought the farm, it already had an acre of Primitivo vines, an old planting from the turn of the century. Even when he had primarily been cultivating cannabis, Ben had always harvested their one acre of Primitivo. The vines produced low yields, but high-quality grapes. Natoma's growing season consisted of warm sunny days and cool nights, thanks to the winds that blew in off the slopes of the mountains in the evenings. This temperature variation allowed the grapes to mature slowly. Also, because the soil was rocky, the vines were forced to grow deep roots in search of water. These factors led to fruit that possessed concentrated flavors and healthy levels of acidity. An oft-noted truism in viticulture: vines that struggle produce better grapes.

Several years ago, Ben began planting additional acreage, experimenting with Rhône-based varietals, which he'd been told did well in the foothills. More recently, he'd planted the new Gamay blocks. He'd been encouraged to plant Gamay by Sloan Howard, Ada's friend from college. Sloan sold enology products to wineries throughout the region and was very well networked. She said Gamay was becoming increasingly popular and, like the Rhône-based varietals, did well in the foothills. Sloan was also the person who had initially connected Ben to his buyers, two large producers who sourced grapes from all over the state.

When he finally had the chance to walk through the vineyard after the fire, he was relieved to see that most of the vines were in good shape. The Primitivo lot was the one exception to this, but the damage there was only on the edge of the parcel. A couple other growers in the region were reporting similar outcomes: their vineyards had acted as natural firebreaks. This was not true of everyone, however, and he had heard that two vineyards west of Ponderosa had been badly burned. He wondered if this was because they had not yet begun irrigating for the season. He had started irrigating about a week before the fire, when some of his vines had begun to show signs of water stress.

He spent some of Tuesday surveying the property and plants. Even though he'd been gone for a week, things were relatively under control. There was still a bit of forage on the hill but it was nearly time to move the sheep to the irrigated pasture. Out in the vineyard, bug pressure continued to be low, due to the dry spring and now, he suspected, the impact of the fire. His biggest concern was, of course, the smoke taint, but he would not be able to test for that until a couple of weeks before harvest. For now, all he could do was farm as though everything was OK, and hope for the best.

The following day, Wick came over with Alfonso's dump truck. He wore a white hazmat suit, goggles, and a P100 respirator that made him look like a giant housefly. Ben brought him a gallon jug of water from the house and a couple of energy bars. They chatted for a bit about Wick's new earbuds, which had a much better battery life than his old earbuds, he explained, and were perfect for days like today, when he was working alone.

"I'm always listening to pods when I work now," he said. "There's so much stuff out there. It's incredible. I love the true crime. The news. You can listen to any news you want. BBC, Japanese news."

After making sure Wick had everything he needed, Ben headed off to the tractor to begin his powdery mildew sprays. He spent the morning working his way through the first two blocks of Barbera. For preventative sprays, at this point in the year, he used a biofungicide derived from a beneficial bacterium, *Bacillus subtilis*. The Barbera in these blocks rested on a shallow quartz vein and usually produced little fruit for him. But this year they were looking particularly healthy. In the coming weeks, he would need to start dropping some fruit, along with any seconds: smaller bunches of grapes that formed a few weeks after the main clusters. Doing this helped the vines focus on ripening their most promising clusters, and led to higher-quality yields.

When he was finished with the second block, he stopped for lunch. Normally, he would walk into the woods a bit, take his break there, but all of the woods along the northern boundary of the property had burned through. Instead, he sat down on the edge of the burnt area, under a roasted oak tree, and unpacked his food: a salami sandwich, salt-and-pepper chips, and three plums for dessert. His ears were buzzing slightly from the vibration of the tractor. It was another pleasant day, the brunt of midsummer not yet upon them. While he ate, lizards and ants traversed an outcropping of quartz in front of him. And for several minutes, deeper in the forest, he watched two deer silently forage among the blackened pine trees. Ben inhaled through his nose. That normal forest smell—of moisture and decaying leaves and duff—was gone. Now it was something else: the muted smell of smoke and burnt wood.

After lunch, he sprayed blocks three and four of the Barbera, and then decided to call it a day. He drove the tractor back down to the edge of the Primitivo lot to check in on Wick. When he arrived, he found a second man in a white suit, goggles, and a respirator.

"I thought I'd help out for a bit," Yoel said, when he saw his father approaching.

"We just did our first dump run," Wick said, pulling out his earbuds.

Their voices were slightly muffled through the respirators.

"You didn't have work?" Ben asked.

"I do," Yoel said, "but I can finish it up later."

"You done?" Wick asked Ben. "Should we have a beer?"

Yoel took off his gear and walked back up to the house with Ben. Wick stayed behind to throw a tarp over the truck. After they had washed up, Ben and Yoel brought a six-pack out to the porch, sat down on the outdoor couch. Wick came up the hill a few minutes later. His face was streaked with sunscreen and he still had one of his earbuds in. When he made it to the porch, he exhaled, and pointed to the earbud.

"You hear about this with the hallucinogens?"

"What?" Ben said.

"Up in Dover," Wick said. "A man has been importing hallucinogenic drugs from Europe through the dark web."

"I don't know."

"I'm telling you, I'm just listening about it right now," he said. "What kind of beers we got here?"

"It's from the new brewery."

"Ah, I love that place."

Yoel handed Wick a beer and he took a seat next to them on an overturned produce box. Ben looked out at the horizon, to the spot where, almost two weeks ago, he had first seen the plume of smoke. Wick began explaining why he had so many dogs at his house. His brother, who lived in Ponderosa, had started volunteering for an organization that brought street dogs from Guatemala and placed them with American families. He'd persuaded Wick to foster the animals while the organization tried to find homes for them.

"I need to figure out something to do about it," he said. "Because it's way too many dogs to have in your house. My brother made it seem like they'd get adopted quicker."

"I might know someone in LA who wants one," Yoel said.

"Well, we've got seven to choose from. I'll send you pictures. They're cute dogs. But too many dogs, for me. It was a goddamn shit show getting them out during the evacuation. I mean, not as bad as you probably had it here."

"It's all a blur," Ben said. "I barely remember it."

For a moment silence fell, all three men lost in their recollections of the evacuation. Then Wick looked over at Ben.

"So what's the outlook with the insurance stuff?"

"Not good. Not enough."

"Shit."

They'd called one of Ada's cousins, who worked in insurance, and ran their policy by her. She'd confirmed Ronaldo's assessment. They would not get more than ten thousand. Without Ada's book, their financial picture was growing increasingly tricky. He and Ada had run the numbers a couple nights ago. With the loan repayments, property taxes, and their regular cost of living, they would just squeak by over the next couple of years. And that was assuming everything went well with the harvest.

"We'll be OK," Ben said. "We just need to have a good couple of years."

"What do you mean have a good couple of years?" Yoel said. "What happens if we don't do well?"

Ben put his hands into the straps of his suspenders.

"Well, we'd probably have to look into selling this place."

For the most part, he thought this was an unlikely outcome. He was confident that they would have a good harvest, and Ada seemed reasonably confident she could complete a manuscript soon.

Yoel seemed dismayed by this news.

"You'd sell the farm?" he said.

Ben was surprised to see concern on his son's face. He hadn't even considered that the idea might be upsetting to him. This farm? The farm that he used to complain about whenever he came up to visit? Ben figured he would have leapt at the prospect of selling it, would have encouraged them to downsize right now, why wait.

"Well, we don't want to," Ben said. "We'll see. We're getting way ahead of ourselves here."

"Would be a damn shame if you lost this place," Wick said. "Everything you did here."

Ben glanced from Wick to Yoel. He had said too much. There was no need for people to worry.

"I shouldn't have even mentioned it," he said. "We're not selling this place. We're going to make it work."

But neither of them seemed particularly reassured.

THAT FRIDAY, Wick told them, he was playing a set at the McEwan's annual Fourth of July party. They had turned the event into a fundraiser, were asking for donations for the volunteer fire department. At Wick's urging, the Hechts decided to go. Ben hadn't been to the McEwan's Fourth of July party in years. This one was going to be their last, Wick explained, because they were moving to San Diego to be closer to their daughter and her newborn. They had recently sold their vineyard to a woman from China who owned a lucrative scarf factory.

The McEwan property was located on a sandstone ridge-line, west of Natoma. They grew Rhône and Provence varietals, and their logo featured a badger. There was some long story about why it featured a badger but Ben couldn't remember it. The party took place on a patio behind the tasting room. There was a bar set up and a small stage with a mic and a keyboard. In the distance, a grove of walnuts and then the ridgeline of grapes. Nothing in this area had burned and the hills were golden, covered in matted dry grass.

The crowd at the party appeared to be a mix of locals and visitors. Ben saw two assistant winemakers he knew, as well as Abe Beringer, the editor of the local paper. Ada quickly found Suzy Greenwood, a friend of hers from Canasta, and the two of them headed over to the bar. Right after they disappeared, Connell McEwan got on stage and gave a brief speech about the fire. He said he was proud of the community for how prepared they'd been, and tremendously grateful to the firefighters who had somehow kept Natoma out of harm's way.

"Now, in honor of all that," he said, "in honor of life, I want you all to get very drunk and enjoy yourselves."

Everyone at the party already appeared to be doing this, which was good to see. There was a sense of collective release, a feeling that they had all been waiting for the moment when it was OK to express joy again and it had finally arrived, in the form of this drunken outdoor gathering. Even Ada's mood appeared to lift for the first time in weeks. She had been working a lot lately, rewriting a new draft. He wasn't sure how it was going, but he was hoping for the best. Today, at the party everything seemed like it might, again, arc toward its best possible outcome.

He grabbed a glass of wine for himself and Yoel and the two of them went looking for Wick. They found him off to the side of the party, sitting at a table, next to a man with a beret. This man was Alfonso Reyes, Wick's friend and songwriting partner. Alfonso had moved to Rose Mountain in the late eighties and converted his property into a wedding venue. Years ago, Ben had served on the county fair board with him. When Alfonso saw Ben, he gave him a hug, told him he was sorry about his barns.

"Thanks so much for letting us use your truck," Ben said.

"Oh, it's no problem," Alfonso said.

Wick pulled a ziplock bag of weed out of his vest pocket and began rolling a joint.

"I rarely use it," Alfonso said. "I bought it when I thought I was going to get into the compost business, but then the wedding stuff really started taking off."

"Did you lose any business from the fire?"

"We had to reschedule two things," Alfonso said.

Wick lit the joint he'd been rolling, took a hit, and handed it to Alfonso.

"I'm good, still full from that last one," he said.

The joint was then offered to Ben. He recognized the smell. It was Cinex, grown from the clone he'd given Wick years ago. He looked over at Yoel.

"Go ahead," Yoel said. "I don't care."

"I'm actually OK," Ben said. "I'm good with this wine."

Wick hit the joint and leaned back in his chair. Alfonso took his hat off and ran his hand through his hair.

"You hear the fair was postponed?" he said. "Till early August."

"I did hear that," Ben said.

"We miss you on the board. Would you ever consider coming back?"

"I don't know," he said. "Been real busy at the farm."

Ben loved the fair but he had no interest in joining the board again. The board commissioner was an old man named Robert Busch, who Ben couldn't stand. He took frequent trips to France and insisted that every board dinner be served on white tablecloths. The board members spent all their time shooting down his ideas, to preserve the quality of the fair, while convincing him that, in fact, his ideas were not being shot down.

"Sure," Alfonso said. "Well, maybe next year you could come back and at least help out with the fruits and veggies contests again. You were so good at that."

"No one runs a fruits and veggie contest like my man," Wick said.

Ben smiled. "I'll think about it."

The conversation shifted toward the fair's postponement. Alfonso said almost all of the fair's entertainers and judges had been able to adjust their schedules. So the show would go on more or less as planned. People were particularly excited about the wheelbarrow contest this year. It was going to be the seventy-fifth anniversary of the contest, and with a victory, Reggie Pyne had the chance to move into second place on the all-time leaderboard.

"He has a knack for turning the corners," Alfonso said. "That's where he really distinguishes himself."

At a certain point, Wick looked down at his watch and said he should probably get on stage. He unclipped his guitar case, which was covered in stickers, including one that said, only, "Futures," and pulled out his instrument.

"I think I'm just the right amount of stoned to go on stage," he observed, and wandered away.

Moments later, he was in front of the microphone, greeting everyone.

"I'm glad to have played this party for the past few years," he said. "What I like about it is the McEwans give me all the wine I want and I get to play in front of this pretty vineyard. I once slept in this vineyard in my pickup truck when my girlfriend and I were fighting. I was doing mushrooms too often, that was what the fight was about. Her points were very legitimate. Anyway, that's a story for another time, probably. This is a song from my new album, which I recorded in Big Sur about a year ago."

The song was about standing in a post office line. Alfonso bobbed his head as Wick began to play. Yoel stood up and walked over to the bar to get another glass of wine. Ben watched as a few younger people approached him, led by Jeremy Laramie. Yoel seemed pleased to see him. Off in the distance, Ben took in the great granite batholith, rising up toward a warm blue sky. Even with the music, he could hear snippets of the conversation between Yoel and the other young people.

At one point, they started talking about the Bookery Café in town. Yoel told them how he had really wanted to work there, when he was younger, because he was trying to save up money for a cross-country road trip. He'd long had this idea for this incredible monthslong journey he was going to take, where he'd buy a cheap sedan, take off with his two best friends, and just see the country. One night he told his parents how he wanted to apply for a job at the Bookery, but they didn't think it was a good plan. He asked them why—didn't it make sense for him to start working and saving for his trip now? To which his mother replied, "Yoel, you're in sixth grade."

A classic Yoel story. Ben found himself chuckling.

AFTER A COUPLE SONGS, Wick called Alfonso up to the stage, and he positioned himself behind the keyboard. Wick then spoke, at length, about how he had initially met Alfonso online, on a forum for local musicians, and how the first time they had hung out, Alfonso had invited him over to his house and introduced him to his OP-1 synthesizer, a truly astonishing instrument, which could make your voice sound like a wind chime, among many other things, and which Wick really recommended for electronic musicians who were just starting out, because it allowed for a lot of musical exploration and also retained a high resale value, in case you decided you wanted to get rid of it. The audience clapped politely after this detail-rich introduction.

Ben enjoyed seeing the two of them perform. It had been a while since he'd been to one of Wick's shows. Wick was so at ease up there, always had been. Ben admired that. Their sound was sort of part–folk music, part–spacey video game soundtrack. Wick had told him earlier that they usually performed with a drummer these days, but that the McEwan's party called for a more stripped-down set. At one point, Ada and Suzy Greenwood walked over and joined Ben at the table. Suzy appeared to have taken Connell McEwan's edict quite seriously. She was slurring her words and kept asking if they were going to be serving brisket.

"I thought they said they'd have a brisket here?" she said. "Didn't they say that?"

Apparently, Suzy Greenwood also needed to head home within the next hour to meet her brother-in-law, who was driving down from Arcata. Ada proposed that the two of them go for a walk.

As Suzy teetered away, Ada leaned in and whispered in Ben's ear, "I think I'm going to have to drive her home."

"How is she already so drunk?" he said. "This is record time for her." Ada smirked, punched his arm.

She came back five minutes later and told Ben she was indeed going to take Suzy home.

"I can do it," Ben said.

"No, you stay here," she said. And then she nodded toward the stage: "Tell Wick he's a star."

Shortly after Ada left, Wick and Alfonso announced a break, and walked back over to the table where Ben was sitting. Moments later, Yoel, Jeremy, and two others—a young man and a young woman—came over to the table too. The young man wore a Rose County Fire T-shirt. The young woman was wearing jeans and dangling red earrings in the shape of cartoon devils.

"Hi, Mr. H.," Jeremy said. "These are my buddies Halle and Paul. We just wanted to say hi to these guys. I mean, say hi to you, too. There's—"

"Paul Brinkers," the young man said, holding out his hand to Wick. "Owner of Brinkers Bar."

"Brinkers Bar?" Alfonso said. "Where's that?"

"It's in town. Just opened this year. I've heard of you guys. I loved the last song you played. So mournful and sweet and yet, still upbeat."

"It reminded me of that song about lighthouses," Halle said. "What's the name of that song?"

She took out her phone to look it up.

"Oh shit, these fucking passcodes," she said. "Nevermind."

"Passcodes?" Yoel said.

"I set all these child locks so I wouldn't waste my life on the internet, but I can never remember the codes."

Paul turned back to Wick and Alfonso.

"Anyway, we've already had the Red Dahlias come play, the Juggernauts. I'm talking to some major players in SF. Going to start having really big talent out there on the regular. I want us to be a big-time tour stop for bands moving through California."

"Forgive him," Halle said. "He thinks he's Bill Graham."

"You guys should come play," Paul said. "Here's my card. We can talk terms any time."

"OK, interesting," Wick said.

He had his ziplock bag of weed out again, was rolling a new joint.

"I'm a songwriter myself too," Paul continued. "I play guitar, keys."

"He's really talented," Jeremy said. "I can vouch for it. He performed, like, a thirty-minute experimental song in high school."

"A lot of it was silence," Paul admitted. "But yeah."

Wick lit his joint, leaned back in his chair, puffed it thoughtfully.

"Well, OK, man, right on," he said. "We're pretty busy right now, I think. Pretty booked up with stuff, but we'll take this card and . . . yeah, thank you."

"Excellent," Paul said. "Call me any time."

Wick passed the joint over to Alfonso. Then he turned to face the young people.

"Out of curiosity," he said, "are any of you interested in adopting a dog?"

"THEY SEEM LIKE a nice crowd," Ben said. They were driving home along Cold Springs Road, windows down, the cool night air streaming in.

"Sure, yeah," he said. "Halle's nice. She works in the cellar at Michael Deliso."

"Oh really?"

"Yeah, she's the assistant winemaker."

"Impressive."

"Yeah, though apparently Deliso is an asshole and drunk all the time."

"Eesh."

The windshield was dirty, reflective in moonlight. Ben tried to clean it with the wiper fluid but there wasn't any left.

"You know," Yoel said, "I don't mind if you smoke pot."

"Really? Cause I just remember the last time you were back, how you got upset when I was smoking with Peter Giroud. At that picnic. A couple of summers ago."

"No, I don't care. I was just annoyed about something else."

"About what?"

"It doesn't matter," Yoel said. "I'm just saying I don't care."

"OK."

"I want us to move forward."

Ben glanced over at his son and then back at the road. He sensed the moment hanging there.

"I know I did some selfish things," he started. "I'm sorry about what happened in LA."

"I really don't care about that," Yoel said.

"I get how it was connected, though, to what happened with the second grow."

Yoel seemed to be processing this admission, evaluating the integrity of it. Then he nodded.

"With the whole second grow," Ben continued, "if I could take that back—"

"I know."

"I just didn't think it through. When I got out, I don't know. I just wanted some money to get jump-started. Everything was falling apart at the farm in the time I was gone. And growing cannabis is what I knew how to do."

"I know," Yoel said again.

"I guess I thought: Well, this is a much smaller operation. I'm not applying for medical, like before. This is just a back-of-the-woods thing and the sheriff is on his way out. But of course I didn't think about you, I didn't think about your mom."

He paused.

"I didn't think about how hard those years were for you," he continued. "When I was away. I know it was hard."

"Dad, it's OK."

"I'm really sorry. And Martin too. I'll never—"

"We don't have to talk to about it." Yoel said. "I just want to move on."

Ben cleared his throat.

"OK," he said.

"OK, good," Yoel said.

There was a brief pause. Then Yoel opened up the glove compartment and took out the container of Swedish tobacco. He handed a packet to his father and put one in his own mouth.

"You like those?" Ben asked.

"Every once in a while," he said. "When I've had a drink or two."

5

STARTING IN THE 1980S, the cultivation of cannabis became a significant part of Natoma's local economy. This was not any kind of secret—everyone knew about it. Some growers would even plant "pencil patches" and donate all the profit from those grows to the local school district. By the late nineties, many growers had gone medical, with the passage of the state's new law, Proposition 215, but others remained underground. The first big farmers to go medical were the Strange brothers, a duo from Long Island, who lived over by Ponderosa. They helped many other growers begin their transition, including the Hechts, who up until 1998 were still selling their product illegally. Many in town viewed the growth of medical cannabis as a positive development. The wine industry didn't care much about grapes from Rose County in those days, and pot was a good cash crop.

But after the murder of He "Bean" Tran, in a botched robbery at his cannabis farm, a group of reactionary activists emerged. They were led by a man named Ed Wallace, who insisted that cannabis was the wrong type of economic development, that it brought crime and violence to the community.

In 1999, during Mary Lopez's first term as mayor, Wallace ran for sheriff and won. He spoke about cannabis during the campaign, but it was not until he was in office that he made his positions clear: pot had no place in the Rose County community. It endangered residents and caused disorder. His arguments were laced with racialized overtones. Tran had been killed, it later emerged, by a group of Vietnamese men from Sacramento, and Wallace began referring to these men as "gang members." He also often spoke about "illegals" wandering through the hills.

Because the state had failed to pass legislation clarifying Proposition 215, different municipalities interpreted the ordinance as they saw fit. Some unlawfully enforced prohibition, while others manipulated zoning restrictions to prevent grows. Wallace adopted an arrest-first policy, raiding properties and sorting out issues of prosecution later. This tactic did not lead to many successful prosecutions—Ben was one of the few growers who was ultimately convicted—but it did scare the community, and during those years, most people who wanted to grow cannabis moved elsewhere.

It was a divisive time in Natoma, and none of them looked back on it with fondness. Those who were around during the timber wars—the disputes with the Wisconsin-California Lumber Company—said it reminded them of that era. At dinners, people stayed away from the subject of the sheriff's office. There were several board of supervisor meetings that ended in shouting and profanity. At one point, Hector's girlfriend, Berenice, called for the sheriff himself to be prosecuted. A resistance grew, and by the time Ben was getting out of jail, Wallace was in the last year of his term, and it was clear he would not be reelected.

This was why, when Ben was released, he didn't think it would be dangerous to develop a small grow in the forest. Wallace was nearly gone and had clearly lost the support of the public. Plus, he had never pursued small grows. He had always hounded the bigger operations, people like Hector, the Mulehorns. Meanwhile families like the Reens, who had been growing a few pot plants on their property for years, went unbothered.

Of course, Ben had been wrong about all this.

Wick was the one to alert Ben that there were cops coming up Mountainview. It was summertime, and Yoel was home from college, working on an apple farm in Dover. They'd spent the morning driving around, looking at used bikes on Craigslist, because Yoel's old bike didn't fit him anymore. They'd stopped at an estate sale too, and Ben had surreptitiously picked up a porcelain doll, surprised Yoel with it. They were slowly getting back to their old, goofy rhythms. It was their first summer together since Ben had gotten out of Lompoc and things still felt a little odd, at times, a little uneasy. Every day it was getting better, though. They had plans, later that week, to host a pig roast in the backyard. Yoel had some friends from college coming up to visit from the Bay Area, and he wanted to show them a good old-fashioned Natoma party.

But that party would never happen. When Wick called about the deputies, Yoel was back in his room, and Ben was eating a chicken salad sandwich at the kitchen table. Wick said he'd been down at the Circle K and he'd seen at least five county cruisers heading up the hill. Ben didn't remember if he said anything else to Wick on that call, or if he even hung up the phone. The next thing he knew he was sprinting toward the bedroom, shouting Ada's name. He didn't find her, but Yoel came bursting in from the other room.

"What's happening?" he said.

Ben told him he needed his help and the two of them ran back toward the chapel. On their way there, they met Ada, who had heard Ben yelling, and come in from the front yard.

"Quick, follow me," he told her.

When they got to the chapel, Ben led them over to the sliding screen closet, next to the antique train tracks. Inside the closet were scores of turkey bags, stuffed with cannabis. Yoel and Ada just stood there, staring at the stash, but there was no time to explain anything. He tucked as many bags as he could under his arms and walked over to the back of the room, where he shoved aside a green velvet couch, and reached down to open the hatch.

The hatch led down a short staircase, into a tiny cement basement. Beneath the house there was a little spring and the previous owners had built a small, square cistern in this basement to tap the water from it. When it rained, water rolled down the hill and into that spring. This was why the yard next to the chapel was always green, and why the calla lilies grew there.

Ben no longer used the cistern, because it had an open top, and there were constantly animals crawling into it and dying. Rats and so forth. There was also arsenic from some previous chicken operation. But when they'd knocked down the old building that had been here, and built the chapel, he had converted the basement into a secret storage unit. There wasn't much down here now, just some metal shelving and a few grow lights. He didn't like to store weed down here long-term, because it was too moist and that moisture sometimes led to mold.

He guessed they had about five minutes to get all of this crop into the basement. After their initial shock, Ada and Yoel had begun to help him move the bags, and together, they made good progress. At a certain point, Martin, the dog, walked into the chapel. He seemed to sense the gravity of the moment, and jogged back and forth from the closet to the hatch with them every time they made a trip, as if he were protecting the product himself.

After a few minutes of moving bags, Ben remembered that there was cash in the closet in their bedroom. He asked Ada if she could go get it, told her it was in a shoebox, above the box of Haggadahs.

"There's cash?" she said. "In our bedroom? Above our Haggadahs?"

"Yes."

She gave him a look that he knew, in that moment, he deeply deserved. But then she hurried off toward the hallway. While she was gone, Martin ran over to the door and began barking. It was at this moment that he realized they were running out of time. If Martin was barking, that meant other people were on the property. The idea came to him in an improvisational flash—as ideas sometimes do, in states of extreme desperation—and at the time, it seemed quite sound.

"Go let him out," Ben told Yoel.

"Martin?"

"Yeah, let him out."

"With the deputies?"

"He'll distract them for a second."

"What? Are you sure?"

"Yeah, it'll be fine."

MARTIN WAS PART-PIT BULL, part–something else, and he barked at everything, despite being entirely harmless and, some might even say, a bit of a coward. Yoel and Ben had adopted him from a shelter in the Central Valley, after he'd been found in an old asparagus cannery, with ten of his siblings. This was the culmination of Yoel's long campaign to convince his parents that he deserved his own dog, which had included, among other things, a written contract outlining the ways in which he would care for the dog himself. As they drove home from the Central Valley, Yoel sat in the back seat with his new dog, petting him and falling in love. That night, when they got home, he named him Martin, after a character in a fantasy series he was obsessed with.

At the time of the raid, Martin was around eight years old, mellow, and suffering from the beginnings of what the vet told them was a degenerative spine condition. For the past several months, he had been on and off steroids, which seemed to help keep the pain down. He could still move well, but he was not as active as he used to be. Martin would never attack a visitor— he had never once done that—but he would certainly bark. Would a loud old pit bull slow the deputies down? Maybe not, but it was worth trying.

Yoel walked over to the door, opened it, and Martin ran outside. They could hear him standing on the porch in front of the chapel, growling, as Ben had expected he would do. The two of them began grabbing turkey bags again, rushing them down to the basement.

Within a few moments they had finished transporting everything. Ada arrived shortly thereafter and brought the shoebox down with her. They all exited the basement, and Ben hastily closed the hatch and pushed the couch back into place. This was all happening in less than a couple of minutes. He knew they were running out of time because the sound of Martin's barks were getting louder. And then, all of the sudden, they heard the scratch of Martin's nails on the wooden porch, a loud bark, and several gunshots.

The Hechts threw open the door and ran outside to find Martin bleeding out on the ground. In the distance, they could see a red-haired deputy, with his gun raised, screaming something about the dog charging him. Ben remembered the deputy had a sort of odd, unplaceable accent. The kind of accent that people have when they've spent a long time overseas. Everything happened so quickly in those moments. He remembered that deputy yelling at him in his odd accent. He remembered seeing Martin about ten yards or so from the porch, blood pooling around him. He remembered Ada screaming and Yoel screaming and he remembered stumbling toward Martin, and falling to his knees beside him.

The body heaving. Martin's eyes darting around in terror. Ben leaned over and the dog glanced at him, a brief touch of hope in his eyes, as if Ben might be able to save him. Martin was gasping for air, but in between the gasps, he licked Ben's hand. One lick, two licks. The most loving of creatures. The red-haired man was still yelling at him, or maybe it was the other deputies, but Ben couldn't really even make out the words. He was focused on Martin, trying to make him comfortable in his last moments. The dog gave one more lick, and then he was gone, no longer breathing.

Ben turned around, at that point, and found Yoel's eyes. He would always remember that look of shock.

THE NEXT THING he knew he was being pulled off the ground and handcuffed. He looked down at his shirt and saw that it was caked in blood and dust. He felt like he was outside of his body, his consciousness hovering somewhere above it all. Ada was handcuffed too, and Ben heard Wallace begin to read them their rights. He was a large man with sharp green eyes and a dumb goatee. As the world started to come back into focus, Ben realized he was surrounded by only county agents. The first time Wallace had raided the property, there had been federal agents. The deputies entered the chapel and began to sweep the house. Wallace told Ben they knew about his grow in the forest, that an agency helicopter had flown over it and taken photos. He remembered looking at Ada, watching her close her eyes as she heard this news, breathe deeply through her nose.

After they had hauled off Martin's corpse, they kept Ada and Ben outside for around a half hour of questioning. Then they were taken to the county jail. The whole time they were at the jail was excruciating. He was worried about Yoel, and what he'd seen. He was worried about going back to Lompoc.

And worst of all, the image of Martin kept coming back to him. The terror in his eyes, the feel of his dry tongue, those last licks.

Later that evening, they were finally released on bail, and Yoel came to pick them up. The look of shock from before had transformed into something else, something hard. Ben tried to talk to him, to ask him what happened to him while they were gone, but Yoel didn't want to discuss any of it. He just said that he'd called his friends, told them not to come up, that the pig roast was canceled. Ada was sitting in the front seat and she put her hand on Yoel's and he let it rest there. There were a million things going through Ben's head at that time but, more than anything, he remembered wanting to make this right for Yoel. Somehow he was going to do that, he thought. Whatever he needed to do, he would do it.

When they got back to the house, Yoel paused in the front yard. The sun was going down, the chill of a Natoma summer night descending. For a few moments, Yoel just stood there, in the cold, staring in the direction of where Martin had been shot. Then he turned around and faced Ben.

"It's always about you," he said, shaking his head. "I can't believe you would do this. After everything we went through, you decided you would grow again?"

"Yoel," he started, "I didn't—"

"I don't want to hear it. You did what you did."

"I didn't think this was a serious risk," Ben said.

Yoel gaped at him.

"It was a risk," he said, nodding over to where Martin had been shot. "Obviously it was a fucking risk."

"Maybe we can talk about this later," Ben said. "We're all in shock, I think."

"Yeah," Yoel said, pausing, weighing his words. "Yeah, I'm not so sure I want to do that."

A PRELIMINARY HEARING was set for a month later, in early September. Even though the deputies had never found his stash, the county claimed they had enough evidence with the aerial footage to press charges. Ben hired the same lawyer who'd handled his first trial. He was a kind man, an ex-hippie who had taken an oath of poverty and frequently defended cannabis cases. To their tremendous relief, he managed to get the charges dismissed, after convincing the judge that the initial helicopter surveillance, which had been conducted without a warrant, constituted an illegal search, and was therefore a violation of the Fourth Amendment. By the time the ruling came down, Yoel was already back at college, in the middle of his senior year. Ben tried to call him to talk to him about what had happened, but he didn't pick up. He left several messages, but Yoel never responded.

Ada was furious with Ben too. Those first few weeks after the raid, he was banished to the guest bedroom. She took a trip with Carole to Mendocino to "get some space." But ultimately, after many hours of conversation, they were able to work their way through things. She came to understand why he'd done what he'd done, even if she thought it was foolish. It was true that the fences on the property were sagging, the roads rutted. It was true that they needed money. He was an idiot for thinking this was the best way to make money, but she understood that he had felt trapped, felt he had no other way of getting back on his feet.

In the ensuing years, Yoel moved to Los Angeles and began building his life there. He got an internship at a production company. He settled into his first apartment, where his bedroom was a converted living room, through which his roommates had to walk to get to the kitchen. And he met Sally, at a Dungeons & Dragons game he coordinated with a few other nerdy friends. Yoel was the dungeon master. On some level, he seemed to be doing OK, but he was also working nonstop. At one point, he developed a stomach ulcer. Ben learned about all of this through Ada. Everything he learned about Yoel he learned through Ada.

Ben and Yoel, by that point, were barely in touch. Ben had tried apologizing many times—at his graduation, when they flew down there to help him move—and Yoel seemed to accept these apologies, but their relationship was never the same. There was an icy tautness to their interactions, a low-level hum of distrust. Sometimes Yoel would come visit them at the farm but usually these visits ended with Yoel asking Ben to go for "a walk" and then picking a fight with him. Eventually there was the summit with Andrew up at Bootjack Lake, and shortly after that, Ben and Ada's visit to Los Angeles. The visit where he cemented himself, in Yoel's words, as "careless and deeply self-involved." The phrase ran through him like a metal stake.

After the visit to Los Angeles, Ada tried to mediate another conversation between the two of them but that went nowhere. Ben began to lose track of his son. He was into this, into that. He wasn't ever happy with his job but he wouldn't leave it. Ada was always talking about how he might quit soon but he never did.

"It's a safe job," she said. "It's comfortable, and I think he wants that right now."

For his part, Ben tried to just carry on, keep himself busy. He threw his energy into the vineyard, planted the new blocks of Gamay. He acquired more animals. The life of the farm absorbed him. He accepted the idea that Yoel didn't want to talk to him. This was just the way it was, he told himself. We don't get to choose everything that happens to us in life.

THE WEDNESDAY AFTER the McEwan's party, Yoel went out with Jeremy, Halle, and Paul, to Paul's bar. And that weekend, he invited all of them over to the farm. They spent the afternoon lounging by the pool, drinking seltzer and reading. It was a hot summer Saturday, the sky popsicle blue and bright. Ben puttered around the house, avoiding the heat and listening to a podcast Wick had recommended about the history of backgammon. At one point, he made some iced coffees and brought them out to the pool. Yoel, Halle, and Paul gratefully accepted them, but Jeremy told him he didn't drink coffee anymore.

"It's better for everyone if I don't," he clarified. "Because of my excitable temperament."

In the late afternoon, when things cooled down, Ben spent some time pulling laterals in one of the sunnier south-facing Primitivo blocks. This helped the vine focus its energy on ripening its grapes, but one had to be careful, because if too much of the canopy was removed, the clusters could get burned by the sun. In general, he was happy with the fruit set in the undamaged sections of the Primitivo lot. Primitivo was known for producing "shot berries": small, poorly developed grapes scattered among the normal-sized grapes. Its fruit was also sometimes too tightly bunched, which created a more favorable environment for certain molds, and led to ripening problems. But neither of these issues were present in this year's crop: the berries were developing more or less evenly, and in loose clusters—a beautiful sight.

There were still no signs of veraison with the Primitivo or with the other varietals, but it might begin any day now. He had continued to drop any seconds and, very soon, he would begin fruit thinning. Across the property, this year's crop looked healthy and robust. He was going to have more grapes for sale than what Torneo and Golden Hill had ordered. When the berries were a little farther along, he would call them to see if they were willing to increase their order. They almost always were. If they didn't, he could look into a different potential buyer. Maybe Tony Fernando, out in Woodside. Tony sourced grapes from all over the state and Ben had sold to him a couple of times. He was fine to work with, though somewhat abrasive. He was very powerful in the industry and aware of that power. His LLC was named I Am God LLC. Ben had found that out when he first sold to him.

When he was finished in the vineyard, Ben walked up past the chicken coop and the irrigated pasture. He loved looking at the irrigated pasture in the summer, that crisp, cool splash of green in the middle of so much brown. The sheep seemed happy, foraging about while Eddie looked on. In the shade of the chapel, he paused and took a drink from the garden hose. Then he held the hose over his head, drenching his hair and scalp with cool water. He was about to head up to the house when he noticed Halle standing by the emu enclosure. She had put on a yellow jumpsuit over her bathing suit and she was carrying a large green tote bag. It seemed like she was on her way out.

"Funny-looking creatures," she said, when she saw him.

"Oh yeah," he said. "They're like dinosaurs."

He stood next to her and, for a moment, the two of them watched the emus bob around the enclosure.

"I still feel jacked up from that coffee," she said. "Might go home and like, organize my storage closet."

She smiled and Ben noticed that one of her front teeth was a different color than the other one, slightly dulled and yellow.

"What made you decide to get emus?"

"I don't know," he said. "I think I was just looking for something new. And I went to the Speedway to check out this fair they were having for solar equipment and started talking to the concession guy and he was telling me about raising emus and how friendly they are, so I just went for it."

"They're friendly?"

"Yeah, they're totally harmless. You want to meet them?"

Ben opened the fence gate and gestured for Halle to follow him. The emus jogged over, thinking Ben might have brought a snack. When they realized he didn't, one of them drifted toward Halle.

"They're endemic to Australia," he said. "The largest birds in Australia. The father actually sits on the eggs. They can grow to be over six feet tall. And strangely, you can't tell their sex until they're fairly old."

This was probably one too many emu facts, he thought. This young woman had not asked for so many emu facts.

"That guy's name is Angelo and that one by you is Kevin," he said, in conclusion.

Halle looked down at Kevin, who was pacing in circles in front of her.

"Charmed," she said to the bird.

Ben reached out to stroke Angelo's neck. The emu recoiled at first, but then calmed and relaxed into his touch.

"Do you have any animals?" Ben asked.

"No," she said. "But we had bearded dragons when I was younger."

"Oh yeah?"

"My brother named his Deion for Deion Sanders. I named mine Loopy for that cartoon character . . . Shoot, what was that cartoon character? She was super creepy."

"I don't know."

"Anyway."

The emus lost interest in their human visitors and began to wander the perimeter of the enclosure. Ben and Halle watched them for a few minutes and walked back outside the gate. It was so hot, the water was already drying on him, creating a cooling sensation. Halle looked at the emu, and then around at the wider farm.

"We walked over to the barns the other day," she continued. "I'm so sorry that happened."

"Thank you," he said. "That's kind of you."

"It's amazing the house survived. I mean, the way it burned around everything else."

"Yeah."

"The vineyard here is so interesting," she continued. "I love that you're growing Gamay and all the Rhône varietals. I traveled through Rhône Valley a few years ago. Mostly I was in Italy, though, doing a sort of half-year apprenticeship thing. I drank so many good wines. In Italy you can get an amazing wine for like five dollars. And an espresso for one dollar. For some reason everything has to be expensive in America, I don't know why."

Out on the road they could hear a truck clanking down the hill, toward town. By sound alone, Ben knew it was Rita McKee's truck. She was an old, black-toothed woman who lived on the other side of the mountain. Halle looked over at the truck as it came into view and then back at Ben.

"Well, I should get going," she said.

"Where are you heading now?"

"You heard of Orion?"

"Orion? As in the cult?"

"It's not really a cult now."

"It's not?"

"No, it broke up. My friends run the vineyard there now, Seba and Yami. They let me use their cellar to work on my own wines last year."

"I've always wondered about that place."

"You and Yoel should come check it out some time."

"It's over by Dutch Flat, right?"

"Exactly," she said. "You're neighbors."

Paul and Jeremy walked out the back gate moments later.

"I thought you already left," Paul said.

"I was waylaid by emus," Halle said.

The group thanked Ben again, and then headed off toward their two cars. Halle in an old station wagon and Paul and Jeremy in a white sedan. They drove down the gravel driveway, dust rising in their wake, and turned out onto Mountainview.

Ben watched them go and then headed back toward the house. A hummingbird buzzed ahead of him, en route to one of Ada's sugar-water feeders. Its throat was bright and red, the color of hot sauce.

He paused up by the porch, looked out at the vineyard. He was glad Halle appreciated the plantings. Maybe she would know a winemaker who would want to buy the place, he thought darkly. Last night, he made their most recent payment on the loan. It had given him a bit of a scare. He hadn't seen their checking account so low in years. And the monthly installments would only be rising from here. Still, there was no reason to panic. They'd worked their way through tight financial situations before. And look at that crop: it was in great shape, better than anything he'd produced the last few seasons.

He walked back into the house feeling reassured. He took off his boots, took off his socks, which were punctured here and there with foxtails. Inside, on the stove, a borscht was simmering. The smell of it was so intense it made his eyes water. Ada was walking around the kitchen with a hand vacuum, going after various fluffy motes of dust, which always seemed to gather around the AC vent. She looked up at him when he entered.

"The way this room accumulates dust is insane," she said. "What is that? What even is dust?"

He laughed, walked over to her, and kissed her on the cheek.

"I don't know," he said.

BEFORE LONG, the Hecht backyard became the regular hangout spot for Yoel's new friends and Ben slowly got to know them. Jeremy lived with his grandmother off of 51. His parents were both out of the picture, his father in the air force and his mother now in Florida with a new husband. He and Paul had been friends since middle school, when they both acted in a musical together. Paul was a year older, short but solidly built, his face spackled with acne scars. In high school, he'd gotten a job at the In-N-Out in Woodside. Soon after graduating, he was promoted to manager, and started making good money. He was scrupulous with his earnings and, over a period of about eight years, somehow saved up enough to open Brinkers. He still loved In-N-Out, ate there once a week, and saw his job there as one of the great formative experiences of his life.

"Showed me how to work," he told Ben at one point. "If I hadn't gotten that job . . . I mean, I was this close to being one of these kids up here who lives at their parents' house and has a jacked-up pickup and a pet rattlesnake, you know what I mean?"

Halle was originally from Chicago but had moved out West for college. In her early twenties, she'd bounced around working for different wineries, in California and briefly in Italy, before settling in Natoma a few years ago, when she was offered the job at Michael Deliso. Though she had moved out here knowing almost no one, she seemed to have built a strong social network. Her closest friends were Paul and Jeremy, who she'd met right when she moved to town, at a Labor Day potluck. But she was also friends with many winemakers and other industry people, with local radio producers and chefs and bartenders.

"We call her the queen," Jeremy told Ben once. "It's kind of a joke but it's also kind of not a joke."

The Queen of Natoma. She had a curious gravity to her, owing, in part, Ben felt, to her unusual style. Every time he saw her she was wearing some surprising new item: that yellow full-body jumpsuit, for example, or a vintage Bulls jersey or, often when by the pool, a dramatically wide white sun visor, which she said had belonged to her grandmother. Her hair was dark and curly, her nose sloping and turned up. When she found something particularly funny, she let out a loud, throaty cackle. This was her mom's cackle, she said. Her mom and dad had apparently come out to visit her recently. They had gone indoor rock climbing together and Halle had tweaked her back jumping off a bouldering wall. She was doing better now, but still trying to take it easy.

Ben enjoyed having all these young people around the farm. They brought a vibrancy with them, wandering in and out of the house, barefoot and smelling of chlorine and wet towels. Occasionally, new people would come over, friends of Halle's usually. Generally speaking, they were lovely folks—the one exception being a guy named Zeke Lunder, who was visiting from San Francisco, and who trapped Ben in a long conversation about the home chef meal-kit start-up he had founded.

Most days, however, it was just the core group hanging out: Jeremy, Paul, Halle, and Yoel. On any given weekend afternoon, Ben would look out the kitchen window and see all of them lounging by the pool. Paul was often on his phone, placing orders for this or that or talking to his only full-time employee, Chris, who he was constantly bothering. Jeremy usually brought weights with him and did an exercise routine under the shade of the elm tree, though, as far as Ben could tell, he never seemed to add any muscle. And Halle liked to sit on a chaise lounge and sketch with a set of pastels. She had studied art in school and rented a studio space in town.

At night, after dinner, they often hung out and watched television in the living room. Halle loved reality TV, particularly this one dating show where all the contestants were secretly paired into couples by matchmaking algorithms, and while residing on a tropical island, had to identify their perfect matches. After Halle and everyone else had watched a few episodes, they would go out on the back patio and talk and drink wine and ash their cigarettes into an old orange coffee can. Ben and Ada mostly left them to their own devices, checking in occasionally to see if they needed anything.

One evening, Halle and Yoel wandered into the kitchen while Ben was pouring himself a glass of wine from the house jug. It was early August now, harvest inching closer.

"Are we too loud out there?" she asked.

"No, not at all." Ben held up the bottle: "Do you guys want some?"

Halle looked at Yoel, who shrugged, and then she said sure.

Ben took out two jam jars and poured them glasses.

"It's not refined stuff," he said.

Yoel picked his glass up and leaned against the counter. Halle took a sip and nodded.

"I actually like it. What kind of yeast are you using?"

"Just a packaged wine yeast."

"Yeah, you can taste that. But you can tell the grapes are good quality. I walked through the vineyard a bit the other day. The fruit is setting nicely. Yoel said you do all the work yourself." Ben looked over at Yoel, surprised that he'd been talking about the farm.

"At harvest I hire two workers," Ben said.

"Still that's a ton of work. But good for the grapes. Who did you study with?"

"No one really," he said. "Just sort of learned as I went."

"Yeah, the vineyard feels that way," she said. "It's kind of homemade looking. And who do you sell to?"

"Torneo and Golden Hill."

"Really?"

"What?"

"Well, they probably just smash up your grapes and throw them in with a bunch of other stuff."

"I think so, yeah."

She got up, held the wine against the white of the fridge to examine its color.

"With a few tweaks," she called back to him, "you could be making something really interesting with this."

"I just follow a little recipe I have," he said. "I don't know much about winemaking."

She was still standing in front of the fridge, inspecting the wine's color. Ben looked over at Yoel again. His gaze was trained on Halle.

LATER THAT EVENING, Ben walked out to the front porch with his book to read a bit before bed. He had a glass of wine with him, and as he read, he found himself thinking of the records he'd lost in the barn. This kind of thing was still happening to him: he'd think he was done processing the loss of everything, and then something would crop up out of nowhere and he'd feel its loss all over again. The record collection was often on his mind. Ben usually only kept a small number of records in active rotation in the house, but every once in a while, he liked to go down to the barn and bring up some new selections.

He'd bought most of the collection at the shop around the corner from Soraya's antiques store. It was owned by a guy named Emilio, who had been the first one to really get him into classical music. He'd never had any interest in classical music, but Emilio had a way of discussing it that really captivated him. He'd talk about Stravinsky showing up in Paris in 1913, scandalizing his audience with *The Rite of Spring*, about Schoenberg's introduction of the twelve-tone technique.

In Lompoc, classical music had been an important part of his life too. On the edge of the prison camp, there was a multidenominational church, which also functioned as a rec room. In the church, there was a piano that inmates were allowed to play. Ben's work raking the eucalyptus trees always brought him past the church, and he would pause there sometimes, if someone was playing, and listen to the music. He could still picture it now: his wooden rake, the eucalyptus leaves on the ground like pale pink moons, and the untutored playing emanating from the church. Those had been some of the more peaceful moments throughout that whole ordeal.

Ben was sitting there, sipping the wine and thinking about Lompoc, when he heard voices coming from the back side of the chapel. Then, moments later, he heard the hollow clack of a Ping-Pong ball against rubber. There was an old table that they kept back there, folded up under the eaves. Yoel must have pulled it out. It seemed like it was just Yoel and Halle playing. At one point, he saw Halle dart out from behind the chapel, in pursuit of a lost ball. After a minute or so of searching, she found it and ran back behind the building.

"You close with your neighbor over that way?" he heard Halle ask.

Ben hadn't been able to hear them well before, but now, for some reason, their voices seemed to be traveling farther.

"Where?"

"Right back there."

"Oh, not really," Yoel said. "Bunch of State of Jefferson freaks."

"Damn, my back's hurting," she said.

"Probably cause you run around in those Converses, you maniac," Yoel said.

"I don't usually run in Converse. I walk in Converse. If you would stop hitting the ball into the goddamn ravine over there I wouldn't have to run after it."

"I'm trying to get it to your backhand. Your backhand is weak."

"My backhand is not weak. You know what's weak is your dumb little serve where you slam the table. Is that really necessary?"

"That's how I get the spin, with the slam."

"Sure."

"I'm going to keep coming at that backhand."

"I welcome it."

"I've got you clocked, Fremont."

"What you're doing is you're poking a bear, and you're going to regret it."

"We'll see," Yoel said.

"OK, enough stalling," she said. "Serve it up."

"10–7."

"10–8."

"Right. 10–8."

Ben decided he should head inside, give them their privacy. As he turned toward the door, he heard a loud clack.

"Ohh!" Halle shouted. "A punishing forehand! I told you. You were poking the bear. What did I tell you?"

ONE DAY, Yoel asked him to go for a walk. Ben's first thought was that he'd done something wrong, and that Yoel was mad at him. Years ago, when Yoel was just out of college, he would come up for the occasional visit. This was before they stopped talking, when things were not good, but not quite as bitter as they would later become. These visits were often saturated with dumb bickering, but the worst fights were usually preceded by Yoel asking Ben to go on a walk. It was his way, Ben thought, of getting out of the house, keeping their battles away from Ada. So when Yoel proposed a walk now, Ben was concerned.

"Is everything OK?" he asked.

"Yeah, it's fine," he said. "Let's actually get way out there. Go hike somewhere."

Yoel didn't seem to have a specific place in mind, wanted to know what Ben would recommend. A hike? Not just a walk down the road? Normally he would have said Studebaker Preserve, but it had been burned badly in the fire. Ben bumbled around for a moment, trying to think of options. He was caught off guard by the request, still uneasy. Eventually, they settled on Comish Lake.

Comish Lake, which was actually a manmade reservoir, was located a few miles northeast of town, off Highway 12. It had been established in the thirties, when the water district rehabilitated an old nineteenth-century mining dam. These days, the lake had a boat ramp, an RV camping ground, and every year, it hosted a junior sailing competition.

The body of water itself was about five miles in circumference and filled with carp. The story went that, many years ago, a German immigrant had brought some carp back from Germany for his fellow immigrants to eat and also released a couple of carp into his pond, who then made it into the river and the rest of the watershed and that's why the lake was filled with carp.

They took the Old Mines trail around the edge of the lake, through a forest of yellow and sugar pine. Dragonflies buzzed past them and other small animals bustled about the forest floor. They were up at a higher elevation here, and Ben could feel it in his lungs. Over on the east side of the lake, they passed an old cabin where one of the park rangers, Ed Dinnuci, lived. He was a member of the Dinucci family, most of whom worked at Dinucci's Homestyle on Broad Street. It was one of the fancier restaurants in town. Ben and Ada used to go there and order the prime rib and martinis after he made a big sale.

The air today was slightly smoky, but not that bad. Not bad enough to stay inside at least. As they began to hike, Ben waited for Yoel to bring up what was bothering him. Usually, right when they started walking, he would get into whatever the issue was. But he seemed mostly interested in talking about Sally. They had just canceled the wedding venue, he said, and had to eat the deposit. But the venue was, fortunately, the only thing they had booked already.

"I still wanted it to work out," he said. "But I wasn't happy in LA. I never felt exactly right about my life down there."

"Did she know that?" Ben asked.

"She knew, yeah," he said. "That was part of the issue. She wanted me to love being down there. We talked about buying a house before the wedding but I just didn't want to do it. Once we got a house, I knew we'd be committed to LA."

Eventually Ben and Yoel rounded a bend and came upon a small rocky cove. There was a picnic bench here and an exposed rusty drainage pipe coming out of the hillside. They stopped for a water break, and then Yoel walked over to the shoreline. He picked up a few rocks, began side-arming them into the water. Two skips. One skip.

"You want to find a flat, saucer-shaped one," Ben said.

Yoel turned around and rolled his eyes at him.

"I know how to skip a rock," he said.

"My bad."

He threw another one. No skips.

"OK, maybe I don't," he said, laughing to himself.

The two of them looked out at the lake, its color blue and then green, changeful under the high alpine sun. To their right, a fleet of small dinghies had come into view, zipping back and forth across the surface of the lake like water skeeters. The kids sailing them were in high school, or maybe younger. It was hard to tell from this distance.

"I still feel terrible about what happened," he said. "I feel guilty."

"Don't feel guilty," Ben said. "If you had stayed together when you weren't meant to be, that would have been even worse."

An older couple walked past on the trail behind them. They were both wearing water sandals and wide-brimmed hats. Yoel waved to them and then looked over at Ben.

"I don't know," he continued. "I don't know what the fuck I'm doing. I have no motivation for work stuff these days."

"You've been taking back-to-back meetings since you graduated," Ben said.

"Yeah. I wasted so much time. I never liked it. I knew I never liked it, but I don't know . . . I kept thinking I'd try something else but I never did."

Yoel squinted toward the horizon, and then looked back at Ben.

"I really don't want to go back to LA," he said.

"Don't go yet, then. Stay as long as you like."

Ben looked over at his son. He thought Yoel had brought him out here to confront him about something. But it turned out he just wanted to talk about his life. He felt the ambient fear that had been with him all day easing up.

"Should we keep going?" Ben asked.

"Sure."

The two of them both looked out at the lake for another moment. One of the dinghies that had been sailing past had somehow capsized. The sailor was hanging onto the edge of the daggerboard, trying, unsuccessfully, to flip it upright.

"Robby," they heard him yell toward one of his fellow sailors. "Robby, dude, come fucking help me."

THE FOLLOWING MORNING, Ben was sitting in the easy chair in the living room, drinking his morning coffee and reading the paper. On the table in front of him, stacks of old papers and magazines, Ada's huge red dictionary. Light pouring in through the living room doors, ferns and other plants hanging from the low wooden beams above him. On the wall beside him, a painting of two cows and a poster from the 1997 Rose County Peach Festival. As he was sitting there, Ada walked into the room with a cup of coffee. She'd just finished a call with her agent, who had, for many years, lived in New York, but who had recently moved to Los Angeles.

"Oy, I'm so stressed," she said.

"What's up?"

He set down the paper and rubbed his nose, felt the gummy leftover adhesive from his nasal strip. He had started wearing them at night last year, after his internist told him the most important thing he could do to extend his longevity was to start breathing through his nose.

"It's just not going well," she said.

He looked over with concern. He was surprised to hear this. The previous weekend, she'd told him and Yoel that she was starting to share the news of the lost manuscript with friends, that they no longer had to keep it a secret. This seemed like a promising sign. And for the past couple of weeks she seemed to be working steadily. She'd been spending much more time in the old computer room, and less time out in the garden.

"But you've been writing so much," he said.

"I can't do it. I was telling Julia just now, I can't recreate it. I can't remember it all."

"You don't need to remember it all. You can rewrite the parts you can't remember."

"I'm telling you, it's not working," she said. "I can't put out something terrible."

"What did Julia say?"

"She says I should take a vacation or something, get away from everything."

"That's a good idea."

"Yeah, with what money?"

"Don't worry about the money."

"How do I not worry about the money, Ben?"

"I mean we'll figure it out," he said. "It's no problem."

Even as he said this, he wasn't sure it was true. It took Ada four-plus years to write a book. If she needed to start on an entirely new manuscript, they were in trouble.

"I just wish I had looked at that table," Ada said. "If I had looked at that table, instead of grabbing the bag, I would have seen it."

"We were in a rush, Ada. We were running from a fire."

"We can't even make it another two years here, Ben. We're going to have to sell."

"Not yet. Let's not jump to any conclusions. You just take a break from writing for now. Give yourself a little space."

"Of all the things to have left behind," she said. Then she groaned, picked up a pillow, and threw it toward the arm of the couch. It bounced off the arm and made a clattering noise as it struck the fireplace grate.

Yoel walked into the room right after she did this. He had clearly just woken up, was holding a coffee cup that said "Happy Hanukkah" and had an image of two children dancing.

"What's happening?" he said.

"Give us a second, honey," Ada said. "I'll come find you in a moment."

6

N SMALL FOOTHILLS towns like Natoma, there was little reliable industry left. Most people worked in a tourism-adjacent vein, or the service industry, or increasingly, in the wine industry. There were some cannabis jobs—though not as many in Natoma as in other regions, because of Wallace's crackdown. And there were still a few logging jobs and some mining jobs too. But across the board, the majority of the work in Rose County was low paying. Most people in town scrapped together their living from several different sources. Fortunately, land in Natoma was still cheap, and the rent was still cheap, and people could get by on less income. Many found this attractive, said it was what drew them to the area in the first place, along with its natural beauty.

But despite these struggles, despite the ever-looming threat of the fires, there was optimism with regard to the town's economy. It probably wouldn't be anything like it had been in the boom days, but it could evolve into something new and different, prosperous in its own way. This had been the campaign message of the current mayor, Rachel LeBlanc, successor to Mary Lopez. Mining was gone, she said, logging more or less gone. It was time to focus on beautifying the town, on turning it into a tourism destination. If they did that, and continued to support the farms and ranches of the region, they could draw money into the community.

LeBlanc had, at one time, been the town drunk, but in a miraculous turn of events, she had sobered up and earned the trust of the entire community. This was the kind of thing that could happen in a town like Natoma. In her first term as mayor, she revitalized several buildings, including the fifty-foot historic fire tower, which had been built in 1866, after a blaze destroyed much of the business section of the town. Electrical difficulties in ringing the bell had forced it to shut down sometime in the thirties. It was opened for a while as a tourist attraction, but in the sixties a car accidentally struck the tower, and it had been closed to visitors since then. Some had been in favor of its demolition, but LeBlanc opted to repair it. Most in town were happy with the result, and felt a great deal of pride when they looked at their old fire tower. LeBlanc then proceeded to renovate a couple of other local landmarks, like the Rose County Historic Trail and the building that housed Gleason's Soda Works. She also became one of the leading proponents of turning the defunct railroad into a tourist excursion train, though no verdict had been rendered on that yet.

In addition to her work rebuilding historic landmarks, LeBlanc had also helped get a bond passed to improve the city's parks. One of the most successful results of that bond measure was the revitalization of Willeaux Park, a small flower garden, which was located a few blocks from Broad Street, right next to the charter school. It had first been established by a man named Jacques Willeaux, a pioneer nurseryman best known for introducing several fruit and nut trees to California. Over the years, it had fallen into disrepair, but with the new funds, the city had turned it into a magnificent garden, a favorite destination for tourists and residents alike.

When Ben was younger, he sometimes used to go to Willeaux Park to sell cannabis. He'd never forget the first person he'd sold to here, a friend of Hector's who went by the name "Sherbert." He bought three pounds, stuffed the turkey bags in the trunk of his Corolla. These days, if Ben came to the flower garden, it was only to relax, or to think, which was why he had come there this afternoon. He wanted to get away from the farm, see if he could tease out some solution to their problems.

So far, he was having no luck. Cannabis was now legal—and he would actually be first in line for permits, as someone formerly incarcerated for growing—but he didn't have anywhere near the cash he'd need to pay for the certification process and invest in a new business. He could try selling off some of his antiques but the market for them was terrible, and half of his stock had burned in the barn, anyway. What other options were left for them? Just hang tough, make it through the next couple of harvests, and hope Ada finished her book soon? That wasn't going to work.

As a kid growing up in the East Bay, his family had struggled with money at times. There were dinners where they only had canned butter beans with bread or onion soup or baked potatoes, which his father called "bulbes." His mother was constantly clipping coupons, finding ways to make their dollars go farther. But it had been a long time since he'd felt that kind of insecurity. As he'd gotten older, his father's small real estate company had done better and, by the time Ben was heading to college, the family was well off. They no longer thought much about what they were putting in their grocery cart. They owned their own home. When their father died, Ben and Andrew even inherited a little money, which Ben had put toward the purchase of the farm.

Yoel mentioned the other day that he wished he could help them pay off some of the debt, but that he didn't have much saved. He'd been spending all his money, he said. Ben told him this was fine, that he should keep whatever savings he had for himself. He could tell Yoel was increasingly nervous about the prospect of losing the farm. He had asked Ben for specifics on the loan, wanted to know what kind of money they'd need to bring in over the next few years. He also seemed to be taking extra interest in the daily activities of the farm, as though he knew it might be his last chance to experience them. He had decided to stay until October. His boss, Jerry, had been very kind to let him continue working remotely, but he needed him back by the fall. If Ben and Ada couldn't figure this out, they might have to put the property up for sale shortly after he left.

Ben was walking through the garden, thinking about all this, when he saw a man sit down on a bench, across from a patch of irises. Was that him? He did a double take and yes, it was definitely him. He looked older, Ben was pleased to see, his hair thin and sparse, like the fur on a squirrel. The former sheriff of Rose County, Ed Wallace, now retired. The man who had upended his life, for no reason, who sent him to jail once and who kept persecuting him even after that. Ben felt a full-body heat taking over him, a feathery thudding in his chest.

Why the hell was this guy here? He was not a man entitled to flowers or peaceful public spaces or anything good. Ben felt a strong urge to approach him. But instead, he pulled his hat lower over his forehead, sat down on a nearby bench. He was probably thirty or forty feet from the sheriff, who was not looking in his direction.

This was the man who had orchestrated the backlash against all the growers in the region, who had wreaked havoc on the county for years. Such an idiotic and destructive legacy he and his small following had left behind. They didn't care that the pot growers invested in the community. They didn't care that legalization was nearly on its way. They just wanted to squash cannabis in Rose County. And they were still fighting to limit its production. Even though the town had thoroughly rejected his vision, Wallace and his cronies continued to try to tamp down any cannabis projects. The agricultural commission, for example, had just debated, last month, whether or not to allow growers to plant industrial hemp. Hemp! A widely cultivated US commodity. That commission was such a mess, manipulated by a few people close to Wallace. It didn't help that the other members on the committee put up little resistance. Two of them really needed to retire, both had Parkinson's, but that was another story.

Ben felt himself growing more and more angry. He heard Ada's voice in his head, *Don't do anything stupid*. This was what she'd said to him when they'd passed the sheriff on the street, outside Danny's Café, years ago. But that was when Wallace was still in office, could still mess with them. Now he was just a common citizen. Now he was a powerless old man. Ben felt a holy rage growing inside him. If this man only knew the suffering he'd caused. The years of fallout between Ben and Yoel. This man had ripped their family apart.

His hip was hurting again and now he was starting to feel dizzy too. Maybe he was dehydrated. He needed to get out of here before he fainted or something. Besides, he didn't want to look at this asshole anymore. But he couldn't not say anything. He couldn't just let the man sit there in peace and look at irises. He didn't deserve that.

Ben stood up, pulled the hat even lower. Then he cupped his hands, and yelled: "Not guilty!"

It was an odd thing to yell, but for whatever reason, it was what came to mind. Wallace looked over at him.

"What?" he said.

Ben started toward Wallace. He wasn't sure what he was going to do. He didn't have a plan for this. As he got closer, he could tell Wallace looked confused. Ben stopped in his tracks. The two men stared at each other and Ben took in his features. A sagging neck, hands folded over one another, covered in wiry black hair. Next to him, a metal cane with black rubber handle.

"How are you doing, sir?" Wallace said.

The anger went out of Ben. The old man didn't even recognize him.

"Ed Wallace," he said, extending his hand. One of his eyes appeared to have become lazy, was looking off to the right.

Ben turned around and walked away. Left him there, with his arm outstretched.

HE WANTED SO badly to fix this situation for Ada. He'd texted his brother to see if he had any ideas, texted Wick too. He had started looking at the job listings in the paper. Maybe there was something out there that he hadn't considered. The other day he'd written the growers' association, to see if they needed any teachers. He knew they had a viticulture training program, connected to the UC extension school. And he could instruct people in grape growing, he'd been doing it for years.

Ben had taught himself everything over the past decade, how to stratify cuttings, how to graft root stock. He knew how to build terraces, how to head train and cordon train. He could talk about the advantages and disadvantages of each strategy. He could talk about how much mycorrhizae to add to the soil, how much calcium and rock phosphate and kelp meal and boron. You needed a lot of boron up here, because the foothills soils were deficient in it.

The people over at the association would know all of this. He didn't need to explain his credentials to them in an email. He'd gone to the meetings for years, and they were familiar with his vineyard.

But none of that had mattered. After a few days, the email arrived, a brief, kind note from Bass Volker, who managed the extension program. He said they were not hiring at the moment, but they'd keep his name on file. They might have openings sometime in the next couple of years. So that was the end of that.

The morning after he got the note from Bass, he woke up early and picked up doughnuts and coffee in town. He came back to the farm and worked hard all day, as if, through the sheer effort of the work, he might find a solution to his problems. By late afternoon, he felt a rasp in his throat and he stopped to look up the AQI. It was 120, fairly nasty stuff. He'd been too distracted by everything to check it before he'd gone outside.

When he got back to the house, he found Yoel in the kitchen, taking a slice of cold pizza out of a Tupperware container. He said that Halle wanted to bring over some wines for Ben to try.

"Why would she do that?" Ben asked.

"I don't know," Yoel said. "She has something she wants to show you."

Halle arrived around seven with an entire case of wine. She said they were natural wines, a loose term that, broadly speaking, meant that no sulfur or other additives had been used to make them. This type of winemaking was not new—in fact, it was really a return to traditional winemaking—but at the moment, there was a burst of interest in it throughout the industry. These bottles Halle had brought over were made by her Argentine friends, Seba and Yami Garcia, who had been making natural wines for years, prior to the industry's burgeoning fascination with it, under their label, Bodega Garcia.

Seba and Yami lived and farmed on the Orion property, which was about a fifteen-minute drive east of the Hecht farm. The property was still owned by the Young World Fellowship, a New Age cult that had emerged in the late seventies and, according to Halle, more or less disbanded a decade ago, after the financial crimes of its founder were exposed. Ben had never visited Orion, but he'd been vaguely aware of YWF as an organization. By the time he and Ada arrived in the foothills, its membership had dwindled, but he knew that, at one time, it had been significant and, on occasion, you would meet someone in town who was a current or former member.

To Ben's understanding, the cult had been reminiscent of other California spiritual collectives from that era, weaving together the teachings of many disparate thinkers and religious practices. Halle confirmed this, and also explained that the cult had been particularly interested in the arts and high culture. Over the years, using its members' annual tithes, YWF had started its own theater company, museum, and restaurant. It had also planted a vineyard: 365 acres of grapes, a massive development by today's standards. Only thirty-three of those acres remained and only twelve of them were actively farmed by the Garcias, who had been granted the right to manage the vineyard by a board that oversaw the cult's remaining assets. Seba and Yami had never been YWF members themselves but apparently they knew one of the members, and this person had recommended them as caretakers. They lived in a winemaker's cottage on the edge of the vineyard, and used the wine cave that was beneath the cottage as their winery. Apparently, Halle had been at Orion during the fire, had stayed there the whole time with the Garcias, waiting it out.

She mentioned all of this to Ben while they sat at the kitchen table. Yoel was leaning against the counter behind them. All three had a jam jar of wine in hand. Halle had just poured out the first wine for them. Its contents were faintly yellow and cloudy and looked, to Ben, like the juice of some tropical fruit. Wine was really a very simple thing, Halle said as they sipped from their jars, but we had made it complicated. It had been industrialized, sterilized, drained of its particularity and character. This was how Michael Deliso made their wines, and she did not like them. She preferred the kind of stuff that the Garcias made. Last year, she had produced a few cases of pétillant naturel, an unfinished wine made from a mixture of red and white grapes. She'd used fruit that she'd scrounged from vineyards that Michael Deliso worked with and produced the wines in the Garcias' wine cave. She wanted to do more of this, to ultimately build out her own label.

"I would have brought you a bottle of the pét nat," she said, "but our friends and family drank it all."

Ben sipped the wine. It tasted clean and energetic, had a slight fizz to it. He was reminded of the first time he smoked the Heinz strain that Hector had been breeding down in Harde Gap. It was an entirely different product, what would later become known as "grape." They hadn't realized weed could smell like that.

"We could make wine like this," Halle said.

Ben looked up at her.

"You're farming really good fruit," she went on, "but then you just give it away to these mass producers."

"Well, we sell it to them."

"And what do you make on it?"

"About fourteen hundred dollars per ton."

"And you get three tons per acre?"

"Less than that."

"I mean, I don't want to pressure you, but you could be making so much more off your crop. I could use the facilities at Orion, bottle the wine, sell it, and we'd split the proceeds. This harvest we'd start with whatever extra grapes you have. I know you'd normally sell those grapes to Torneo or whatever but you'd give them to me instead. If it worked, we could build a label out from there."

She paused.

"I think we could make something really good," she said.

He was immediately sold. This would buy them time. This would take the pressure off. It all felt so perfect, as if someone had understood what he needed, and delivered it to him wrapped in a bow. He would need to talk it over with Ada of course, but it sounded great. He swished the wine in his glass, held it up against the white of the fridge, like Halle had done, to examine its color. Then he turned to his son.

"What do you think?" he asked.

"What do I think?" Yoel said. "It was my idea."

"It's a great idea," Ben said.

Yoel looked at Halle: "This guy loves a risky venture," he said, nodding at Ben.

But he was smiling as he said it.

THAT NIGHT, he and Ada discussed the project, and she said she was in favor of it. She'd tried one of the wines Halle had left and absolutely loved it. Also, somewhat relatedly, she'd recently heard an interview with an oceanographer, who said that whenever you are faced with a serious life decision, you should always move in the direction of change.

"Why was the oceanographer giving life advice?" Ben asked.

"I don't know exactly," she said. "But he had lots of good advice."

So a couple of days later, Ben and Halle made plans to visit Orion, to see the cellar and meet the Garcias. Halle picked him up in the morning, in her station wagon, and they headed up Rose Mountain. While she drove, she played a CD by a harpist folksinger. The singer's voice was sweet but kind of shrill and childish. Apparently, she had grown up in Natoma, but now lived in New York and was married to a famous comedian. Halle said she had loved her stuff for years, and knowing that she had been born in Natoma was one of the first things that had attracted her to the area. This was all news to Ben, who hadn't known that there were any famous musicians from Natoma, harpist or otherwise.

Halle was an aggressive driver, a little too aggressive for Ben's liking, but she didn't seem out of control. She whipped up the mountain, then slalomed down the other side of it, toward Sherwood Road. Her car was cluttered, the back seat strewn with books: botany texts, winemaking manuals, and a history of the Russian Revolution. It also smelled quite strongly of lavender. At first Ben thought it was some kind of air freshener, but then Halle explained that she had spilled a bottle of the lavender solvent she used for her oil paintings all over the back seat.

"It was a real bummer," she said. "Because that shit is expensive."

Which, by the way, she continued, she wanted to talk through some of her thinking on costs with him. Her vision, she said, was to keep all her wines under fifteen dollars. This was both a philosophical position and a business strategy. She wanted regular people to be able to drink the wines she made—the way anyone could drink good wine in Italy—and also, there just weren't many good, affordable bottles on the market. Most bottles that were fifteen dollars or less were mass produced by big wineries, who could take advantage of economies of scale. But because of their unique positioning, with their free access to Orion's facilities, she felt they could make it work. Ultimately, she wanted to mainstream their label, get it into a major supermarket or two. Few natural wine producers had done that, but it was where real money could be made.

As they drove, she again laid out the math for him. Packaging, she estimated, would cost around $1.30 per bottle. This included bottles, cork, and the labels, which she would design herself. She didn't really think they'd need a foil. Foils were kind of out, stylistically speaking. As far as fermentation, they would use the stainless steel tanks at Orion. There would be some other ancillary costs, but to start, they'd sell directly to the consumer, cutting out any middlemen. If everything worked out, she thought they could make about eleven dollars per bottle. And if you estimated that, per ton of grapes, they'd get around 720 bottles of wine (or sixty cases), they were looking at approximately twenty grand in profits each—much more than what Ben would've made selling those excess grapes to Torneo or Golden Hill.

"That all sounds good to me," he said.

They had turned left on Sherwood Road and then left again onto a winding paved driveway.

"We'll keep everything simple," Halle said. "That's what Seba and Yami have really shown me. Just keep things simple."

A few minutes later, out the window, Ben began to see the hilly vineyards of Orion appearing. They drove under a lichen-covered stone gate, passed bronze statues of centaurs and winged gods. Off to their right there was a grove of citrus trees and, beyond that, cows picking their way across a brown hillside. The vineyard itself was huge but largely unkempt. In general, the whole place had a sort of abandoned feeling to it. After a few minutes, they arrived at a roundabout, at the center of which was a circular fountain, its water tessellating blue under the bright sun. Straight ahead, higher up on the hill, Ben could see a series of large neoclassical structures. But Halle did not head toward them. She turned right at the roundabout, following a road that dropped downhill, through a forested section of the property.

The winery was a two-story building, situated at the foot of a hillside, and surrounded by old eucalyptus trees and spiky conifers. On the first floor were the actual winemaking facilities and above that were Seba and Yami's living quarters. Halle led him through a small wooden door and into the main room, which had high ceilings and was filled with winemaking equipment: steel fermenting tanks, a white plastic de-stemming rack, open-top bins. Halle explained that most of the wine here was made by foot stomping in the bins. This allowed the vineyard's indigenous yeasts to drive fermentation. The interior of the winery was larger than it appeared from the outside. The air was cool and smelled like stone. At the far end of the room, there were two framed posters of French cognac labels.

Ben followed Halle down a short flight of stairs, into the cellar where the oak barrels were kept. Along the side of the stairs there was a wide hose, which Halle explained was used to pump wine from the cellar up to the tanks above for bottling. Down below they found Yami standing in front of a barrel, a stirring rod in her hand. She was younger than Ben had expected, probably in her late thirties, with a wide face and moonlike eyes. She was wearing overalls and hiking boots and she had a hand-rolled cigarette tucked behind her ear. Halle gave her a hug and then gestured toward Ben.

"This is the guy from the farm I was telling you about," she said.

"Oh yes," Yami said. "I'm sorry about your barns."

"Thank you," Ben said. He felt like there was something else he should've said in that moment but he wasn't sure what.

"We drove over to Mountainview to look at the burn scar the other day," she said. "Crazy what happened."

He looked around the cellar. It wasn't the tidiest space in the world. In the corner of the room, there was a bike covered in cobwebs, two messy bookshelves. They reminded him of the bookshelves in the Lompoc law library, which were always in disarray, the books constantly being taken, never returned.

Ben nodded at the stirring rod: "What are you doing here?"

"Just stirring the lees, the dead yeast cells."

She dipped the rod into the barrel and began rotating it, as if she were churning butter. There was a crisp, studied confidence to her movements.

"Where's Seba?" Halle asked.

"He's out fruit dropping."

"It's so hot though."

"He's trying to get that done so he can sanitize the tanks tomorrow. And then we've got our table at the fair on Saturday, you know, so it's busy. Busy week."

"Oh, I forgot the fair is this weekend," Halle said. "I could help out with that."

"You could?"

"I think so."

"You should come too," Yami said, looking at Ben. "We mostly just sit around and drink wine," she added, with a conspiratorial nod.

"I can do that," he said.

"Is the ferment stuck?" Halle asked, nodding at the barrel in front of Yami.

"No, no we're just trying to give it a little more texture."

"Got it," Halle said. "Well, we'll get out of your hair. I think we're going to walk around for a bit. I want to show Ben the vineyard."

"Of course, enjoy. If you see Seba, tell him to come inside before he passes out." She turned back to Ben. "Great to meet you. We're looking forward to the wines you and Halle are going to make."

"Me too."

"We think she's the best," Yami said. "We would make her the president if we could."

Halle was gathering her hair with both hands, wrapping it with a hair tie.

"Glad I can count on your vote," she said.

THEY LEFT THE WINERY, walked out into the vineyard, through a block of Syrah. It was a messy, wild block, filled with the life of the surrounding forest in a way that reminded Ben of his own property. Spiderwebs clung to the grape leaves and orange butterflies flitted in and out of the rows. The heat of the day was rising and the short grasses were dry and crisp beneath their feet. Halle pointed to the ridge on the other end of the vineyard.

"We could see the smoke billowing up from over there," she said. "But it never moved across that part of the canyon."

They continued onward, through the vines, which were heavy with fruit. Periodically, as they walked, Halle would pick one of the grapes and taste it. Ben followed her lead, sampling the Syrah, which was approaching ripeness. The soils here were comprised of rich clay and loam, Halle explained, with some decomposed granite. The grapes had a dusky blue color and tasted cool and refreshing. Ben was struck by the sheer scale of what had been planted here, though clearly not all of it was under active cultivation.

"Do you ever run into people from the Fellowship on the property?" he asked.

"Not really," Halle said. "There's no one here. There's a couple guys who look after the main section of the property, those buildings you could see on our way in, but we don't go up there."

"It must have taken a ton of labor to plant all this."

"Oh yeah, they had hundreds of members working on it, and volunteers coming in from all over."

They had exited the block of Syrah, were now moving through a section of Chardonnay. As they walked, Halle told him about what had first gotten her interested in winemaking. She'd been living in Berkeley and had gone to see a Georgian winemaker speak at the university. He was from the Kakheti region of the country, near Tbilisi, and he talked about the way in which the practice of winemaking decentered the individual. It was like midwifery, he said, if done right. You took what the land was able to give and you allowed it to express itself. She found his talk interesting, but what really transformed her life was the tasting that took place afterward.

Halle had always liked drinking wine, but she had really only ever had cheap, mass-produced wines. On the weekend, she might pick up a six- or seven-dollar bottle at the corner store, and she was happy with that, because that was what she knew. She was aware that many people cared a lot about wine, but that whole world had always seemed snobby and highfalutin to her. After she tried the Georgian's wines, however, she realized that there was way more to wine than she had ever imagined. The wines were light bodied and had visible sediment. There was a surprising dimensionality to them, an earthy, lively flavor. Drinking those wines made her feel like she was connected to something ancient and elemental. She became obsessed with that feeling, and she knew, then, that she wanted to make wine.

As she advanced through the winemaking world, however, she realized that very few people were making the kinds of wines that the Georgian winemaker did. This was true in terms of the taste of the wines and in terms of the way they were produced. Most people in California were making heavy, oaky, high-alcohol wines. And the grapes for these wines were mainly farmed in an industrial fashion: the soil doctored, the vines sprayed with chemicals and pruned by machines. This was no midwifery. In the cellar, the manipulations were even more intense: the grapes were fined and filtered, centrifuged and racked, oxygenated and pumped with preservatives. It was not until she met Seba and Yami that she saw something closer to the kind of winemaking she had wanted to practice.

"What I've come to believe," she said, "is that the less controlled things are, both in the vineyard and the cellar, the more interesting the wines will be."

When they got to the edge of the Chardonnay, Halle turned back and headed down one of the wider paths along the edge of the forest. She was hoping they'd run into Seba so she could introduce them but she didn't know where he was. They were back at the car a few minutes later. Halle had left the windows down and she reached through one of them, pulled out a water bottle from the back seat. She took a sip and then handed it to Ben.

"There are dangers involved here, obviously," Halle said. "I just want to be really clear on that."

The two of them got in the car and Halle started the engine. Ben grabbed his seatbelt and singed his hand on the hot metal buckle. The AC was on but it only blew warm air. Halle plugged her phone into a charger, set it down on her lap, and then looked over at Ben.

"Because I should tell you that the last time we tried this we did have an . . . an issue."

"What do you mean?"

"You know how I told you we had a pét nat last year?"

"Yes."

"Well we also had a Cab Franc, but we had some problems and it got all vinegary."

"All of it?"

"All of it," she said. "I feel like I learned from the experience but . . . I just wanted you to know, in case it ever comes up with Seba or Yami. I don't want you to feel duped. I just want everything on the table before we start."

He could tell she had been fearing this moment all day. She shifted uncomfortably. Perhaps she felt she had exposed herself as a fraud. But if anything, he was touched by her candor.

"Because I do really want to do this," she continued. "I believe in myself. I'm ready for my own label. My boss would laugh at that but Seba and Yami believe in me, and I know I can do it. It's so hard to break into this industry as a winemaker and Michael's never going to give me a chance to really put my imprint on anything over there."

He looked down at the water bottle, noticed it had the sticker of Yoel's college on it.

"Is this Yoel's?" he asked.

"Yeah, he left it in here the other day."

She unlocked her phone, then locked it again and set it on the dashboard.

"He was so excited when he had the idea," she said. "I've never heard him like that."

"Well," Ben said, "maybe he'll head up our marketing department."

She looked up at him. From his years in cannabis, he knew that it was not every day that you met someone you trusted. But she had won him over at the start and she had never really even come close to losing him.

"So you're not out?" she said.

"No, I'm in."

They shook hands. The deal was done. They were partners.

WHEN THEY GOT BACK to the farm, they saw Yoel sitting on the porch with his laptop. Halle did a U-turn at the end of the driveway, by the chapel, and pulled up in front of the house. She put the car in park, rolled down her window, and killed the engine.

"Returning your father from his cult visit," she called out.

Ben leaned over and smiled at his son.

"It was great," he said. "I want you to come next time. Just for one informational session."

Yoel set his laptop on the ground, walked toward the car.

"My American vignerons," he said. "How were the facilities?"

"A+," Ben said.

"You guys just missed Jeremy," Yoel said. "He was stopping by to pick up his dumbbells. He left them here again."

"I think we need to just buy him a set to keep here," Halle said.

"He said there's some band playing tonight at Brinkers."

"Oh yeah, you should come," Halle said.

"I don't know," he said. "I think I've got to work late."

"Come on," she said.

"What's the band?"

"Some friend of Paul's friend from college."

"Compelling."

"I'll buy your first drink."

Ben watched a kind of softness take over his son.

"How about all my drinks?" Yoel said. And then, after a beat: "I'll see how things are looking around six."

Ben got out of the car, walked around to the other side where his son was standing, and handed him his water bottle.

"It was in Halle's car," he said.

"Oh good."

"Everyone's just trading objects back and forth, aren't they?" Halle said.

"Actually, that reminds me," Yoel said. "Hang on one second."

He disappeared into the house and reemerged moments later.

"I picked this up at the bookstore the other day. It was in their half-off bin. I remember you saying you liked her."

It was a coffee-table book of paintings by an artist whose name Ben didn't recognize.

"Oh, that's so sweet," Halle said. "Thank you."

She opened the book on her lap and flipped through the first few pages.

"I love her," she said. "She is such a weirdo. My mom thinks her work is grotesque—which I get, but I just love it."

She looked back up at him.

"Thank you for this," she said. "See you later tonight?"

"Yeah," Yoel said.

"And you're both coming to the fair, right?"

Yoel nodded and then Halle looked over at Ben.

"Wouldn't miss it," he said.

7

A T THE FAIR, there was a Ferris wheel and a teacup ride and the Zipper. There were funnel cakes and nachos and shawarma and shaved ice. There was a library bookmobile, a US Forest Service booth, and a county history tent. Outside the history tent, there was an old man raking coals over a pit for his blacksmithing demonstration, sweating and talking about different kinds of miner's picks. And then there was the main stage, over by the Zipper, where Ben and Ada paused, under the shade of an umbrella, to look at a map of the fair. While they stood there, the board of supervisors representative for District Five, Elon Horace, got on stage and read the Opening Proclamation of the Rose County Fair, which featured a list of the highest-grossing agricultural products in the county (apples, livestock, and grapes, in that order) and a warning about dehydration.

"You need something to hydrate you out here," Elon said. "Personally, I drink vitamin C salts, about three or four per day. That's probably more than is necessary. The truth of the matter is that I like the taste. I drink the orange flavor, and highly recommend it. But regardless of flavor, you need to be drinking something, because it's hot. That's straight from the desk of the board of supervisors."

After conferring for a moment, Ben and Ada decided to head over to the Garcias' table, in the beer and wine tent. Yoel would already be there with Halle. He'd come over earlier in the morning to help her set up. Ben also wanted to check out the fruits and veggies contest, which was on the other side of the fairgrounds, but he figured he could do that later. So they headed off down the main thoroughfare, some kind of cumbia echoing over the loudspeakers, its tinny rhythms punctuated, on occasion, by a shriek from the Zipper. Over by the back lawn, Guy Matthews was filming a live recording of his nature and history public access program. They paused for a moment and listened to him hold forth on the subject of infested timber. Western pine beetles, he explained, only ate the cambium layer of infested trees. So the wood inside was actually totally fine. He had brought a giant board of infested pinewood as a demonstration of this and, every few minutes, he would hold it up to the audience like a sacred tablet.

"See?" he kept saying. "This is really perfectly fine wood."

Even though it was only 2 P.M., the beer and wine tent was bustling with fairgoers. There were probably around fifty wineries and breweries tabling, and they were all giving out tastings and selling drinks and bottles. Ben and Ada passed through the beer section of the tent first, pausing briefly to check out the results of the county home brew contest. The winning beers had all been placed on a white table, along with their blue ribbons. Champions had been awarded by type of beer: sour, stout, wheat, pilsner. There was also a mysterious category called "historical beer." Ben looked around, briefly, to see if anyone could explain to him what this was, but no one seemed to be working the award table.

They continued on, into the wine section of the tent. It took them a few minutes to find the Garcias' table, which was located in the back corner of the tent, next to a table for a credit card company, one of several paid advertisement tables placed throughout the fair. Yami recognized Ben and waved him over. Their table was arrayed with open wine bottles and a couple fliers and there was a banner hanging from its front that said BODEGA GARCIA. Ben introduced Ada to Yami while Seba finished up a sale to their right. When he was done, he turned to face them.

"Not a great spot this year," he said, "I don't know who we wronged on the fair board."

He wore thick wire spectacles, cuffed jeans, and a thin, worn T-shirt that said something in Italian. Yami told them that Yoel and Halle were off picking up food, but that they'd be back soon. Then she gestured toward the several foldout chairs behind the table and invited them to sit down. Once they were settled, Seba prepared a maté with hot water from his thermos and handed it to Ben. He asked him if he'd tried maté before and he said yes, years ago, when he'd worked with a trimmer from Argentina. Ben sipped the hot, bitter tea until the straw made a soft slurping sound and then handed it back to Seba. He refilled the maté and handed it to Ada.

"You are a novelist, is that correct?" he asked.

"Seba loves to read novels," Yami said.

"I started a book club up here, for a while," he said. "With a couple other wine people. But it fell apart."

"No one was reading the books," Yami said. "They just wanted to get drunk."

"Yeah."

"Seba lost control over his own creation."

"I can't make them read the book," Seba said. "What am I supposed to do? Read the book for them?"

He pressed his thumb to his index and middle finger and shook his hand at Yami. She laughed and said something in Spanish that Ben couldn't understand. Then she refilled the maté, handed it back to Ben. The conversation returned to Ada's work. Ben watched her closely, knowing how fraught the subject was at the moment. But she simply spoke about her last book, gave a general overview of its plot. Seba said he was going to buy it. Then the conversation moved on, with Seba mentioning the name of an Argentine novelist, whose book he had just read and enjoyed. Apparently, the author was from the same neighborhood in Buenos Aires that Seba was from, which, he admitted, had perhaps made him overly partial to the book. Sections of the story were set in his neighborhood.

"She included this Arabic empanada shop," he said. "Which, that's how you know she knows what she's talking about. Cause that's a really local place. Only locals know it."

"It's true," Yami said.

"I think you would like that book, actually," Seba said.

"Me?" Yami said. "No, no. For me only science and history. He's always trying to push fiction on me. I don't read fiction . . . No offense," she added, winking at Ada.

Ada smiled. She said she actually knew the book Seba was talking about, had a translation of it back at the house. From here they began to discuss translation and what that process had been like for Ada, as an author. All the while, as they talked, they were passing the maté back and forth. By the time Ben finished his third round, he was feeling energized, almost euphoric. Soon, Yoel and Halle rounded the corner, grinning about something, juggling four hot dogs and waffle fries between them.

"Ah, we would've got you some if we knew you were here already!" Halle said, fries falling to the ground.

"We'll give them wine instead," Seba said.

He uncorked their Sauvignon Blanc–Viognier blend and poured out paper cups for everyone. The blend had been made as a cofermentation—they did all their blends as cofermentations.

"We think this makes things better integrated," Seba explained.

Then he opened a Mourvèdre-Syrah blend, which also included a small percentage of Counoise. They liked Counoise, Yami said, for its ability to add a bit of acid to a blend.

"It's like squeezing some lemon onto a dish of food," she told them.

Next came a blend of Tannat, Syrah, and Grenache. And finally, their straight-up Syrah and their straight-up Primitivo. No one was able to drink at the pace Seba was pouring so they set their paper cups at their feet. Yami turned on a mini speaker and chose a playlist that Ben saw was titled "Boppin Good." Periodically, a customer would approach the table and ask for a tasting. Seba would gamely pour out a few wines and answer any of their questions. Sometimes the customers were already familiar with the Garcias' wines and purchased a bottle or two without sampling anything. The most popular wine seemed to be the Tannat blend, which they called "Blue in Green." Like many of the Garcias' wines, Ben learned, it was featured on the wine list of several high-profile Bay Area restaurants.

At one point, a middle-aged man in khakis and a collared shirt approached the table. He said he worked as a winemaker just outside Napa.

"Ah, well you get the industry discount then," Seba said, pouring him a large tasting of the Sauvignon Blanc–Viognier blend. The man stuck his nose into the cup, inhaled deeply, and then took a sip of the wine.

"So you guys are doing that natural thing," he said.

"Well, yes," Seba said, "but we don't like labels really. We are just trying to express the land where our grapes are grown, which is right near here, actually."

The man took another sip. "I hope you don't take offense to this, but I think the whole thing's a scam."

"I think there are probably some scammers out there, yes," Seba said.

"It's just, you're not using all the tools at your disposal to make a great wine, you know? And like, what is it? There's no definition. It's a marketing fad."

"We haven't done anything because of marketing."

"Well, maybe not you guys, but other people have. I don't mean to be rude, I just have strong opinions about the whole thing."

"What fun would wine be without opinions?" Seba said.

The man tried a couple more wines, thanked Seba, and continued on to a different table. Once he was out of earshot, Seba turned around to the group and smiled.

"He did not like the wine," he said.

.   .   .

THEY SPENT THE REST of the afternoon at the Garcias' table, talking and drinking. Ben learned that Seba and Yami had both come to the US for college. They had met in their late twenties, in San Francisco, at a party for expat Argentines. Ben also found out that Yami did astrology charts and that Seba loved Iowa. This was where he'd studied, as an exchange student, in the nineties. He still had lots of Iowan friends, he said, who he stayed in touch with via video chat.

At one point, a woman at a distant table began waving at Yami and she waved back.

"Is that a friend?" Ben asked.

"No," she said. "People here are just friendly."

Then she looked back over at the woman, who was still waving energetically at her.

"Ah, no, she is a friend," Yami said. "We know her."

Oddly, the Garcias reminded Ben of the Mulehorns, growers who had lived on the other side of 99. Something about the way their banter merged together, the way they teased each other. It made him feel close to Garcias, even though he hardly knew them. The Mulehorns had been one of his favorite old couples. They'd shown him how to cut terraces, how to buy bonemeal at the old tallow works, how to camouflage your grow with army surplus tarps. He hadn't talked to them in years. They'd moved up north to retire, somewhere on the Oregon coast.

After Ben finished his flight of wines, he reverted to maté, knowing that he would need to drive sometime in the next few hours. Everyone else, however, kept drinking. Someone raised the volume on the speaker and more people continued to arrive at the table, pulling up chairs or perching on coolers. Jeremy eventually showed up, along with Paul, who was in a bit of a mood because someone had mocked him while he was attempting one of the basketball shooting contests on the main concourse.

"I know I'm a good shooter," he told everyone, after relaying the story. "I have good form."

"You have a good follow-through," Jeremy said.

"Yeah, so, you know, whatever, bad shooting day."

"Everyone has a bad day."

At a certain point, Wick texted Ben to see if he was at the fair and Ben invited him over to the Garcias' table. When he arrived, Ben introduced him to Yami and Seba, who poured him a cup of wine. Wick pulled up a chair between Yoel and Ben and sat down. Across from them, Halle was telling a story that had something to do with the qigong class her mother taught in Illinois. Seba and Yami, meanwhile, were standing in front of the table, talking to another winemaker friend of theirs, who had just stopped by.

"So these are the people farming at the cult place," Wick said, nodding toward them.

"Yeah."

"I knew some people who were a part of that group. Mary Hammack. Carol Hammack. Also, Jerome Hentley. You know him? Lives in town now. Had a big mouse problem at his place last year, actually. The problem was he didn't follow any directions, in terms of not leaving food out, checking your surfaces. Shouldn't have taken as long to get it under control as it did. But we did, yeah, we got it in check. I like this wine."

Ben looked over at Yoel. He seemed particularly happy to see Wick. The two of them had clearly bonded during those few days when they were cleaning up the wreckage of the barns.

"So what have you been up to?" Yoel asked him. "It's been a minute since you stopped by."

"Well, just working, you know," Wick said. "And looking after the dogs. But this month things are leveling out, I think. Going to have some more time this month."

"That's nice."

"I'm sorry," Paul said, leaning over toward Wick. "But did you say you're not so busy next month?"

"Paul, you already harassed him enough at the last gathering," Halle said.

"Paul Brinkers," Paul said, extending his hand to Wick.

"No, yeah, I remember you," Wick said. "You have the bar. How's it going over there?"

"Pretty good," Paul said, and then he looked over at Jeremy, who nodded in agreement.

"Definitely better," Jeremy said.

"Better?" Wick asked.

"Better than it used to be," Jeremy said. "Good, I mean, it's pretty good, I think, in terms of bars, and establishments of the like, in this phase of the business plans, of the strategy—"

Paul glared at Jeremy who promptly stopped speaking. Wick nodded and sipped his wine.

"Well, I'm glad to hear that," he said.

"For the past couple of shows, we haven't had the kind of turn out we want," Paul said. "But I think it's cause the bands were out-of-towners, you know? We just need to get people in the door with someone they know, and then they'll be like, 'Oh, hey, this is a cool place.'"

"I got you," Wick said.

"That's why it would be so great if you guys could come play one night," Paul said. "If you have the time."

"I think we could do that, yeah."

"Really?"

"Yeah."

"You've got my card so you can just call me whenever and we can talk details. Do you need another card?"

"Yeah, probably," Wick said. "Why don't you give me another one."

Wick took the card from Paul and stuck it in his breast pocket.

"Make sure you book him before October 5th," Yoel said, "cause I want to come."

"You leave October 5th?" Paul asked.

"Yeah, have to be back in LA on the 6th."

"Well, that's plenty of time," Paul said. "We can definitely make that happen on our end. Does that work for you, Wick?"

"I need to talk to Alfonso," he said, "but hopefully, yeah. This guy deserves a send-off."

ADA AND BEN drove home as the sun was setting, the light soft and orange on the distant granite peaks. The temperature was cooler now, the alpine winds blowing down the slopes, across the foothills, and out toward the hot valley floor. Ada was coming down from all the wine drinking. They talked briefly about the Garcias but then she grew tired and fell asleep. Ben drove past the liquor store, its neon sign blinking in the night. Two loggers stood in the parking lot, orange hard hats in hand, smoking cigarettes. You saw fewer loggers than you used to, but they were still around, and their union still had some sway over the town's politics.

Ben eased past the co-op and the bookstore and the movie theater, where a small line was queuing up for that evening's showing. He was enjoying being out and driving around so he decided to take the long way to 51. He turned left on Prospect Street, which headed over the river, and into the north side of town. The streets here were wide and leafy, the homes a hodge-podge of different architectural styles: nonsymmetrical Queen Annes with cupolas and turrets, Dutch cottages, sturdy Colonial Revivals. There were a few churches on this side of town, along with B'nai Tikvah, one of the only synagogues in the region. The Hechts had been members there since they moved to Natoma. When Yoel was in Sunday school, Ben would go to services with him every week. They would stay for the bagel brunch for about a half hour afterward, and then sneak off to watch the one-o'clock 49ers game.

Eventually he made it back out to 51, headed past the feed store and the massage and wellness clinic and the old hotel, which appeared to be at capacity, its restaurant patio filled with diners. He wished they could go out for a meal there, but they couldn't afford it. They could barely afford olive oil. At least they had come into some wine today. Yami had sent them home with an entire case. The bottles clinked against each other now in the back seat as he accelerated onto the highway.

By the time he got to Mountainview, darkness had descended. He drove slowly, his window down, all around the sounds of the forest settling into night, everything quieting, everything smelling of cold pine and oak. Up and down the hill the vineyards were ripe with fruit, harvest just around the corner. It was going to be a busy month, but tonight would be quiet and easy. Tonight he would make mint tea and lie in bed and read—or maybe he would draw a bath. That sounded nice. Up ahead of him the farmhouse came into view, yellow light leaking from its windows. They'd left a light on for Harriet and George, who would be waiting for them at the front door, delirious with doggish joy. He pulled up the gravel driveway and parked in front of the chapel. He put his hand on Ada's arm to wake her.

"We're home," he said.

She rubbed her eyes and looked around for a moment. Then she reached into her pocket and took out her phone.

"Oh," she said.

8

MOST OF THE PEOPLE who lived in Natoma understood that wildfire was essential for a forest. They knew that it helped return nutrients to the soil and that certain species were adapted to its presence. Many knew that Native peoples had, for generations, cultivated wildfire throughout the region. But they also knew that things had been changing. They saw the smoke, which descended for days, sometimes weeks, at a time. They read about the catastrophic fires in other towns, about the dry lightning storms and the rainless pyroclouds. Not all fires were bad, but it was hard to tell which ones were good anymore.

The fires seemed to move in different ways now. They burned hotter, burned larger, burned at higher elevations. Fire season itself lasted longer. People who had once thought they understood the parameters of how fire worked in the landscape now saw it as unpredictable. It was hard not to feel like you were watching an unraveling. It was hard not to wonder where the bottom was. Was this the year they figured out what could and could not happen? Or would the next fire, once again, surprise them?

In response to this unpredictability, the utility company had begun shutting off power whenever they deemed there to be heightened fire risk. This was good in the sense that it reduced the likelihood of an ignition, but it came with its own set of challenges. For people like the Hechts, who had a large generator, it wasn't so bad. But others were not as fortunate. Many lost their air conditioning, lost their internet, or in some serious cases, lost the functionality of important medical equipment. The hospital was always flooded with extra patients during an outage. The local coffee shops were full of customers camping out to charge their devices. At the hardware store, people shopped for battery-powered lanterns, for candles, for portable radios.

It would be one thing if these outages were happening only occasionally. But over the past few years, the town was having to deal with several of them a summer. It was good that the utility company was trying to prevent fires, everyone agreed, but this was clearly not a viable long-term solution. Many advocated for more prescribed burns, for a return to the Native practices that reduced the fuel on the forest floor, thereby preventing dangerous fires. And some of this was done. But it was difficult to fully implement this strategy. Property owners often did not want burns on or near their property. Others opposed the burns because they caused air pollution. And then there were difficulties in coordinating agencies across the region, procuring resources. In the end, the forest floors remained overly thick with bushes and small trees and the utility company, terrified of new incidents, continued to cut the power.

According to the alert Ada received, this most recent power outage could last anywhere from one to three days. Heavy winds and hot temperatures were expected during this period of time. "Prime conditions for a fire," a utility company representative said on the news. That was the problem these days, for the utility company, for the residents of Natoma, for everyone: the conditions were always prime for a fire.

In the morning, over coffee, Yoel asked if it was OK for Halle to stay in the guest bedroom during the outages. She could go to Seba and Yami's, Yoel said, but she had to stay on the couch if she went there. Ben wiped his mustache with the back of his hand, said that seemed fine to him. There was obviously something romantic developing between the two of them. They were spending so much time together. Ben thought it was sweet, but he wasn't going to say anything about it. Not until Yoel brought it up himself. As he was thinking about this, Ada walked into the room.

"Can someone look over these royalty statements with me?" she said. "I just want to make sure they didn't miss anything."

"I'll look at it," Yoel said.

The two of them sat down at the kitchen counter together and Yoel began to scrutinize the statements. Ada didn't get much in royalties anymore—the occasional check from the fresco book, usually a couple thousand dollars a year. Ben looked over Yoel's shoulder as he ran through the numbers on the PDF. There were lines for e-book and paperback, lines for income and expenses and returns.

After several minutes of review, Yoel concluded that the statements were up-to-date: Ada wasn't owed anything. As he broke the news, a call came through on his phone. He took it out and stared blankly at it for a few moments. Ben could see Yoel's boss's name, but Yoel silenced the phone, put it back in his pocket.

"Shouldn't your agent be checking this?" Yoel said.

"She said she did, but I just wanted to double-check," Ada said. She shut one eye, pressed her palm to her forehead. "Fuck, I have such a headache right now." Ben and Yoel watched her in silence for a few seconds.

"It's probably cause you've been staring at this boring document," Yoel said. His phone was buzzing again. Yoel took it out and silenced it. Ben saw that it was once again his boss.

"Why don't we go for a quick walk?" Yoel said.

"I'm just going to go lie down," Ada said.

"No, come on, we're going to go for a walk."

Yoel put his arm around his mother and helped her up. Then he slammed shut her computer and the two of them walked over to the doorway to put on shoes.

"You want to come?" Yoel asked Ben.

"No, you two go," he told him. "I'm going to get started in the vineyard."

After Yoel finished putting on his shoes, he came back over and set his phone on top of Ada's computer, punched Ben in the shoulder, and walked out the door. Through the kitchen window, Ben watched the two of them head down the driveway and out onto Mountainview.

HE SPENT THE REST of the day picking samples to test for smoke taint. The more he read about it, the more confident he was that it wouldn't be an issue, given the timing of the fire and how immature the berries had been at that point in the season. But still, it needed to be done. Like everyone else in the county, he was doing many small fermentations, testing clusters from each block. He conducted these fermentations in blue plastic buckets, which he kept on the cooler side of the chapel. It was an involved process because, about five times a day, the crushed grapes needed to be stirred. After five days, if all went well, he would have a small sample of wine from each cluster. The samples would then be shipped off to the lab, where they could be tested for smoke taint markers.

Outside in the vineyard, in between the rows, the tarweed was blooming yellow. It clung to his socks and the air was full of its spicy odor. As he picked clusters, he imagined the possibility of another fire. Just the other day he'd read about a new fire in Clear Lake, their second big one of the season. Another fire in Rose County would be devastating. He tried not to linger on these kinds of thoughts, tried to bring his attention to the work at hand, but it was difficult.

Later that afternoon, as he was heading back up to the chapel in the four-wheeler, he saw Halle's car in the driveway. He unloaded the grapes he'd just picked and then walked down the passageway that led from the chapel into the kitchen. Halle had the door of the fridge open, was rearranging things. She said she had come by to drop off some food from her fridge, which would have gone bad during the outage.

"Yoel said it was OK," she said.

"Oh yeah, that's fine," Ben said.

Looking at the fridge, he was reminded of the day they returned home after the fire, of the putrid smell, the frantic surveying of the property. Halle closed the door of the fridge and looked at Ben.

"You OK?" she said.

"What? Oh yeah, I'm fine. It's just . . . it was hot out."

She nodded. He could feel a faint twinge in his rib.

"You heard any updates?" she asked.

"Power's going to be out later in the afternoon. Yoel said there could be winds up to seventy miles per hour."

She sighed.

"Do you know where you'll evacuate to?"

"Back to my brother's, I think. You could come there too."

"Oh, thanks. I have some friends in San Francisco I can stay with too. Wine people. They live in Potrero."

"That's good."

"Yeah, it's far but it'll work."

"It is far," he said.

"I get so . . . It's just so disappointing. I was already having a hard week and now this."

"What's going on?"

"It's just a bunch of stuff at work. I know it's difficult for everyone right now. I don't mean to complain."

He thought about Ada this morning. When she came back from her walk with Yoel, she'd gone straight to work in the garden.

"It's a hard time," he said.

"Seems like right now we're dependent on the wind."

"That's what I'm hearing too."

She looked down at her phone, quickly responded to a text, and then looked back at Ben.

"If there's another fire right now our harvest is fucked," she said.

The previous week he'd made another payment, the checking account dwindling ever lower. He was used to boom-and-bust cycles, that was always how it had been with cannabis too. You started in March, had to wait all the way till November to find out what your return was. Then you took that huge influx of cash and, if you were Ben, for example, you bought stained glass and lumber to build a huge chapel next to your house. Or you bought a brand-new tractor. Or you put solar panels on the roof.

He had grown accustomed to having that kind of money to play with in those years. It had been fun, he had enjoyed it, but he didn't need to live like that anymore. All he wanted was to make enough to keep the farm, to take the pressure off of Ada, allow her to write in peace. She was struggling a lot lately. This morning was not the first time he'd seen it. There was the stress of the book, the stress of their finances, the ambient stress of the fires. At night, she said, she sometimes awoke with a copper taste in her mouth. She would remain awake, staring up at the ceiling. It wasn't like her.

Halle walked over to the kitchen counter, where he had been standing, and the two of them gazed out at the garden. Just another month and they would be through the harvest. That wasn't so improbable, was it? In the distance, a lone chicken wandered along the stone pathway. They watched it come and go. Then Halle nodded toward one of the apple trees by the front porch. Beneath the tree there was a plastic container of apples Ada had picked earlier that day.

"Those any good?" Halle asked.

"Yeah."

"I'm gonna go eat one," she said, and walked away.

THAT NIGHT THE WIND charged down from the mountains in great, swelling runs. Its most powerful gusts caused the windows of the house to tremble, just like they'd done on the night of the fire. The power had gone out at around seven in the evening, while they were eating dinner: two pizzas from the brewery that Halle had picked up after work. Lying in bed now, he could hear the familiar low hum of the generator, though it was often drowned out by the noise of the wind.

He put on Wick's backgammon podcast for a bit but, after an hour of listening, he still felt agitated. He decided to go read in the living room. The other night he'd started the Argentine novel that Seba recommended. He settled into the easy chair, put his phone on the table in front of him, in case any alerts came through, and opened the book to the second chapter. The story took place in the nineties and its protagonist was a conceited mathematician.

He had only been reading for a few minutes when Yoel walked into the room. He had a tissue in his hand and he was wearing blue pajama pants. He blew his nose and then leaned against the back of the couch.

"Can't sleep with that wind," he said.

"You nervous?"

"A bit."

"Me too." Ben stood up. "How about pancakes?" he said.

He walked into the kitchen and set his book on the counter. While he whipped up some batter, Yoel picked up the book and began flipping through it.

"So the mathematician is blinded?" he asked.

"What? No, not yet. Don't spoil it," he said, reaching for the book. Yoel turned away, shielding it while he leafed further.

"Hang on, let me just get to the last page here and figure it out for you—"

He opened his mouth, about to read.

"Don't do it," Ben said.

Yoel looked at him, raised his eyebrows, then closed the book.

"Impossible," Ben said, grinning.

Ben reached up to take one of the cast irons down from over the stove.

"My dad used to make pancakes for us when we couldn't sleep sometimes. Your grandpa Alvie."

"What was he like?"

"Oh, I wish you could have met him. He would have loved you. He loved people who had great work ethic, like you. And you two could have played golf together."

"He liked golf?"

"Yeah, after golf he and his friend Goldberg always went to the snack bar for gribenes. Fried chicken skin with onion."

"Gross."

"It was an acquired taste."

Ben poured out a splash of oil, watched its clear bloom spread to the edge of the pan.

"Mom wanted to know if you made the appointment with the dentist," Ben said.

"Not yet, but I will."

"You don't have a dentist down there?"

"No, I need to get one. I just haven't had the time."

Ben turned around to face Yoel, who had taken a seat at the table. At the mention of his mother, he had grown slightly more serious.

"Can I ask you something?" he said. "Is Mom OK?"

He was tapping the spine of the book on the table, blinking slightly.

Ben paused for a moment before answering. He wanted Yoel to not worry, but he also wanted to be truthful with him.

"Well, I think she's struggling a bit," Ben said.

Yoel brought his hand to his chin, began to stroke his beard. He had grown out a short beard in the past few weeks. It was brown, with specks of red here and there.

"It's just so fucked," he said, tugging on the beard.

"Yeah, it is," Ben said.

He turned back to the pan, spooned some batter into it. The air filled with the scent of fried dough. They were silent as Ben fried up the pancakes. When he was done, he brought two heaping plates to the table, set one in front of Yoel.

Outside the wind roared and roared. Yoel looked down at his pancakes.

"Sometimes," he said. "I'll think I've spotted the manuscript somewhere. I know it sounds crazy. But like, I'll walk into the living room and for a second, I'll think I see it in the corner of the room or something."

He knifed a tab of butter onto the top of his pancakes, drenched them in syrup.

"I know that sounds crazy," he said, forking off his first bite. "But it keeps happening."

THE FOLLOWING EVENING, in the chapel, Halle and Ben discussed plans for harvest. Yoel was down at Brinkers helping Paul record an ad for the radio. He had initially been going for a kind of smear campaign against the owners of the other bars in town, but Yoel was able to steer him away from this. They had settled on a pretty generic bit of copy. Yoel also convinced him to say that he would donate 1 percent of proceeds to the Rotary. People in Natoma loved the Rotary.

Yoel had said he'd be back after dinner but the recording was obviously taking longer than expected. Halle and Ben sat at the worktable with their laptops. Above them, dried herbs hanging, chamomile and nettle, which Ben used to make compost tea. He had just shown Halle the fermentations he was working on, which were almost ready to be shipped off to the lab to test for smoke taint. Outside the wind had calmed, but there was still a red flag warning throughout the county. Earlier that day, Ben had read an article in the paper that said power would likely be restored overnight, assuming no new fires broke out.

Halle had opened a bottle made by another young local winemaker she liked, a guy named Wendell. It was a white blend, primarily featuring Verdelho, a Portuguese varietal that had long been grown in the foothills. Wendell had given her a box of these wines last year: they were all shiners, unlabeled bottles, which couldn't be sold. Apparently Wendell's labeler had broken at some point, and that's why he'd ended up with all these shiners.

Halle had tried one of the bottles right after Wendell had gifted her the box, and she'd enjoyed it. It was obvious the grapes had been pressed to oak—that flavor was clear. Beyond the Verdelho, though, she was not sure what other grapes were in the blend. Wendell hadn't told her. Ben asked what she thought.

"Couldn't even guess," she said, laughing. "Sémillon? Chardonnay?" This was something Ben admired about Halle. She took herself seriously, had real ambition, but she never faked it, never acted like she knew something when she didn't.

As they sipped the wine, they discussed their first pick, the Gamay, which would take place sometime the week after next. Halle said Paul and Jeremy would help with picking, in exchange for some wine on the other end of things. Yoel and Ada had volunteered to help too, and Ben was also going to reach out to Wick. With that crew, they probably wouldn't need to hire any additional help.

Ben would operate the tractor through the rows and also transport the grapes using a rented trailer. He would go to the Torneo facility first, to drop off the grapes he'd allotted to them, and then head to Orion, where Seba and Yami would be waiting for him. This second leg was where things might get dicey because, under the warm sun, the grapes could begin to ferment en route. But they figured that if they started picking at 3 A.M., there would be plenty of time to make both of these deliveries, before the heat of the day really ramped up.

Halle had actually wanted Ben to pick the grapes earlier, when they were around twenty-two Brix. She wanted to make lighter wines, and the lower the sugar in the grapes when picked, the lower the alcohol content in the finished wine. But Torneo would not allow this: the lowest they would go, Brix-wise, was twenty-four, so this was what they settled on for the pick. It would have been too complicated, they agreed, to do two separate picks. Halle was still excited about the possibilities for the wine. With the Gamay, she was going to make a vin de soif, an easy, thirst-quenching drinking wine. With the Syrah and Grenache, she was going to make a Rhône-style blend. She was also going to produce a piquette, a very light, wine-adjacent beverage that was made by adding water to the grape pomace, or the grapes that were left over after the first pressing. This drink had been around since antiquity, and was often consumed by field workers and their families, who couldn't afford wines made from a first pressing.

After they had wrapped up their meeting, Ben corked the bottle and handed it back to Halle.

"I sent a bottle of this down to my grandmother," she said. "She didn't like it."

Halle's grandmother was ninety and lived in Palm Desert. The two of them were very close. Halle had been close to her grandfather too. He had operated a successful track lighting company for many years but had since passed away.

"She's nervous about all this stuff with the fires," Halle continued. "My parents too."

"Makes sense," Ben said. "How are you feeling?"

"OK," she said. "Will definitely be better when this passes. I've been having what I've started to refer to as 'pillowcase moments,' where I look around my room and think about what I could grab and stuff into a pillowcase in fifteen minutes. You know, the stuff that you don't keep in your bugout bag but that you'd try to take with you, the pictures and so forth."

"I do something similar, but for me it's the animals. I'll start thinking about which ones I'm going to grab first, where I'll put them. It's a whole process. Makes me stressed out just thinking about it."

"I bet," Halle said. She looked down at her phone, checked the time. "Well, I'm going to go watch some TV," she continued. "Try to take my mind off all this."

Then her phone began to buzz.

"Oh shit," she said.

"What?"

"It's Michael, hang on."

She picked up the phone and Ben could hear the sound of an irritated voice on the other end.

"But it's ten o'clock and there's a red flag warning," Halle said.

The sound of the voice again. Halle looked over at Ben and rolled her eyes.

"Uh huh," she replied. "OK, yeah. I'll come. OK, yeah, see you soon."

She hung up and then explained that she needed to go meet Michael at the winery.

"It can't wait?" Ben asked.

"With Michael it can never wait," Halle said.

He felt sleep deprived from the previous night, but he didn't want her to have to go over there alone. It was way out in a pretty remote part of the county.

"Let me come with you," he said. "What if something sparks while you're out there?"

"I'm OK, it's fine."

"No, please let me come with. I'll keep you company."

She closed her laptop, put it under her arm. Then she turned and looked out the window.

"I just wanted to spend the rest of the night watching people find their algorithmically matched partners," she sighed.

AS HALLE DROVE along 51, Ben looked out at the dark, cool forest. The wind was driving up the canyon, gaining velocity as it squeezed through the ravines. It was a different kind of wind. Normally, in the summer, the hot air rose during the day and pulled in air eastward, from the valley. The cold air then went back west at night and into the early morning. But this was all reversed. The wind was coming from the west at night, sometimes even from the north, and it was a strong wind. If there was any other kind of ignition, a blaze would grow easily.

Michael Deliso Winery was located just west of town, near the trailhead for Aum's Loop. Ben and Ada sometimes hiked along this trail, which had been developed out of the Toledo Ditch, a canal built by Chinese workers in the nineteenth century in order to deliver high-pressure water for hydraulic mining. Along the west side of the trail, there were several wooden flumes, which had been used to transport lumber, and one of these flumes crossed right over the Michael Deliso parking lot. As a result, Michael Deliso had incorporated flume iconography into their label, which featured a man shooting downhill in a flume boat, a placid look on his face.

Of all the wineries in the region, Michael Deliso was the oldest and most prestigious. Ben had gone tasting there with Ada's folks years ago, when they came to visit. What little Ben knew about Michael Deliso, he had learned from the local paper. He knew Deliso had studied at UC Davis, that he came from a winemaking family, who had been farming in the foothills for half a century. And he knew Deliso had been one of the leading opponents of the plan to revive the Yellow Daisy Mine, which was located a couple miles away from his property.

When they got to the entrance to the winery, Halle typed in a keypad code to open the swinging metal gates. The gardens along the driveway were lit with low light and immaculately landscaped. Rose bushes and native grasses and large egg-shaped urns. At the end of the driveway there was a parking lot, which was empty, except for one lone Tesla, presumably Deliso's. Deliso himself was standing in front of the cellar's antique iron doors, a mop in hand. He looked to be around Ben's age, though perhaps a bit older. He wore a fleece vest over a checkered dress shirt, a hat that said, "Ponderosa Bocce Club."

"Finally," he said. There was a distinct drag to his voice, and his eyes looked swollen. Or maybe that was just the way his eyes always were. He seemed to not register Ben's presence, but simply turned around and strode inside. Halle and Ben followed after him. Entering the cellar Ben saw towering racks of oak barrels, a forklift that could be used to reach them. There were also presses, pumps, hoses everywhere. All the equipment was shiny and new, nothing like what was in the Garcias' cellar. Deliso set down his mop, picked up a glass of wine that had been resting on a barrel, and took a sip. He swished the wine around in his mouth, made a sound like he was sucking it through his teeth, swallowed, and then turned to face Halle.

"I can't deal with you anymore," he said.

"Is there an issue with one of the barrels?" she asked.

"What?" Deliso said, looking off at some point in the distance.

"Is there an issue with one of the barrels?" Halle repeated. "Or something we need to deal with? I figured it was an emergency."

Deliso did not respond but simply turned and walked away through the cellar. Ben had seen this type of character a thousand times. He glanced at Halle.

"Let's get going," he said. "This guy's gone."

"I know," she said. "Let me just see—"

"Over here!" Deliso roared.

They turned and saw him standing by one of the cellar's drains.

"Over here!" he repeated. "Come look at this."

Halle walked over, Ben following. He watched as Deliso got down on one knee. Next to the drain, he picked up a wrinkled grape skin.

"What the fuck is this," he said, holding it up. "Tell me what the fuck this is."

"I've been getting everything ready for harvest," Halle said. "I worked twelve hours yesterday checking all the equipment, cleaning, dealing with the sparkling—"

"Well, you didn't clean this. First grapes of the year and I already find this in a drain?"

"It's one skin."

"We're going to get flies because of this, Halle. Bacteria. This is not up to our standards. This is not acceptable."

"Come on," Ben said. "Time to go."

"Why are you here?" Deliso asked.

"He's my friend," Halle said.

Deliso breathed through his nose.

"Not close to our standards," he said.

"We're going to go," Halle said. "But I'll see you tomorrow."

"Do you know what it's taken me to build this place from the ground up?" Deliso said, still on one knee, holding the grape skin between his thumb and forefinger. "The sweat I have poured into this name. And you just treat it like shit. You really don't fucking care."

Halle didn't respond.

"The floor drains need to be cleaned completely," he continued. "With peroxy. Every day. They need to be thoroughly scrubbed out. You know this."

He was staring at Halle now. Ben could see fear in her eyes.

"Do you not know this? Answer me. How many times have we talked about these being completely cleaned every day?"

"We've talked about it."

"So fucking lazy," he snarled.

"That's enough," Ben said.

Deliso looked up at him.

"That's enough," Ben repeated. "Here look." He reached out and snatched the grape skin from Deliso's hand, put it in his pocket.

"Problem solved," he said. "We're leaving now."

ON THE CAR ride home, Halle seemed dazed. She kept reaching up with her free hand, tucking her hair behind her ears. Outside the wind was still blowing. They rolled the windows down and the air smelled like rock and sunbaked fir needles. As Halle pulled back out onto 51, Ben cleared his throat.

"You can't reason with a person when they're like that," he said.

"No yeah, I know."

"When a person gets to that point, it's all over. There's no point in having any kind of dialogue."

"Last time he got drunk, he told me we needed to reinvent the whole brand, go for something more modern and stylish. We were out at dinner. He said we were going to 'shoot this thing to the moon.' He was acting like he was some blockchain

CEO or something. The next morning he didn't remember any of it. He was hungover and screamed at me about putting the brooms back in the wrong place. He's not going to remember any of this, he never does."

"Probably not."

"Another time—I'm not kidding you—he literally fell asleep with his head on the side of a barrel. He came in and he wanted me to take him around to taste everything and he fell asleep on a barrel while he was listening to see if it was still fermenting."

They were approaching town from the west now, passing the liquor store that sold wild jerky. Halle shook her head.

"It wasn't always this bad," she said. "It's gotten worse. I'm sorry you had to see that."

"You're sorry?" Ben said. "I'm sorry you're dealing with that."

"I know but what am I going to do? He's so well connected. I've already put in so much time with him, put up with so much shit. I want to at least be able to get what I need from him. I can't just bounce and ruin the relationship."

Ben nodded.

"But I'm not staying there much longer," she continued. "I wish I could just focus on our thing. Be done with him. Soon, once we get our production up."

He looked over at Halle, his sweet partner. She was tucking her hair behind her ear again. Michael Deliso was not going to get her down. He wouldn't let it happen.

"We're going to crush that guy," Ben said. "No doubt in my mind. Just absolutely run him out of his business."

She glanced over at him and he winked. Then she looked back at the road, a smirk growing at the corner of her mouth.

"It will be biblical," he said. "He's going to come running to us begging for mercy."

"With his ugly bocce club hat in his hand," she said.

"And we will say, 'Sir, in the wine business, there is no mercy.'"

She raised a finger.

"And even after his business is ruined," she said, "a great many pestilences will befall his house."

"Yes."

"Lizards in his winery. Frogs? Was it frogs? I haven't read the Bible in a while."

"I think it's frogs," he said.

"Frogs everywhere! A hail of dried grape skins!"

She smacked the wheel and they both laughed. They had just passed the town, were heading toward the 51 bridge. There were no other cars around. Halle flicked on her high beams, and the sides of the road bloomed into ghostly view.

"Yeah," she murmured. "One more harvest."

AFTER THE OUTAGES ENDED, Halle moved back to her apartment. But, in the following weeks, they continued to see her around the farm all the time. She and Yoel seemed to be hanging out nonstop. In the past, even on weekends, Yoel would spend a lot of time working. He would read scripts or edit beat sheets or sometimes even take calls from Jerry. But he was doing less of this. Instead, he was staying up till 3 A.M. watching a six-hour Italian movie with Halle. Or the two of them were meeting at Brinkers or Orion or Danny's Café. One weekend, they went camping high up in the mountains, at Triangle Peak.

And so, when he finally told them, one night at dinner, that he had a crush on Halle, they were unsurprised. Both Ben and Ada had long suspected this, had talked about it. The surprise, however, was that Yoel's feelings were not reciprocated. Apparently, he and Halle had gotten drunk one night on the camping trip and Yoel had confessed his crush to her. She'd told him that she deeply valued their friendship but didn't think she had romantic feelings toward him.

Yoel's affect was muted as he relayed this to Ben and Ada, resolute. The reality was, he said, he probably wasn't ready to start a new relationship anyway, given how recently he and Sally had separated. But the feelings were there. What could he do? He told them he appreciated how honest Halle had been with him, and that they had resolved to stay friends.

"We're handling it like adults," Yoel said. "Don't worry. Nothing's going to get weird."

And the truth was, their friendship didn't seem to take a hit at all. Halle continued to come over to the farm after work almost every day, and she usually stayed for dinner. Ben remembered that kind of dynamic, a deep friendship that tottered on the edge of romance. He'd had a few of those and sometimes, the broaching of romance almost brought you closer, cleared the air. It allowed the connection to take its more natural form. This seemed to be what was happening with Halle and Yoel.

One weekend, around this time, Ben's brother came up to visit. Andrew said Jenny had wanted to come too, but she had to stay home because her mother was in the hospital, recovering from getting a pacemaker installed. The day he arrived, Ben took him up to the top of the hill, showed him the burn scar, explained what it was like coming back to the house after the fire. Then they went back down to the patio and opened a bottle of wine. Ben caught him up on everything that had happened the whole summer: the project with Halle, the latest on Ada's manuscript. He told him how good things had been with Yoel lately, and Andrew seemed relieved to hear this. It was so nice having his brother here. He was such a settling presence. Though it was a little jarring to see him take in the destruction of the fire. Ben had grown accustomed to the dry, ashy landscape, but looking at it with his brother, he saw it through new eyes.

"And they cut the power again?" Andrew said.

"We had fifty-mile-per-hour gusts."

"Jesus."

The next morning they had breakfast with Ada and Yoel, and then the whole family dispersed to their tasks of the day. Ada to her office, and the three Hecht men to the vineyard. They needed to fix part of the fence near the Primitivo lot. A bear had come through there the other night, squashed the fence, and proceeded to eat some of their grapes. Growers in the region were reporting an irregular number of issues with bears. The thinking was that, because there were so many fires deeper in the forest, the bears needed to come down from their higher-altitude summer homes in search of food. It was possible the bear would just come along and squash the fence again, but Ben hoped if they built it up a little higher, it would be OK. The best thing to do would be to install a fully electrified fence, but he didn't have the time or money to do that at the moment.

After they were outside for about a half hour, Ben heard the sound of Ada's leaf blower—a signal only he likely recognized. He felt a momentary nervousness overtake him, thinking about

Ada and the state of her book. Yoel seemed slightly off-balance too. He was talking to Andrew about Halle, who, he said, was supposed to come over that afternoon. He breezed over the part about having a crush on her, but did mention it. Mostly he told Andrew about the kind of wine she made. Andrew said he'd heard of natural wine but never tried it. At a certain point, Yoel looked down at his phone.

"Ah, she's not coming," he said, staring at the phone. "Too bad. Wanted you to meet her."

"Maybe another time," Andrew said.

"She's hungover." Yoel looked up from his phone. "Guess she, um, had a good time last night," he said.

"What was last night?" Ben said.

"She was out on a date."

"Oh," Ben said. Some sort of bug landed on the strap of his suspenders and he flicked it off. "Anyone we know?"

"Lonnie Harris."

Ben remembered the name, though he hadn't seen the kid in years. He'd gone to high school with Yoel.

"He was the kid who played college football, right?" he asked.

"Yeah, I guess she likes jocks," Yoel said.

"It wasn't meant to be," Andrew said. "Probably wouldn't have worked anyway, with you down in LA and her up here."

"Yeah."

"So it's all good."

"Yeah."

It took them a few hours to finish the fence, but they were able to get it done before the heat of the day really kicked in. It was supposed to be another triple-digit afternoon, their second in a row. Hopefully it would cool off a bit after that. In the summer, they always hit triple digits at some point, but ideally it didn't happen too often, otherwise the grapes got baked.

Back inside, Yoel headed off to his room. Andrew and Ben sat down in the living room, opened beers, and put on Wick's new record, which Ben had bought at the McEwan's party.

"I don't miss that age," Andrew said, nodding toward Yoel's room. "Too much heartbreak."

They listened to the album and talked about old friends, people from their Berkeley days, when the two of them lived in a co-op together. It was barely a co-op, only nine members—more like a big, shared house. Ben had lived there before Hawaii and it had been a crash pad for him when he'd come back. After he moved up to Natoma, it also became his most consistently reliable zone of commerce. He would post up in the co-op for a few days and sell until he'd exhausted his product. People would hear he was in town and swing by the house. Andrew wasn't living in the co-op at that point. He'd moved out before Ben.

After they had been talking for a little while, Andrew stood up.

"I brought you something," he said.

He walked into the guest bedroom, and emerged moments later with a manila file.

"What is this?" Ben said.

He opened the file, saw a printout of an article about his case. The headline: "Orchard-Like Pot Plants Seized in Natoma."

"Look in the back," Andrew said.

Ben rifled through the papers and saw a photocopy of one of his letters to Ada. It was one of the longer ones, around six pages. He leafed through the letter and then got to another one. There were at least three other letters here, and a couple of letters that Ada had written to him.

"It was my research files from the documentary," Andrew said. "I found it when I was cleaning out our basement the other day."

He looked up at his brother.

"Thank you for this," he said. "Thank you."

It wasn't Ada's manuscript. It wasn't every letter. But it was something. A piece of his life, returned.

9

THEY WERE HEARING, now, that it was already the biggest and most expensive wildfire season in the state's history. The Clear Lake fire was still growing, and there were other blazes in Plumas County and in the southern part of the state. They read about them in the paper. The forest service didn't have enough firefighters to work the blazes so outside contractors were being brought in. These private contractors were more expensive but the forest service didn't have any other options. They needed all the help they could get. Helicopters and air tankers and hotshot crews were descending from all over the nation.

There was talk now, too, that the insurance companies might pull out soon, might simply stop providing new insurance for homes in fire-prone regions. If this happened their homes would all lose their value. The people of Natoma read about this in the paper too. The papers these days, national and local, were filled with terrifying news. Some mornings, it was too much to open them. At birthday parties, hosts took them off the table, shoved them into a cabinet, out of sight.

"Let's get that depressing stuff out of here," they said.

There was only so much they could take. They talked to each other of the fatigue, of the fear. To have this thing hanging over you, it crushed the spirit. Some took practical actions: they joined volunteer-firefighting groups, installed sprinkler systems on their roofs. Others covered their ears, decided that it wasn't really that big of an issue, that the media was blowing it out of proportion. But most of them did take it seriously. Most of them woke in the morning and looked at the horizon and looked at the calendar and prayed.

On the best of days, during the fire season, it was often on their minds. But when there were outages, when they knew a red flag warning was posted, it was particularly bad. You just hoped no one did anything stupid. You hoped there was no one out there starting a campfire, no one driving through town from out of state, with no idea where they were, throwing a cigarette out their window. In the evenings, they thought twice about having a second drink, or putting themselves in any kind of vulnerable situation. You didn't want to be the person who was drunk or on a sleeping pill when the evacuation orders came through. Those were the people who got stuck in their houses. They'd read about those people.

After Andrew left, there was the threat of another outage, but the windstorm never came, and the outage was canceled. With some trepidation, and the knowledge that there was still at least another month of fire season, they let themselves feel some sense of relief. Ben was now in the vineyard every day with his spectrometer, testing for Brix. Halle was doing the same thing for Michael Deliso, in their vineyards. She was stopping by the farm less now, with all the work she had, but for the most part, she and Yoel seemed to be on normal terms. Ben hadn't heard the name Lonnie Harris mentioned again.

Temperatures returned to the low nineties, the Brix on everything steadily moving higher. He was still giving the grapes some water at night, and for the most part, his irrigation well appeared to be holding out. Because of the dry winter, the water table was lower, and the well had started to show some signs that it was reaching its limits. Hopefully, right after harvest was complete, they'd get a big drenching, to refill the wells, and quell any fire risk. If there wasn't solid rainfall, he would have to make an adjustment the following year, and perhaps consider not cultivating certain blocks of the vineyard.

One day, after he was finished with his work, he walked over to the irrigation well to check its levels. He had a system for doing this that involved a long strand of radiant heating tubing, a pressure gauge, and a bike pump. Wick had devised this system, which he'd apparently read about on an internet forum. The well was located on the south edge of the old Primitivo block, in a manzanita thicket. For several years in a row, he had cleared a pathway through the manzanita, to better access the well. But today, upon arriving, he noticed that there were tiny, two-inch shrubs all over the path again. Manzanita was incredibly vigorous and hard to remove. The best thing would be to get these little ones now, while they were still young, before they became thicker and more deeply rooted. But the idea of going at it with his pruning shears again sounded exhausting. Maybe he should just let the manzanita win. What was laziness and what was just accepting reality? It was hard to tell sometimes.

When he was done checking the well, he walked back up to the house. He sat down at the kitchen table to read his email and found that he had letters from both Torneo and Golden Hill. He opened the Torneo message first. The lab had just sent them the results of Ben's test fermentations:

"Due to the impact of excessive heat, ash, and smoke caused by the Bennett fire, and after careful analysis of officially submitted test fermentations, we have determined that the grapes from Hecht Vineyard will not meet the applicable Quality Standards and other requirements as stipulated in the force majeure clause of our agreement."

It was signed by their vice president of operations. He opened the Golden Hill email next and found an almost identical message. They were rejecting his grapes. He had considered this possibility but, the truth was, he had never really thought there was any chance of it happening. All of the smoke exposure had happened before veraison. The crop should have been fine. He reopened the Golden Hill letter, looked again at the attached report from the lab. The chance of someone else accepting these grapes, at this point, after they had been rejected by two other wineries, was next to nothing.

He walked out to the truck, grabbed a packet of Swedish tobacco from the glove compartment, put it in his mouth. Then he headed back to the front porch. It was almost dinnertime. Yoel was still in his room working. Ada was in town for a doctor's appointment but she would be back soon. A bunch of black flies were flying in circles in the cool shade of the porch, orbiting nothing. He took a seat on the couch and looked out at the chapel.

This was an entirely different sort of catastrophe. Without the money from Torneo and Golden Hill, they wouldn't be able to make their loan repayments for the rest of the year. And there was no chance of Halle's wines bailing them out either. Once she saw the results of these test fermentations, she wouldn't want the grapes either. He knew there were certain enology products winemakers could use to combat smoke taint—compounds made from potato proteins and so forth—but Halle wouldn't want to use anything like that. My god, he couldn't believe it. It was actually happening. They were going to lose the farm. After all this. It was unbelievable.

He wondered how many other grape growers were dealing with similar problems. This was the kind of thing that could put others out of business too. He had never actually tasted a smoke tainted wine, though he'd heard from others that it was pretty awful, like licking a burnt cigar. The crazy thing was his grapes did not taste bad at all. And neither had the test fermentations he'd tried—maybe a slight hint of smokiness, but that was sometimes a natural flavor profile, especially in Syrah. Still, he knew that smoke taint often took months to develop. Just because a grape tasted OK off the vine didn't mean it hadn't been affected.

After sitting on the porch for a few minutes, he headed back inside. Yoel was in the kitchen now, cooking himself an omelet.

"Was there bleach on one of these sponges?" he said, nodding at the sink. "I started to wash something with it and it smelled like bleach."

"Yeah, Mom keeps one of those for counters. The bottom one."

"Oh, I didn't realize that."

Yoel tentatively prodded the edge of the omelet with his spatula, testing its stiffness. Ben reached under the sink, pulled out the house jug, and poured himself a glass of wine.

"You want a glass?"

"I'm good," Yoel said. He flipped and plated the omelet, and then looked back at his dad. "Everything OK?"

Ben started to explain the situation but before he had said more than a few sentences, Ada walked in the door. She was wearing a light shawl and straw hat. She took off the hat and hung it on a hook by the door.

"There's smoke taint," Yoel said.

"What?" she said. "Oh no."

"They're rejecting everything," Ben said.

"There's nothing to be done?"

"I'll try calling around tomorrow, but probably not."

"What about Sloan?" she said. "Could Sloan help?"

"I'll call her, but I doubt it."

"Oh no."

Ben noticed he was clenching his jaw and he tried to loosen it. His hip was hurting again too. Was his hip pain psychosomatic? Well, whatever, it didn't matter, it was hurting. He walked over to the kitchen table with his glass of wine and sat down. Ada joined him, put her hand on top of his. Yoel came over a few moments later with his omelet and the three of them sat there together. The last light of day moved easy through the casement windows. Outside the sound of some bird in the elm tree, making a noise like a squeaking hinge.

"I'm going to write the San Andreans about this," Yoel said.

Ben vaguely recognized the name, but he couldn't remember from where.

"The who?" Ben said.

"Oh, I only told Mom about this, I guess," he said. "It's a group of activists I've been talking to."

"They could help?" Ada asked.

"Maybe."

"I'll call Sloan tomorrow," Ben said. "What are they called? The San Andreans?"

"Yeah, like the fault line," Yoel said. "Halle introduced me to them. They do a lot of stuff: actions, mutual aid."

"I see."

"I mean, I don't know what they could do, but it's at least worth telling them about."

"Sure," Ben said. "I'd welcome any help, at this point."

Ben looked around the kitchen and then over toward the living room. In his mind, he began to imagine packing up everything in here. Where would you even start?

Ada picked up his glass of wine and took a sip.

"I had a dream about this," she said. "But I didn't want to give any keinehoras."

"What happened in the dream?" Ben asked.

She sighed.

"The thing we're all afraid is going to happen," she said.

YOEL WROTE HIS mysterious activist friends that night but it seemed they wouldn't be able to help. They were planning a big day of actions soon, they said, and they were putting all their focus into that. Ben hadn't held out much hope for their assistance anyway. What were they going to do? Pay off the loan on the farm? Ben didn't get the sense that it was a very large organization, or an organization with any money really. Yoel said there were around sixty or so active members, and others who were less active. They all used aliases with each other, though some had met in person. At first the group had sounded potentially sketchy but Yoel told him that they were good people. Ben didn't have too much time to worry about it anyway. He needed to figure out what to do with his crop.

The next day he called Halle first thing in the morning, told her the news. She was clearly disappointed, but he could tell she was trying to remain positive. She said she'd heard about a few other growers in Ponderosa having issues. Seba and Yami, on the other hand, had just gotten their tests back, and everything looked OK for them. Halle said she was going to talk things over with a few people and get back to him. She asked him to send her the reports. They spoke for a few minutes about the unpredictability of the whole situation, how the proximity of the fire to Ben's property was probably to blame.

He spent the rest of the day reaching out to other wineries and winemakers, without any success. *There were some issues with smoke taint?* they said. *What kind of issues?* The assistant winemaker at Rose Cellar told him he'd received inquiries from the other growers in Ponderosa whose grapes had also been compromised. That was over a week ago and the assistant winemaker had heard that they still hadn't been able to unload their grapes. Ben was several steps behind them. The finality of the situation was beginning to dawn on him.

At the end of the day, he eventually got a hold of Sloan Howard, his last real hope. Sloan had helped connect him with Torneo and Golden Hill and she was well respected in the industry. Maybe, with Sloan's word, someone would be willing to take a chance on the compromised grapes. When she picked up, Ben could tell Sloan was in her truck, out on the road somewhere. Much of her job revolved around visiting the different winemakers she worked with, seeing how things were going for them, if they needed any more of her yeasts or enzymes or lab equipment. Most of her clients were in wine country and the foothills, but she also worked with wineries on the Central Coast, which was where she was today, she said, heading to meet a friend for dinner.

"Well, I won't keep you for long," Ben said.

"It's OK, I've got a second."

Ben briefly relayed the situation. He had his computer open in front of him, with the results from the tests, in case Sloan wanted specific numbers. But she didn't ask for the data.

"I wish I could help you," she said, "but there's just no demand. Hard enough selling good grapes right now."

"I understand."

"If you've got the guaiacol and 4-methylguaiacol, they're just going to pass. You should look into insurance for next year."

"Yeah."

"I know it's pricey for someone small like you, but other people are starting to do it. This is just the reality of things."

"So you don't . . . there's not anyone who you think might be short?"

"No, not that I know of."

"Or anyone who . . . maybe just with your recommendation . . ."

"I'm sorry, Ben."

"No, yeah, OK. No problem. We'll figure it out."

"I wish I could help," Sloan said. "I don't know if it's any solace but it's not just you guys, you know. I was just up in Clear Lake the other day and they're having another fire up there now. You've heard about that one?"

"Yeah."

"So they're going to have a ton of problems with smoke taint up there, cause now we're basically into harvest. Anyway, I'm just saying . . . insurance is probably a good idea, from here on out."

"I'll look into it."

"Say hi to Ada for me, OK?"

"I will."

ADA WALKED INTO the kitchen after he had just finished the call with Sloan. He didn't need to say much. She could tell what he'd learned.

"Let's go for a walk," she said.

Harriet and George were wandering around the property somewhere so Ada and Ben just left by themselves. They hiked up through the Barbera, to a promontory at the top of the hill. There was a small granite boulder here, covered in patches of rust-colored lichen. This was where they had stood, years ago, just after buying the property. Before the new house was built, before Ben started growing anything. They had stood here, right after closing the deal, and looked out at all that grassy hill. Now the hill was covered with Barbera but before that it had been grass. Tall grass. For all those years when it was grass, they had never mown it. Even though it crept down the hill, right up to the edge of the house. They hadn't thought about that kind of thing then. Not at the beginning.

Ada reached down to her ankle, pulled a burr out of her sock, stood back up again.

"I haven't been able to get started on any writing," she said.

"It will come."

"Maybe."

"I still think you need to get out of town for a bit."

"Too expensive."

"It's worth spending a little money on."

"We don't have a little money to spend."

"We'll get it sorted," he said. "We will. We'll find a way to get through this year and then . . . I don't know."

He paused and looked out at the horizon. It was so hot out, the countryside quiet. All the animals were off somewhere, resting in the cool shade.

"People always wanted weed," he said. "You never had any issues with selling weed. Drive it down to Berkeley, boom, cash in hand."

"Boom, cash in hand and you'd go blow it on something ridiculous."

"True."

She looked over at him.

"We can't sell this place, Ben," she said. "It's going to break my heart."

"We're not there yet," he said, though he didn't really believe this anymore.

They continued up the hill, turned left, and headed out onto the road. They were going to walk over to the stone bridge on Berry Road and then turn around. As they were making their way up Mountainview, they saw James Thompson approaching from above. He was wearing shorts and a shirt that looked like it wicked sweat well. He was with his dog again and, when he reached them, the dog, who was wet from having swam in some unknown body of water, nuzzled up against Ben's leg, soaking his pants.

"Oh, come here," James said. "Sorry about that."

"That's all right," Ben said.

They spoke for a few minutes about the coming harvest. James told them many of the bigger wineries he worked with were having trouble scheduling picks, because of labor shortages.

"People are lazy these days," he said. "They only work when they want to."

"Well, harvesting is hard work," Ada said. "And migrant workers have been exploited for years."

"Work is work," he said. "That's how I see it. You should be happy if you got it."

They stepped off to the side of the road to let a car pass. Two women in floppy hats in a convertible, presumably on their way to a tasting somewhere.

"You end up having any issues with smoke taint?" James asked.

"We did, yeah," Ben said. "We do."

"You have crop insurance?"

Ben shook his head.

"Too bad."

"You don't know anyone who might be looking to buy?" Ada asked.

James grimaced.

"It's high-quality stuff," Ada said.

"But it tested for smoke taint. No one is going to take that."

"I heard some people have different thresholds, though."

"Listen, I'm telling you no one is going to take that stuff. We're rejecting anything that registers even an ounce of smoke taint."

"It's just," Ada said, "the farmer gets left with nothing in that case. The contracts are so unfair in that way."

"I recognize the situation you all are in," he said. "But I don't make the rules."

"But we could do it differently."

"I don't think so."

"This is a new situation we're all in. We need to adjust how we do things."

"I think it works well how we're currently doing it," James said.

There was something cold and vague in his voice, as though he thought his words were going to be quoted in an article.

"This is the way everyone does it," he said.

"Yes, I understand," Ada said. "Well, we're going to keep going. But you have a nice rest of your day."

She nodded to him and they continued on their walk. Ben didn't say anything for a while. When they turned onto Berry Road, he began rolling his shoulders, stretching them out as he walked.

"What a piece of shit," he said.

THE NEXT COUPLE OF days were slow and depressing. He read more about smoke taint online, even though reading wouldn't do much for him at this point. He looked into selling the antique toy railroad track, which he'd kept in the chapel for years, one of the only valuable antiques that had survived. And he went for a couple long walks in the neighborhood by himself. On one of these walks, he encountered all of Rita McKee's sheep in the middle of the road with no one around. He managed to guide them off the road and over toward her property. When he got home, he told Ada about it.

"I think she's starting to get a little batty," Ada said. "You know, a couple months ago she wanted me to go to court for her. She came by and was talking about how animal control was after her for one of her horses."

"Yikes."

"I told her, 'I'm not a vet. I can't testify.'"

On Wednesday afternoon he drove into town to buy groceries. After he was done at the co-op, he decided to pick up a sandwich for lunch across the street at Ander's. Inside, the store smelled like refrigerators and cold cheese. A high school student was working the register, wearing ear gauges and a black sweatshirt. She seemed to be cultivating a look of casual intimidation. Ben ordered a salami sandwich and a seltzer. While he was waiting for his sandwich, he scanned the store for Ander, but he didn't see him. He did notice Rudy, however, who was sitting at one of the counters, a bag of chips and a sandwich in front of him.

"All right, Ben?" he said.

"Doing OK, yeah."

"Ready for harvest I imagine."

"Well, not exactly."

Again he relayed the situation.

"I heard that was happening to some people," Rudy said. "That's a shame."

"Yeah," Ben said. "Hopefully can find something else to work on."

"All that fruit lost, though."

"Yeah, it's not great."

"The birds will be happy."

Two women with bandanas and jean jackets entered the store and began to peruse the chalkboard menu. For some reason, Ander's store had become a hot spot for motorcyclists touring the foothills. You almost always saw them here on the weekends. Rudy glanced over at the riders and then back at Ben.

"I don't mean to overstep," he said, "but do you have any interest in working at the co-op? We're pretty shorthanded."

"Oh."

"Yeah, they say they're going to need help in the fall. Two of our best guys are leaving. Minimum wage, but it's an easy job. Friendly people. Well, you know most of them. You're in there all the time."

Ben nodded.

"If you're interested, give me a call," Rudy said. "You don't have my number, do you?"

He gave Ben the number and Ben entered it into his phone.

"I could see you looking nice in one of these," Rudy said.

He pointed to his co-op T-shirt, which had his name stitched on the left-hand side in loopy red letters.

"Right, thank you," Ben said. "I'll think on it."

"No problem. Another thing is they give you a really good discount at the store. I save a lot that way. Lot of stuff that I would never buy that I buy now, because the discount is so good. Fancy nuts and so forth."

Ben heard the high school student calling his name.

"That's me," he said.

"OK," Rudy said. "You think on it."

"Appreciate it," Ben said, nodding at him.

He walked past the two riders, grabbed his sandwich, and on his way out, nodded to Rudy one more time.

Back at the house, he spent the rest of the afternoon tinkering around in the vegetable garden. Yoel and Ada were gone, out for a hike somewhere. At about four o'clock, he decided to retire. He opened a beer and headed out to the porch with the radio. His shirt was still sweaty but in the shade of the porch the sweat felt cool and good. He turned on the classical station, took out his phone, and did some quick calculations. He wanted to see what he would make annually at the co-op. It was barely enough to get by. And what would happen to the vineyard? Would they just let it go untended? No, that would just depress him. What was the point of staying on the farm if he couldn't even work it? Better to sell this place and start fresh somewhere else. Benicia maybe. Somewhere in the Delta. Homes were cheap out there.

He put away his phone, looked out across the driveway. Some cat he didn't recognize was lounging in their blackberry bushes. He watched it slowly stalk a squirrel under the apple tree and then, finally make its move. The squirrel darted up into the branches of the apple tree, and began issuing a chattering noise, mocking the cat. The cat slunk away, back into the bushes, to prepare a second assault. Confident now, in its ability to outmaneuver the cat, the squirrel edged back down the tree, toward the ground. Ben turned the radio louder, waited for the next skirmish. As he was sitting there, his phone rang. It was Halle. He picked up the call and walked inside.

She said she'd shared the smoke taint reports with Seba and he'd just had a chance to look at them. They were over at the winery together right now and the two of them had put Ben on speaker phone.

"I don't know," Seba said. "I mean, I look at these numbers, and they're not that bad. You know, the science of this is not exact. You're not tasting any smoke in the grape or the fermentation. The exposure happened before veraison. I think that all bodes pretty well."

"Why would they reject them then?"

Ben was holding the phone flat in front of his face, pacing back and forth in the kitchen.

"Well, could be inventory management," Seba said. "The market's slowing. Maybe they want to draw back on production."

"Really?"

"I'm not sure, but these markers. All I'm saying is these markers do not intimidate me."

"You would make wine with these grapes?"

"I would make wine with them."

He had stopped pacing, was staring out the kitchen window at the blackberry bushes. The cat was gone. There was silence on the other end of the line. He felt a surge of adrenaline, could barely get the words out.

"I guess . . ." he said. "I mean, no pressure, but Halle, do you want everything?"

HE WROTE RUDY to decline the offer and thank him. He wrote Wick and everyone else to tell them the pick was back on. There were still many ways this could go wrong, but he was filled with a sense of optimism. If Halle was able to sell most of the wines, Ben would likely quadruple a normal year's income from growing. Their previous plan had been tentative, more of a light side project. But now all the parties involved were more committed. They were both going to invest labor and energy in harvesting, and Halle would also have to increase her personal upfront investment in corks, bottles, labels, and so on. If there had been more time to deliberate, perhaps one of them would have bailed. But the decision had to be made in a matter of days. The fruit was ripe. It was full steam ahead into harvest.

The day before the Gamay pick, they went to bed at 6 P.M., while it was still light out. Of course, none of them could fall asleep at that time so when they woke, at 3 A.M., in the cold darkness, they had not slept more than a few hours. In the kitchen, Ben put on a pot of coffee and Ada began to make oatmeal. Yoel wandered in moments later, already wearing his headlamp. The day before, Ben had picked up items for lunch: tuna salad, focaccia bread, and several cheeses. He'd also made an almond cake. He packed these items into a cooler, along with a couple thermoses of coffee.

Soon their volunteer pickers began to arrive: Halle first, then Jeremy and Paul, and finally Wick. Ben handed them cups of coffee as they stepped inside, and small, curved harvesting knives. Wick, Halle, and Paul had their own headlamps but Jeremy didn't. Ben went over to the chapel to fetch him one. The orange water cooler was sitting by the door, ready to be loaded onto the tractor. He made a note to himself not to forget to do this. His mind was still mostly blank, but the coffee was starting to kick in. When he got back to the kitchen, he poured himself another coffee and looked around the room. Somehow, in the intervening minute he'd been gone, Wick had fallen asleep at the kitchen table.

"Come on, buddy," he said. "Time to get going."

Outside, on the porch, the pickers all grabbed grape bins. Briefly, they discussed the plan for the day. Everyone except for Jeremy had harvested grapes before so not much needed to be explained to them. Jeremy, however, had a lot of follow-up questions. Halle and Ben took turns responding to him and then, after a few minutes, Halle said it would probably be best if he just worked by her side for the first part of the day. Jeremy seemed pleased with this solution and with that, the pickers headed out into the blocks of Gamay. Ben walked over to the tractor and attached the small flatbed trailer to the back of it. Then he loaded the water and food cooler, along with several grape bins, and drove off toward the rest of the group.

All of the vines in Ben's vineyard were head trained, trellised to a single wooden stake. This style of planting was common in the Rhône Valley and in some older California vineyards. It wasn't tidy looking, but it allowed the vines to generate a large, bush-like canopy, which protected the grapes from the ample foothills sunshine. As they made their way through the rows, the pickers had to reach through this canopy to get to the Gamay, which glimmered darkly in the light of their headlamps. Once they had a full bin of fruit, they carried it over to Ben, who sifted through it, picking out any detritus, and then poured it into the bins on the trailer.

For the next few hours they worked quietly, diligently, pausing only to take a drink from the water cooler. Around six thirty, the first light of day emerged, a soft gray light, and they decided to take a break. They sat down in the grass and ate the almond cake and drank coffee. They were nearly done with the pick, slightly ahead of schedule. Once Ben had finished his slice of cake, he got in the tractor and drove back up the hill to dump the grapes that were in his bins. He had been doing this periodically throughout the morning, bringing all the grapes up to the larger rented trailer, which was parked alongside the driveway, in the shade of an oak tree.

He was in the process of emptying the bins when Jeremy emerged from the vineyard. He had a loping walk, his head stretched out before him like a turtle's.

"Just need to use the bathroom," he said, grinning widely.

"Go for it, the door's open."

He walked past Ben and into the house. Ben finished unloading the rest of the grapes and then brought over a hose to refill the cooler. He had just turned the hose off and was preparing to head back into the vineyard when Jeremy walked out of the front door. He made his way over to Ben and stood next to him.

"Man, this is just so inspirational out here," he said. "I am loving this."

"That's great," Ben said. "We're very glad to have your help."

"At first I was a bit nervous, you know, but now I'm into it, and I'm just cutting those grapes and smelling the smells and having all these ideas. Like a lot of creative ideas, I think. Normally, I'm not a creative person. Normally, I just go to work and say, 'What is the SKU on that? What is the SKU on this?'

But I feel so invigorated out here. Like, I was thinking, you guys don't have a name for your wine label yet, do you?"

"No."

"So I was thinking up all these names, like: Scrimscrapple Wines."

Ben nodded.

"OK, you don't like that one. I've got others. How about: Williwaw Wines, Squabble Wines, Ding Dong Dust Up Wines, Rainchain Wines, Horrorshow Wines, Rigmarole Wines."

"Those are . . ." Ben cleared his throat, "very creative ideas. Those are very creative."

"You think so?"

"Yeah, I'll want to check with Halle, you know, but thank you for the recommendations."

"Also, Fracture Wines and Charleyhorse Wines. I'll keep thinking on it too."

Jeremy looked out at the vineyard and then back at Ben.

"Man, what a day," he said.

BEN MADE IT to Orion around noon, and the fruit in the trailer was promptly unloaded, weighed, and covered with a bedsheet. They put some dry ice in there to cool down the grapes too, so they didn't start fermenting. Halle hadn't arrived yet—she'd needed to go check on something for Michael Deliso—so they paused to wait for her. Once she showed up, the grapes were de-stemmed and pushed into big open vats. Yami put on an album by an Argentine rock band from the eighties while everyone else stripped down to their bare legs. Together, they stepped into the vats and began stomping the grapes to the sound of the music.

Halle was stomping in a vat in between Jeremy and Ben. This style of maceration, Ben heard her explain to Jeremy, was called "pigeage" in French, or "punching down." Once enough juice was released by their stomping, the indigenous yeasts of the vineyard and the cellar would begin the process of fermentation, converting the sugar from the grapes into alcohol. In the coming days, as the fermentation process continued, heat and carbon dioxide would be released, pushing the skins back to the surface of the vat, creating what was referred to as a "cap." This cap would need to be pushed down with a long pole.

No matter what color a grape's skin was, Halle continued, its juice was always clear. The color in a wine was actually determined by the length of time it spent soaking with its skins. The longer the skins were left in, the darker the wine would become. Skin contact also affected flavor, increasing a wine's richness and its level of tannins. Wines with a lot of skin contact were considered heavily "extracted," and though extracted wines had long been popular in California, they were not the kind of wines Halle was interested in making. She would be leaving this Gamay with its skins for eight days, before transferring it to a stainless steel tank, to age for six months. This would, she hoped, produce a light and drinkable final product.

When they had finished stomping, they stepped out of the vats and hosed off their legs. Seba brought out dinner, a hearty sausage and white bean stew that he had prepared upstairs. Yami opened a bottle of the Garcias' Mourvèdre-Syrah blend and a bottle of the Tannat blend. They poured the wine into small ceramic coffee cups, passed them around the room. Through the open door, the smell of eucalyptus filtered into the room, crisp and minty.

After they finished the meal, they continued to sit around on the cool floor of the winery, talking and drinking wine. Ben knew it was getting late, but he felt outside of time, like the day was eternal. It reminded him of the old days, of the endless hours they spent trimming and hanging out in the chapel. Ada leaned her head on his shoulder. Halle told them about her first harvest, when she cut off a chunk of her finger while trying to clip a cluster from the back of a Muscat vine. She held up the misshapen finger, to *oohs* and *aahs*. More harvest stories ensued. Then the conversation turned to the question of where to get the best breakfast sandwich in town. Ada said Danny's Café, but Paul disagreed, said he had "canceled" Danny's Café.

"You've canceled it?" Seba asked. "You don't like the Natoma Fry?"

The Natoma Fry was a local dish featuring a mixture of eggs, bacon, and oysters, which miners had, allegedly, ordered after striking it rich. Danny's Café made a well-known version of it.

"The Natoma Fry?" Paul said. "No, I think it's a horrible meal from the nineteenth century. See, this is the problem. I love this town but it's too stuck in the past. I think the past is interesting, you know, but we need to keep moving forward. That's what Brinkers Bar is trying to do."

"Here we go," Yami said.

"I'm just saying."

"Yeah, we hear you."

"Plus," Paul continued. "The guy who runs Danny's is a jerk."

"Erik Oiler?"

"Yeah, doesn't support local people, jacks up his prices to rip off tourists."

There was a pause.

"I can't say about the café," Wick said, "but I will tell you, when I was selling those sheep pelts in town? You remember this, Ben, when Alfonso and I came into all those sheep pelts. This was probably 1998. When we were selling those sheep pelts, he was very critical of us having a table in the town square. Kept being like: 'These smell. You need to get these out of here. It's bad for business.'"

"See what I'm talking about?" Paul said.

At some point during this conversation, Jeremy had begun wandering around the winery by himself. He was now several feet away from the group, looking down on one of the fermentations they had recently begun, muttering to himself.

"Scrapple Wines," he said, "Apple Wines, *Crab*-apple Wines . . ."

Halle looked over at him.

"What are you doing over there?" she said.

"I'm thinking about some different names for the wine."

"You're drunk," Paul said.

"No, I've had some good ideas. Ben, didn't I have some good ideas earlier?"

Ben nodded, gave him a thumbs-up.

"Purple Wines, Thirst Wines, First Vine Wines . . ."

"Think it's time for me to take this guy home," Paul said.

Halle walked over to Jeremy and looked down at the vat with him. Jeremy continued to riff.

"Pearl Wines, Burl Wines, Big Wines. Big Smoke Wines."

"No," Halle said. "No smoke wines. We don't want any smoke in these wines."

"OK, well what about Word Wines? Or World Wines. Or maybe San An Wines. What about that? San An. After the San Andreans. I mean they really stand for something, you know. Who is more inspiring than them?"

Over the past week or so, Ben had noticed that the young people were constantly referencing the San Andreans. Maybe it was one of those things where once you learned the name of something, you started hearing it everywhere. Or maybe it had just become a more frequent topic of conversation.

"I don't think we can just steal the name," Halle said.

"You don't think they'd be honored?" he said. "I don't know, I've never met any of them. You would know better."

Jeremy paused. Ben watched a kind of poise overtake him. He was looking off into the distance, over the top of their heads.

"OK, here's an idea," he said. "You know how they always talk about the fifty rules on the message boards? Half of them are jokes, right? But what's the thing that gets mentioned most? Rule 43. 'Don't forget what brought you here.' What if we were to call it Rule 43 Wines? Sort of an homage to them. You want a name to connect back to something important, you know? And when I think about Rule 43, I think about moving from a place of awareness and conviction. Of seeing how it's all connected and there's not really a 'them' out there. I mean, when I was out picking today, I could just see it. How good it can still be, how I'm a part of everything. Couldn't you feel that? It's so easy to get discouraged but it doesn't have to be that way. I feel like my mindset has been changing around that. It's been changing in a lot of ways, I think. Like I'm just seeing things more clearly now, living through all of this. I can see what's important, you know? Do you guys feel like that, like you're changing? I know I'm changing."

"Yeah, you've become a sentimental drunk," Paul said.

"Maybe," Jeremy said, nodding philosophically. "Maybe."

There was a moment of silence.

"Rule 43 Wines," Halle said. "I kinda like it."

She turned to Ben: "What do you think?"

"I'm into it."

"You are?" Jeremy said.

"Yeah."

Jeremy looked back down at the fermentation.

"Hell yeah," he said.

10

ALL ACROSS THE COUNTY, the grape harvest continued. On the Hecht farm it went Primitivo, Barbera, Syrah, and finally, Grenache. Yoel and Halle pitched in, Ada and Jeremy and Wick too. In the mornings, Halle would go over to Orion, take a quick survey of the fermentations they had going, punch down what needed to be punched down, and drain what needed to be drained. Sometimes, if she was otherwise occupied by work for Michael Deliso, Ben would go over and do this for her. At first it was easy to keep track of things, but as more grapes came in and the number of fermentations increased, a more careful accounting was required. They left notes for each other on a blackboard in the cellar. If she had time, Halle would also draw a cartoon on the board, a series they began referring to as "Garage Cat," because all of the drawings were of a cat drinking wine alone in his garage.

In addition to the Gamay, Halle had processed the old-vine Primitivo and Barbera using pigeage. For the Grenache and the Syrah, she had opted for a method called carbonic maceration. This technique, which was developed in the Beaujolais region of France, was distinct from other forms of winemaking because it allowed the fermentation to start within the skin of the grape, while the grape was still intact. To begin, whole clusters of grapes were dropped into a tank and the top was sealed. As fermentation began to occur within the grapes, pressure built, and eventually, the berries burst open, releasing their fermenting juice into the tank. This type of fermentation tended to give the wine a smoother flavor.

Because of the concern about smoke taint, Halle was draining off the juice from the carbonic maceration every day, into another tank, where it continued its fermentation. As a general principle, with both the carbonic and pigeage processes, Halle was trying to leave the skins in her fermentations for as little time as possible. This was in part a stylistic preference, but it was also a calculated precaution: the compounds that produced smoke taint were primarily present in the skins of the grapes. The less time they spent in with the fermentations, the less likely it was that the resultant juices would develop smoky flavors.

If worst came to worst, Yami told Ben, Halle would likely be able to blend her way out of certain issues.

"It's smart the way she's doing it," Yami said. "Because you have all these separate elements now, and you'll be able to combine them to get what you want."

Things were going according to plan but there was still a lot of uncertainty. How would the wines be reviewed? How would they sell? Or worst of all, what if despite all these safeguards, the wines still developed smoke taint? This precarity hung over the work, compounded by the daily precarity of fire season. Every morning they looked out the window to assess the smoke, checked their air quality apps. For a couple of days, it was too smoky to go outside, and they had to reschedule their picks. In the evenings, when the work was done, they made sure to fill up their gas tanks before heading home. Some of them bought extra gas canisters to carry with them. They kept water jugs in their cars and blankets and other emergency supplies. They talked with each other about these precautions. They talked about evacuation routes, about what roads had been busy during the last evacuation. If they were at Orion when the fire broke, they would likely head down Bennett Road and out toward Smith Flat from there. If they were at the Hechts' property, they would go down Mountainview and then to 51.

And over the course of the harvest, a new conversation began to emerge too. It was largely led by Halle and Yoel, but they were all a part of it. The origins of the conversation were simple, really: they had been forced to look at something terrifying, and they could not unsee it. So what were they going to do about it?

The San Andreans often came up in this context. They were organizing protests across the state, across the whole West. Ben was still just getting a sense of who they were, though he knew they communicated through a private online forum. Yoel had shown it to him once. According to Yoel, their goal was to impede the fossil fuel industry with consistent, targeted interventions. Halle had also, at various points, explained elements of their philosophy to him. She said they rejected the idea that individual purchases would save us, didn't care if you owned a hybrid. "Owning a hybrid is fine," she told him, "but what matters is people building real, formidable power." Because at the end of the day, she said, this was about power. The industry would only come to the table if they were forced to.

Most recently, the San Andreans had disrupted a shareholders' meeting of a large oil company. Their next action was going to be a blockade of gas delivery trucks in numerous cities. Yoel and Halle were leading an arm of the blockade in Natoma. As part of their planning for the action, they sometimes met with a small group of San Andreans at a nearby walnut farm. The San Andreans were all meeting like this, in small groups around the region, each group planning its own action. Ben could tell Halle and Yoel were committed to the work. At night, even after the grueling, hot labor of the harvest, they would still somehow drag themselves out of the house to get to the walnut farm.

One evening, after coming back from a meeting, they joined Ben for a glass of wine in the kitchen. Yoel seemed exhausted. Pretty soon after he finished his glass, he said he needed to go to bed. Halle, however, asked if Ben would stay up and drink another one with her. She always wanted the night to keep going, and Ben enjoyed staying up with her. So after Yoel left, they poured two more glasses. They were drinking the Garcias' Tannat blend, one of the bottles they'd brought home from the fair.

"Your son is something else," she said, shaking her head, pushing the glass over to him.

"How do you mean?"

"Made this speech tonight that had the whole room jumping like something out of the . . . what was that called? From AP US? The Second Great Awakening. It was like watching some kind of revivalist preacher."

"About the fires?"

"It was about the fires. About the history of different protest movements. I don't know. He just has a way of winding you in. It's good, our group needs a leader."

"I figured you were the leader," he said.

"Well, don't get me wrong, I hold my own sway. But I prefer to stay a little more behind the scenes. I'm more of a connector of people."

"The queen."

"Oh god, did Jeremy tell you that? It's literally only him who's ever called me that."

"Was he at the meeting?"

"Yeah, he was there, Paul too. They're more into it now that Yoel is there," she said. "I don't know what it is. He just has a way of rallying people."

Ben leaned forward, put his elbows on the table to rest his back. Through the screen door, out beyond the back patio, the moon glowed bright above the shadowy woods.

"So what's going to happen when he goes back to LA?" he asked.

"Well hopefully he doesn't. See if I can't make a case for him to stay. He wants to quit his job anyway." She paused. "You know what was actually the most impactful moment?" she said, lowering her voice. "When he spoke about his mom."

She nodded in the direction of Ada's temporary office.

"The hard time she's having," Halle said. "I didn't realize what had happened with the book. I was so sorry to hear that. It just . . . the people in the room, their hearts went out to her."

Ben looked in the direction of the office and then back at Halle.

"Yeah," he said. "It's been tough."

"I can't even imagine."

EVERYONE WHO WAS working with them that summer felt the effects of the fire threat, though each individual engaged with it in their own way, for reasons that were sometimes logical and sometimes mysterious. Ada, for her part, was continuing to struggle. He couldn't remember when it started exactly, but she began to need Xanax to go to bed. She was also having trouble getting up in the mornings. Ben wasn't sure what to do to help her. She said she'd begun looking for a therapist but hadn't found a good one. When Ben got out from Lompoc, they had both started taking Xanax to deal with the stress, but at a certain point, they decided to wean themselves off it. Then they started drinking house wine too much so they went sober for a few months. After that, things had gotten better.

So it was concerning that she had started using Xanax again. And even more concerning that she needed the pills to go to bed—this was what really scared Ben. He told her this, and she seemed to hear him. Eventually, she found a therapist, a woman in the city, who had been recommended by Carole. She began having sessions on the phone. She began taking the pills less. But her mood remained low, muted, and Ben could tell that the stress of the fire threat weighed heavily on her. Some of the things she did were sensible: photographing their furniture, uploading documents to the cloud. But others betrayed unhealthy levels of anxiety. One morning, for example, she nearly had a panic attack after smelling smoke from the bagel Yoel was making. And another day, she wrote a post online, when she was on Xanax, that was riddled with typos.

It was actually a reasonable post, in which she was trying to advise people to look out for trees on their property that had been killed by bark beetles. The dry weather had weakened many trees, made them susceptible to bark beetles, who killed the trees over time, turning them into dangerous dry tinder. But the way it was written, with all the typos, had made her sound crazy. Her agent called her about it and she took it down. After that, she truly swore off the Xanax, flushed it down the toilet, but the experience shattered her confidence even more. She had lost all motivation, she said, wasn't even able to sit down and try to write anymore.

Ben had never seen her in a state like this, and neither had Yoel. The other night, when she started talking about the novel, Ben noticed her hands were shaking. She went on for a while about how she had lost the ability to follow the mystery of the thing, how it was all completely broken, and maybe it was best if she never published anything again. She was deep in the abyss. Increasingly, Ben felt she needed to get out of town. He thought this would help her get some perspective on it all. But she insisted they had no money to spend on travel and refused to plan anything.

"I'll be fine," she would say, without enthusiasm. "I'll figure it out."

Meanwhile, the harvest carried on. For the most part, Ben worked long days—twelve hours, sometimes more. The Garcias worked the same kinds of hours over in their vineyard. It was arduous work, the weather getting hotter and drier every week. But occasionally there were days off too, and a group of them would head down to Ernie's Bar, on the river, to swim, or they would hike Aum's Loop. One day they all went to the weekend flea market together.

Sometimes, on a day off, Yami would host tastings in the morning at Orion. She did these tastings under an oak tree, in front of the vineyard. The setup was simple: six chairs and a plank laid over two wine barrels. Often, she had a bowl of walnuts from one of the trees on their property, and a nutcracker for the guests to use. She would pour five or six of the Garcias' wines and sleepily sip her mug of coffee while chatting with the visitors about what they were tasting. If one of the visitors bought a bottle of wine, their tasting became free.

One morning, Yami called over to Ben in the middle of a tasting. He was heading into the winery to check on the fermentations. It was a particularly nice day, one large cloud above them like a scrap of white fleece. He joined her behind the plank and she introduced him, talked about his property, and what he was growing.

"Ben does almost everything by himself," she said. "He lives up by Rose Mountain."

Ben looked out at the visitors. They were two couples from the city. One of the men was dressed as an outdoorsman, had a backpack with lots of clips on it. He raised his hand and looked over at Ben.

"Your wife is a famous writer, right?" he asked.

"Ada Hecht, yes."

"I've got a friend who knows her. I'm from Oakland."

"Oh, OK, that's where I grew up."

"I liked that book she wrote about Nevada."

"Oh yeah."

"We read it in our reading group. I have a reading group with some coworkers."

"That's great."

"How is she doing?"

"How is she? She's fine."

"Really?"

"What do you mean?"

"I heard that she might be sort of . . . I just heard she was having a hard time."

"What, no?"

"I mean the post she made—that was pretty bizarre."

Ben suddenly saw what the man was insinuating. He cleared his throat but it came out more like a growl.

"You don't know what you're talking about," he said.

"I'm not trying to be offensive," the man said. "I was just curious. I mean we read her books, you know. It's natural to be curious about her."

"OK, this tasting is over," Yami said. "Thank you for coming."

"It was just a question."

"We don't tolerate that kind of disrespect here," she said. "You're here at our home, and as soon as you disrespect it, you're gone."

"Jesus, people are so thin-skinned these days."

The man picked up his backpack and looked over at the woman next to him, presumably his partner, who looked shocked and ashamed.

"Thank you, sorry," she said to Yami.

Yami nodded once. The group headed off toward their car. Yami and Ben stood there for a moment, watching them go. Then he took out his phone and began searching Ada's name. What did people know? Was this just one guy or was there some kind of larger conversation about Ada happening? He searched for news articles, checked a couple different social media accounts, but he didn't see anything. If people were talking, at least, it was a relatively confined conversation. He looked up at Yami.

"I think I'm done with tastings for the year," she said.

DURING HARVEST, the whole family began spending more time at Orion. They lent a hand with the Garcias' picks, as a kind of trade for all the ways in which the Garcias were helping them out. In general, there was a spirit of collectivity that suffused Orion during harvest. Other local winemakers often stopped in to use the Garcias' grape press or borrow some other machine or tool. Most of them were younger, like Halle, and couldn't yet afford their own equipment. Ben met Wendell, the young man whose wines Halle had shared with him, and another emerging winemaker named Sharon, who farmed several high-altitude parcels on forest service land.

Usually, in the evenings, the Garcias would invite whoever was around to stay for dinner. Halle, Jeremy, and Paul often came to these meals, and sometimes Wick too. Seba was always the lead cook but the others would help him with whatever he had planned: warm garlic orzo pasta with parmesan and parsley, or shakshuka with fresh summer tomatoes and feta cheese. They often stayed past sunset, chatting in the cellar, in the low light. The light in the cellar was always low—not because the Garcias wanted to set an ambience, but because the old wiring in the building couldn't handle anything brighter than a forty-watt bulb.

One night, after one of these dinners, Ada and Ben headed home early. The sky outside was a muted gold, and as they drove, they watched the sun set over the granite scarps of Rose Mountain. The air was hazy, had been for the last few days. There was a growing blaze up near Webberville and some of the smoke was drifting down into Natoma. Webberville was a midsize mountain town known for its dairy production and its tight-knit community of Swiss immigrant families. They had all been following the developments of the fire closely. So far it was about four thousand acres, mostly burning through unpopulated forested areas. If it kept growing, however, it might begin to threaten the ranches outside Webberville and then the town itself.

Ben turned onto Sherwood Road, the wheel of the truck sticky from harvest. Ada switched the radio from the classical station to the community radio station, KWMR. She did this almost every time she got in the truck, said classical music made her feel like she was in a nursing home. At this hour, the community radio station was broadcasting its classifieds show, where people called in to advertise items they were selling. Motorcycles, dining tables, two pocket hoses with a nozzle. They listened for a few minutes and then Ada lowered the volume, looked over at Ben.

"I heard from Donatella yesterday," she said.

"You did? About what?"

"She has a free cabin in Amargo for the next month."

Amargo was a small desert town, on the east side of the mountains. It was pretty close to the state line and well known for its natural hot springs. Ada had stayed there for a couple of months when she was working on her last book. She had fallen in love with the place, and befriended a number of its residents, including a woman named Donatella, who owned a property with several cabins on it.

"That's amazing," Ben said.

"I don't know if I should go, though," she said. "There's so much happening here."

Ben tugged at the collar of his T-shirt. The whole thing was stiff with grape juice. All of his work clothes were stiff and stained at this point.

"I think it would be really good for you," he said.

"I know you do."

They were driving along Sherwood, past roaming cows and outcroppings of serpentine rock. Growing around the rocks you could see manzanita, chamise, leather oak. Soils that developed on serpentine rock were toxic to most plant life so only certain species could survive near it.

"I really like this part of the valley," Ada said. "It has such a different look to it."

"Hang on, what about this Donatella thing?"

"What about it?"

"You're not going to do it?"

"I'm not writing anything right now. What am I going to do? Go down there and be alone?"

"Maybe you'd start writing something new."

"Did you know that the miners used to associate serpentine with gold?" she said. "They always looked for serpentine to try to figure out where they should set up their claims."

"I did know that."

"Just interesting, I thought,"

"Don't change the subject."

He turned onto Mountainview and started to climb up the backside of Rose Mountain. Through the window the air was warm and balsam scented. Off to his left, two golden eagles swooped low and long across the sky. He looked over at her. He rarely put his foot down. She was looking straight ahead at the road. She must have sensed that he wasn't going to let it drop, because before he said anything else, she spoke up.

"OK, I'll do it," she said. "I'll do it."

SEVERAL DAYS LATER, she stood on the porch, mask on, bags already packed into the Toyota. The sky was blue but hazy, a filtered blue, and a daytime moon was visible over the hills. Readings said the AQI was around 100, or unhealthy for those with certain health conditions. Some people thought this meant they could go out without masks, but those who had read more about the smoke understood that a full day of 100 AQI was equivalent to inhaling a quarter pack of cigarettes. Sure, you might feel OK for that day, if you didn't have a health condition, but if you did that every day for an entire summer? For years?

Ben had checked the AQI out in the desert and it was as fresh as could be, in the single digits. The heat in Natoma had yet to break, the land growing more parched every day. Earlier that week, when the AQI had been a little lower, they'd gone for a hike at Comish Lake. He'd never seen the water levels so depleted, rings of green muck extending out in concentric circles toward the shore. Sections of the reservoir were so low that it now resembled more of a creek than a lake. They said they were beginning to pump in water from other reservoirs, higher up in the mountains, to keep it somewhat full.

"I'm nervous about going down there," she said. She was applying sunscreen to her face and neck. "You want some?"

"I'm OK," Ben said. "Where's Yoel?"

"He said he'd be out in a second."

"I think it's great that you're going, I really do."

"I'm just worried I'm going to get down there and still be stuck—and also be alone too."

"C'mere," he said. She turned toward him and he took her face in his hands. With his thumb, he rubbed in a streak of sunscreen under her eye. She smiled and it was that same old Ada smile, eternal and true.

"You have nothing to fear," he said. "You are so creative that you can turn anything to your advantage. You will turn this to your advantage too. Eventually, you will."

"I hope so."

He kissed her and then pulled back to look at her again. There were a couple more streaks of sunscreen on her forehead so he rubbed those in too.

"All good now," he said.

Yoel walked through the door moments later, and the two of them turned to face him.

"I'm sorry I'm going to miss your goodbye party," Ada said.

"Oh, don't worry about it."

Yoel was wearing a blue T-shirt that said "La Paz, Mexico." His arms looked tan and muscled from working the harvest.

"What's the weather down there?" he asked.

"Hot," she said, "but could start cooling off any week now. Did you make the appointment with the dentist?"

"I will," he said. "Don't worry about it."

"OK, good."

"And go put on some masks if you're going to stay out here."

"I'm not," Yoel said. "I'm going right back inside after you leave. Is this you telling us you'll miss us?"

"Yes."

She smiled and hugged both of them. Then she stepped back and rummaged through her bag. She pulled out her hat first, then kept looking for something else. Ben started to smile even before she found it.

"Oh my god," she said. From the bag, she extracted a tiny porcelain doll. It had tangled red hair, milky blue skin, and one of its eyes was missing.

"Got it at the flea market the other day," he said. "Little gift for the road."

"I can't believe you're still buying those," Yoel said.

"That is a really good one, you have to admit."

Ada looked at him and shook her head, smiling.

"You are such a freak," she said.

FOR A TOWN of its size, Natoma had a large number of bars. There was the Golden Nugget, which had a popular Irish breakfast, and the Stork, which had a decent patio. There was also Coyote Bar, which Ben had never really gone to, and the Peso, where most of the farmworkers drank. Ben's favorite bar was Gorka's, which served a strong Basque drink called a Picon Punch, but which was rarely open, because its owner, Gorka, was often out hunting.

Given the number of other drinking establishments, it was not surprising to Ben that Paul was having a difficult time drawing customers. As far as he could tell, Paul's business plan rested on the idea that he would be able to pull in crowds with musical guests. Ben wasn't informed enough to know if this was a wise proposition or not. There were a couple other venues in town that also featured live music, but Ben didn't know how active they were, or how well they were doing. It had been a long time since he'd gone out in town.

The night of Wick's show, they were late leaving the house. Yoel had gotten wrapped up in a phone call with his boss. He'd told Ben recently that he was almost positive he was going to leave the company. He was planning to give notice when he got back to LA. He had some savings he could live off for a while, but he said he'd rather know what he was doing next before he quit.

By the time they got out the door, it was almost dark. In the distance Ben could hear the bleating of the sheep as they bedded down for the night with Eddie. He backed down the driveway and turned onto Mountainview. Yoel, who, like his mother, hated classical music, switched over to the community radio station. It was presenting a program called Money Matters, which they listened to all the way down the hill. The program's main focus seemed to be the devaluation of the dollar, and its host kept describing hypothetical scenarios that involved laundromats. Apparently, he had previously owned a laundromat.

"You really prefer this to music?" Ben said, as they turned onto Center Street.

Yoel ignored him.

"Look at all these people," he said. "How fun."

It was Saturday night in Natoma, the streets buzzing with action in the modest way that a town like Natoma is capable of buzzing.

They parked off Center Street and then walked over to Paul's bar, which was across the street from the cheese shop, and next door to a hair salon. At night, the downtown area had a particularly cozy feel to it. The streets were lit by old gas lamps, which were authentic nineteenth-century relics, though their mantles had been replaced and they had been given light-sensitive on-off switches. Residents and visitors walked along the great granite curbsides, past restaurants and offices and hotels with signs that said ROOMS TO LET. On the second floor of many of the old Victorian buildings, bay windows overlooked the street, their curtains wrapped in tidy triangles. And in the background, when the noise of the street died down, one could make out the sound of the creek as it rushed beneath Prospect Street.

By the time they arrived at the bar, there was a long line to get in. A man Ben didn't recognize was standing in front of the door, checking IDs. Ben did recognize the woman in front of them though: Lisa Vermont. Lisa owned the Cornish pasty shop in town and also ran the volunteer senior firewood program. She was standing alongside her husband, George Vermont, a short man, who was somewhat hard of hearing.

"George, honey," Lisa said. "Look, it's the Hechts."

George shuffled to face them. "Hello," he said.

"It's been ages," Lisa said. "Where's Ada?"

"She's on a retreat," Ben said.

"Good for her."

Yoel had caught the eye of Jeremy, who was at the front of the line, next to the bouncer. He told the Vermonts it was good to see them, and walked over to Jeremy to say hello.

"How is the firewood stuff going?" Ben asked, after Yoel had left.

"Oh, we are all ready," Lisa said. "We have about one hundred and twenty cords of wood at Elgin Crayton's house."

"That sounds promising," Ben said.

"Very promising indeed."

Ben looked behind Lisa Vermont and noticed that the line had already grown a bit. The crowd was a mix of older and younger people, a fairly representative cross section of the town: he saw two teachers from the local high school, one of the town's three lawyers, and that young woman who had started her own online cake business. Eloise . . . what was it? Eloise something. He also noticed Rudy, and they waved to each other. He looked back at Lisa Vermont.

"How did you hear about this show?" Ben asked.

"Well, I love seeing Wick's band play," she said. "I try to go to all of their shows. I follow them on social media. All you have to do is 'like' the page and then it tells you when they're playing shows. I can show you how if you want. George doesn't like social media because he thinks it's narcissistic but I think it's kind of useful."

"Everyone in this generation is narcissistic," George said.

"Not everyone, honey."

George squinted into the near distance, did not respond.

Ben looked ahead toward the front of the line, which was moving slowly, and then back at Lisa.

"This is a nice crowd," he said.

"Oh yeah," she said, "they're getting more and more popular. That song 'Grass Growing.' You know that song? 'Grass growing, nah nah nah nah,' I play that song probably every day. He's a silly guy but he's so talented. You really need to like their page. It gives you all the updates. Plus what I like is it will recommend other musicians you might like too, that are similar. I find a lot of good songs that way, lot of good YouTube performances."

"I'll check it out," Ben said.

Lisa hummed Wick's song to herself for a few more seconds, and then she turned back toward him.

"Do you know anything about this bar?" she said. "I heard the drinks are overpriced."

THE CENTERPIECE OF Brinkers Bar was, undoubtedly, the taxidermy polar bear to the right of the entrance. It was set up inside glass casing, poised upright, and illuminated by two spotlights. In front of the glass was a plaque that read: "World Record Class Polar Bear. Shot by J. P. Millner out of Kotzebue, Alaska, in April 1963. Taxidermy obtained in Spokane, Washington." Behind the bear was a fake plastic snowbank and a bloodied plastic seal, which it seemed, the polar bear was meant to have killed.

"Sort of gruesome," Yoel said.

They left the polar bear and Yoel toured Ben around the rest of the space. There was a long oak bar running down the left side of the room, a pool table and several booths on the right side, and at the far end of the room, a drum set on a low stage. The walls were densely ornamented, mostly covered in Thomas

Wilson prints. Wilson was a popular painter of pastoral scenes, who had lived in Natoma from the nineties until his death a few years ago. Though he was commercially very successful, his work was widely scorned in the art world, viewed as excessively sentimental. It was not uncommon to see Wilson images around Natoma and there was still a gallery of his paintings in town, though Ben had never seen an entire establishment decorated with prints of his work. Stacked on top of each other like this, they did have an over-the-top, kitschy effect. Ben was still taking in the whole scene when someone called over to them from a dim wooden booth. It was Seba, sitting by himself. He was wearing a dressy green shirt, the sleeves rolled up, the collar unbuttoned. On the table in front of him there were a couple beer glasses and a half-empty pitcher.

"You look nice," Yoel said.

"Come, sit," he said. "Yami's in the bathroom. Want a beer?"

"I'll take a beer," Ben said.

"I need some food first," Yoel said. "You want anything?" he asked Ben.

"I trust your judgment."

After he left, Seba poured him a glass of beer from the pitcher.

"Ada not coming?"

"She left for Amargo the other day."

"Oh good, Yami was telling me about that. How is it going down there?"

"Good, I think. But I haven't really heard much. She's been settling in."

Yoel arrived back at the table a few moments later, Yami shortly after that. Halle and Jeremy then emerged from the door to the right of the stage, said hi to everyone, and took a seat in the booth behind them. Over on the jukebox, someone had put on a depressing old miner's song. A woman at the bar was protesting this choice, yelling: "Boo! Boo! I boo this selection!" Then the lights were dimmed and a small crowd of people drifted toward the front of the stage. Wick came out wearing a secondhand suit, his hair tucked into a purple bandana. Following him onto the stage was Alfonso, with his keyboard, and then the drummer, who Ben didn't recognize. All three had mics. They didn't say anything, just went right into their first song, the song Lisa Vermont had mentioned outside and the song that clearly everyone loved.

"Grass growing, from the bottom, in the field where we saw the caravan . . ."

There were lots of harmonies and each singer sang one of the verses. At one point, Alfonso took a solo on the keys. All three vocalists joined together for the final chorus and then Wick looked over at the drummer, who nodded back at him, and with a flourish of cymbals, brought the song to its close. They went into another song and Ben found himself wishing that Ada were here with him. She would have loved this. He wondered if he'd been right in his advice. Maybe it would be better for her to be back here with them.

He took out his phone, snapped a picture of Wick, and texted it to her.

"Everyone misses you terribly," he wrote. "Me especially."

She texted back immediately, which meant she was in her cabin. There was little service in Amargo so Ada could only receive texts if she was on the cabin Wi-Fi.

"I miss YOU," she said. "Looks so fun."

"How is it going?"

"It's going so, so great," she said. "I rule."

"Yes, you do!!!!"

"I had all these ideas on the drive down. It just feels different."

"That's incredible."

"Send my love to everyone. Talk tomorrow?"

"Sounds good," Ben wrote. "I love you."

The relief he felt was hard to describe. He picked up his beer, took a sip. Then he pulled his phone back out, reread the conversation. Her tone had entirely shifted. Thank god for Donatella. He'd never met the woman but god bless her. He felt emotion welling up inside him. He pictured Ada, on the ground, on her hands and knees, searching through the rubble. He pictured her on the morning after she spoke to her agent, the lost look in her eyes. They had been through so much this summer. To know that she had found even a moment of peace, down in the desert, it filled him with joy.

"Are you OK?" Seba asked him.

He looked up and wiped his eyes.

"Yeah," he said. "I'm just happy."

THE BAND PLAYED for another hour. Many of the songs were up-tempo versions of the songs Alfonso and Wick had played at the McEwan's but others were entirely new to Ben. At a certain point in the set, Wick paused to address the audience. His suit jacket was unbuttoned and his white dress shirt was already sweaty. He put his hand over his eyes like a visor and squinted out at the crowd.

"Good to see you all," he said. "Good to see everyone. Thank you for coming out."

He looked over to his left, toward the booths lining the far side of the bar.

"I see my friend Ben over there, and Seba. Hey, you two. Where's Yoel? In case anyone didn't know, this show is for Yoel."

Yoel raised his hand.

"There he is. Shout out to Yoel. The whole point of this show is to say goodbye to Yoel. I've known Yoel since he was fourteen. Thirteen? So he's leaving town but he'll be back. He always comes back. Anyway, he's got something he wants to say so Yoel, come on up here."

The audience cheered and whistled. Yoel stood up and walked over to the stage.

"OK," Alfonso said, leaning into his mic, "everyone give it up for Yoel."

Ben hadn't realized Yoel was going to make some sort of speech. He was still feeling slightly raw from the exchange with Ada and seeing Yoel up on stage brought another rush of emotion. Yoel took the mic from Wick with confidence. His hair had grown long over the summer, was starting to resemble the hairdo Ben had worn back in his antiquing days. From the loud applause in the room, it seemed like a lot of people here already knew him.

"Thank you all for coming out tonight," he said. "I know some of you are aware of this but to those of you that aren't, we're planning an action against the gas companies next week. We've got to put a stop to what's happening to this place, what's happening to every place, and we want you to join us. They're trying to make this all about individual responsibility, but we're not going to fix things by carpooling to work or composting. We need to move quickly, as a group. We need to make the cost of doing business so difficult that they have to change, on a scale that matters."

He paused. The crowd had gone quiet, the music had been lowered.

"If we stay on the path we're on, we're gonna be refugees. You, me, my family, everyone we know. That's the way it'll go. This bar, the schools we went to, the whole town—it'll be gone. So what we're doing next week, we don't really have a choice, as far as I'm concerned. We have to do it."

A few murmurs from the audience. You could feel the energy in Yoel's voice, the emotion.

Sometimes Ben had felt like his son was too sensitive. A grape with no skin. But he could see now that this was his most beautiful, most enduring gift.

"I invite you to join us," Yoel continued. "I'll be here for the rest of the night. You can come up and find me, if you like. Thanks so much. And don't forget to buy Wick's album."

The crowd roared when Yoel hopped down from the stage. As he walked over to the bar, a few young people Ben didn't recognize approached him. Halle also came over and touched him on the arm. Yoel leaned toward her and the two of them locked eyes. Ben looked away.

The band played one more song, and then exited stage left, into Paul's office. After several minutes of persistent cheering, they emerged from the office and played two more songs, slower songs, including one Wick had written years ago, about a summer he'd spent trimming with Ben. "Up in the chapel," one of the verses went, "up in the chapel, there's the stained glass light."

Once the show was truly over and the band had disappeared into Paul's office again, Ben walked over to the bar, which was being tended by Paul and one other bartender. They were currently dealing with the end-of-show rush to settle tabs so Ben hung back. He was in no hurry. He looked up at the television behind the bar. Guy Matthews's program was on with closed-captioning. He was talking about how Natoma used to be called Coyoteville, because of the mining method known as "coyoteing," which had been developed there. He was just beginning to describe this method when Ben felt a hand on his shoulder. He turned around to see Wick.

"Let me get your drink," he said. "Paul gave me all these drink tickets."

"Hey, you guys were amazing," he said, leaning in to be heard over the crowd. "I mean really great."

Wick had changed out of his suit, into a dry T-shirt and jeans.

"Helps when you've got a good crowd like that."

Paul noticed Wick and walked over to them.

"So good, man," he said. "So good. You see how this place is jumping? What can I get you? You got the drink tickets, right?"

"Thanks, yeah, let me get that beer from the brewery and whatever he wants."

After Paul left to get the beers, Wick looked up at the television.

"Ah man, I love this show," he said. "You seen that one he did about the Mormon Emigrant Trail?"

"No."

"Good stuff."

Ben smiled and Wick smiled and they looked back at the television. Paul returned moments later with their beers. He followed their gaze up to the screen and noticed what was playing.

"Chris," he called across the bar. "Chris! This is the kind of shit I don't ever want on in here."

Chris didn't seem to hear him over the noise of the bar, or was simply ignoring him.

"Always need to do it myself," Paul muttered and wandered away.

Ben and Wick both picked up their beers and continued watching the television.

"Life was uncomfortable and harsh in the placer mines," Guy Matthews said, standing before a mound of dirt. "There was little fresh food and, after a grueling day of manual labor, miners often had to sleep in wet overalls that reeked of bacon grease and sweat."

"Goddamn," Ben said. "That would have been a no for me."

Wick turned away from the television, looked toward the front door. Yoel was standing there now, surrounded by a group of people. Ben followed his gaze. He couldn't hear what was being said but he could see the whole group was listening to Yoel talk. Halle was there but aside from her, Ben didn't recognize any of the others. They seemed young mostly, younger even than Yoel.

It was not hard to understand the appeal of Halle and Yoel. They weren't single-minded zealots, had none of the exclusionary posturing that so often tinged activist leaders. There was a smile about them, a glamour.

"That son of yours has the gift," Wick said.

"He does," Ben said. "I don't know where that came from."

"Do you worry about it?"

"About what?"

"What might happen to him, getting involved like this."

Ben didn't say anything. The truth was, he hadn't considered the ways Yoel's organizing might make him vulnerable.

"Person like that," Wick said, nodding in Yoel's direction. "That's who they come for."

Ben watched his son. Someone in the crowd seemed to be asking him a question. The crowd seemed to be growing.

"I'm sure he'll be OK," Wick said.

"Yeah."

"Great thing they're trying to do."

Wick clinked glasses with Ben and headed back off toward the booth. Ben looked over at Yoel again. Of all the things he had expected this summer, this was not one of them. Wick's comment was concerning but it passed right through him. The pride he felt washed it away. He wished Ada could be here to see this. He would just have to remember it all. He would have to remember what it looked like and felt like, and tell her about it tomorrow.

11

IT SEEMED AS THOUGH the heat was just going to keep going up and up, as though fall would never come. A nervous energy had descended upon the town, tensions rising. Young men made macho proclamations about staying to fight the fire, if and when it came. It was like war—no one wanted to say they hadn't done their part, hadn't been there for the battle.

All across the county, ranchers ripped fire lines around their properties with D8s. People readied their pumps, if they had them, their fire hoses and totes of water. They mowed the grass and weeds around their homes, cleared any dry slash. Many signed up for an emergency alert system, which let you know when a fire ignited. It was an annoying system, which also constantly sent alerts about missing seniors or police activity, but it was apparently the quickest fire alert system, so they put up with it.

At the Hecht farm, final plans for the blockade were being discussed. Ben was going to attend but not take part in the protest. It was too risky for him to be involved, given his criminal record. Their protest would target the gas station off 99. It was the biggest station in town. All of the protests were targeting large gas stations, because they received daily fuel deliveries. Yoel and Halle had scouted the station, knew that the fuel truck would be arriving sometime around 10 A.M. Their plan was to head it off on the stretch of 99 that ran along the Carey's apple farm.

The day before the protest, a group of them went down to the river to unwind. Ben, Yoel, Halle, Jeremy. It was a slow day on the river and nothing was wrong with anything. They set down their things near the Highway 51 bridge, next to a young family who said they were visiting from the South Bay. They had a small girl and they had brought a blow-up flamingo for her to sit on. The father waded into the eddy closest to them and held onto the girl, who sat on top of the flamingo gazing at everything around her: the giant granite boulders and the emerald green water and the bridge in the distance, that one long curve of cement.

Ben set up his folding chair and opened their yellow beach umbrella. Yoel laid out his towel and began sunscreening his arms. He really had gotten a lot stronger from working the harvest. Ben felt stronger too and rested, having done very little since Wick's show. There were still a few postharvest tasks that needed to be dealt with but they had now more or less entered the off-season. With any luck, autumn would soon be upon them. Cool temperatures and wild mushrooms and rain. His favorite time of the year.

Once their sunscreen dried and they had warmed up a bit, Halle and Yoel waded into the water. In the center of the river there were some gentle rapids but along the edges there were mostly calm pools and inlets, ideal for lounging. Yoel found a flat rock to lean against while Halle swam out into the middle of the river. The current nudged her slightly downstream but she was able to make it all the way across. She waved back toward Yoel from the other side.

"Now you go," she yelled.

Yoel squinted over at her. "Sure, sure be there in a sec," he called back.

"Come on," she said.

"OK, fine."

He pushed into the water, swam in her direction. A group of four college-aged guys were rock hopping their way upstream, shirtless but wearing hydration packs. The family of three next to them were now passing a container of hummus and carrots back and forth. The dad looked a bit like Ben's old acquaintance PJ, one of the guys he'd gotten to know in Lompoc. He'd owned a chain of rug stores and had been serving time for tax evasion. They'd stayed in touch once Ben was transferred to the halfway house, but after that, they'd stopped writing each other. That was the way it was with all the people he'd met in Lompoc. You always said you were going to stay in touch after, that you'd visit each other once you were out, but it seldom happened.

Jeremy had opened his chair next to Ben's, pulled out a tablet, and begun reading. After less than a minute, he turned to Ben.

"I'm glad we're doing this," he said. "Getting out here before tomorrow."

"It's nice."

"I'm not going to lie, I'm a little nervous. Do you have any advice?"

"Well," Ben thought for a moment. "I would just not do anything you don't feel comfortable doing."

"That's good advice. No one's said that to me yet. That's like, really good advice. You're the first person to say that."

"Thank you."

"Thank *you*."

Jeremy picked up his tablet, started to read, and then fifteen seconds later, put it down on his lap again.

"I'm still feeling kind of . . . hyped up?" he said. "I can't really focus on this book. I get like this sometimes. Just really amped up. My grandma used to call it 'Double Jeremy' cause I have the energy of two Jeremys."

"Why don't we get in the water?" Ben said.

"Yeah, OK."

They tiptoed along the rocks, to a small pool slightly downstream from them. The water was chilly at first but then their bodies grew used to it. Across the way, Ben could see a couple of wood-frame cabins with shake roofs. A soft wind blew across everything, rippling the water, and bringing with it the spicy smell of fir trees. Jeremy dunked his head in the river. When he emerged, he whipped his head back to get his hair out of his eyes.

"Feeling better?" Ben said.

"Yeah, definitely."

Jeremy looked off toward the other bank of the river and then back at Ben.

"Can I ask you something?" he said. He stood up and the water came up to his waist.

Ben nodded.

"How did you know you wanted to be a dad? Cause I think about it sometimes for myself. Like could I do it? It seems like so much pressure."

"It is. And it can be hard."

"It was hard for you?"

"Oh, all the time. Of course."

"You guys just seem like such a perfect family to me."

"Well, we've had our difficulties. Everyone does."

"See that's where I don't think I could trust myself," Jeremy said. "Like, things get hard, and I just freak the fuck out. I lost two jobs like that, ask Paul about it. So when I think about having a kid, I don't know. I'm just not sure I trust myself. Like the commitment is so extreme. Your whole life. You know what I mean? Once it happens, you can never go back. You're always a dad for the rest of your life."

Ben was leaning against the back of a smooth piece of granite. He slid down it into the water, until his chest was submerged, his neck, and only his head remained above the water.

"I think if I could talk to my younger self about it," he said. "I would just tell him that there are going to be storms, and sometimes the storms get intense. And there's not always a reason for them. It feels like you did something wrong but sometimes there are just storms passing through. And the thing to remember, the thing I sometimes forgot, is that they always come to an end. Everything has an ending. If you keep that in mind, when you're in a storm, even the really bad ones, you can keep your head about you."

"I don't know," Jeremy said. "I don't know if I could."

"I think you could, Jeremy. I think you'd be a great dad."

"You mean it?"

"Yeah, definitely."

Jeremy smiled, clearly pleased with this.

Ben stayed in the water for a few more minutes and then he climbed up the rock that he'd been leaning against. He found a body-shaped crevice and lay there to dry out. Jeremy followed him onto the rock and took a seat next to him. At a certain point, Ben pushed himself up on his elbows, looked out across the river. Some squirrel was rustling a pine tree along the opposite bank. A man drifted past them in a wooden canoe. And off in the distance, further downstream, he saw Yoel and Halle sitting on a rock together. They were holding hands. Jeremy had followed his gaze, and he looked over at Ben, smiling.

"Yeah," he said. "That just started happening."

WHEN THEY GOT BACK to the farm, Ben joked with Yoel about Halle. He was so happy for them. He wanted to know what had changed for Halle but Yoel said he wasn't exactly sure. They'd just gotten to know each other better, he said, working side by side the whole summer.

"No more Lonnie Harris, I guess," Ben said.

"Oh, he's been out of the picture a while."

On the phone later that night, he told Ada about the new couple and she was excited too. It seemed like things were still going well down in Amargo. She wouldn't say what she was working on but that was typical. That was normal Ada. It was so good to hear her sounding normal.

The following day, the day of the protest, was especially windy. Was it the start of the Junction winds? It was hard to say. It was a little early in the season. Ben drove over to the Carey's apple farm by himself. There was already a small crowd gathering there. He parked away from the crowd, along the side of the road, and climbed up to a berm, from which he'd be able to watch everything. Most of the protestors were already there. Some of them had driven cars, but others appeared to have biked or walked over from town.

On the berm there was a small boulder, which he leaned back against. It was a beautiful day, nothing above but the clear blue vault of the heavens. On the hillside below him, a hare scampered through the dry grass. And, off to his right, there was a beautiful old California redbud tree. They were very slow growing so this one must have been incredibly old. The leaves hadn't started to turn red yet, were still waiting for the onset of the cold.

He looked at his phone and saw that it was almost ten. For a moment, he wondered if Halle and Yoel mistimed the approach of the delivery. Where had they gotten that information from anyway? But then, moments later, there it was, approaching from the south: a silver tanker, gleaming in the foothills sunshine. It had red and white stripes running along its side, an exhaust pipe in the front, like one perked ear. The group of protestors fanned out across the road, formed a line, and began waving their arms. Emerging too, for the first time, was another group of people, all of them masked, like bank robbers, with beanies over their heads, slits poked for their eyes. There were probably six of them or so, and from his build, and the pants he was wearing, Ben could tell Yoel was one of them.

He watched as the masked protestors joined the other protestors on the street. The tanker slowed as it approached and then came to a stop. At this point, the protestors linked arms and sat down. The tanker did not move. Cars began to pile up on either side of the road. They started to honk. One man got out of his van and began screaming at the protestors and some of them yelled back at him. Ben couldn't hear exactly what was being said with all the wind. The driver of the tanker got out of his vehicle too, stood with his hands on his hips and stared at the protestors. Then he took out his phone, appeared to be making a call.

After he hung up the phone, he walked back toward the tanker. The guy from the van walked over to him and the two of them entered into a conversation. Sirens could be heard approaching. They were not so far from the police station. The driver of the tanker turned around and looked in the direction of the sirens, and the moment he did this, Yoel stood up. He was probably ten feet away from the tanker and he sprinted toward it, with some kind of instrument in hand. It all happened so fast but, within a matter of moments, Yoel had smashed the windshield and the passenger side window of the tanker. The driver ran toward him but he was too slow, and Yoel sprinted off, into the orchard. At the same time, a few of the other masked protestors also sprinted off into the orchard, scattering quickly, like minnows in shallow water.

The police cars pulled up moments later. The driver and the man who he'd been talking to, the guy in the van, gesticulated wildly toward the apple orchard. Two of the cops ran off in the direction he had pointed. More patrol cars were arriving now. Ben recognized a couple of the deputies, including the red-haired man. He had approached the protestors now, was moving down the line, placing their hands behind their backs, and cuffing them with white plastic cuffs. The driver of the tanker was still screaming at the cops, motioning toward the apple orchard. Two more cops wandered in the direction that Yoel had run, but returned moments later. Soon all the cops were back. They did not have Yoel. They did not have anyone. They'd all escaped.

Ben realized he'd been holding his breath for who knew how long. Suddenly, it occurred to him that he needed to get out of here. What if the cops started searching the area more widely? What if they found him, up on this berm, and thought he had been involved somehow? It wasn't safe to stay in the area. He waited one more moment, to make sure Yoel had really gotten away. Out on the road, he saw the trucker talking to a cop, making a gesture of pulling a beanie down over his head. The cop was taking notes. On the ground next to them, broken glass like blue snow.

HALLE CALLED HIM later that evening, told him that Yoel was safe, but that she couldn't say anything more. She said she would come over the following morning. But then the morning came and the afternoon too and she still hadn't shown up. He texted her to check in and eventually she responded.

"Sorry," she wrote. "Running into all sorts of delays."

In the meantime, he had been able to get a hold of Ada. He knew from his experiences with the criminal justice system that it was unwise to put anything in writing to her and, out of an abundance of caution, he didn't really want to say anything on the phone either. His old lawyer had mentioned to him once: "the only safe place to have a conversation is in person—and even then you need to be aware of your surroundings." A little paranoid, maybe, but Ben wanted to be extra careful. He didn't know where Yoel was, or what was happening, apart from Halle's assurances that he was safe.

"I can't get into details," he said. "But look at the local paper online."

He waited while she read. There was nothing in the article that specified Yoel's role in the encounter, but she knew enough to pick up what he was putting down.

"Is he safe?" she asked.

"Yes."

"I'm coming home now."

While he waited for Halle to come over, Ben reread the article from the local paper. It said that several of the protestors had been arrested and that the police were seeking information regarding the suspect who had bashed the windows of the tanker. Charges of terrorism could be applicable. Federal charges. For a second time, those lines sent a chill through him. He had to remind himself of his call with Halle the other night. She had assured him that Yoel was safe, that no one knew it was him and no one was going to talk.

There had been four actions across the state, the paper went on, and two in Nevada. They all bore a similar profile: people blocked the pathway of a gas delivery and then either smashed the windows of the gas tanker or, in one case, the windows of a cop car that came to clear the road. There had been over ninety arrests. A couple national papers had also published articles, both of them referring to the San Andreans as a "shadowy regional militant organization." They noted that the San Andreans had issued a manifesto to accompany the protests but they never quoted the manifesto. This was surprising because it was not hard to find. It had taken Ben only a couple of minutes of searching online.

"We have known about this issue for decades," it began, "and for decades, we have watched in despair, as those in power refuse to do anything, despite knowing what must be done. If you ask today's fossil fuel executives if something must be done, they all say yes, but they do nothing. The forces at play are too entrenched. These people hate the work their companies do and yet even they cannot stop them. We have created a monster."

It went on to say that the problem had reached such a moment of crisis, that extreme measures were necessary. The San Andreans vowed to disrupt the infrastructure of the fossil fuel industry in ways that made it increasingly costly to do business. There was a distinction between violence to human beings, they stated, and violence to property. At this moment, given the amount of time we had left to solve this problem, violence to property was not only justified, it was noble and moral, an act of grace. The manifesto then went on to cite many other historical examples of property damage, which were justified and beneficial. In their closing arguments, they made it clear that they wished no ill will to those whose property it damaged. In fact, they clarified, "we love those whose property we are damaging, and we hope they will reassess their role in all of this destruction, and join us in our fight."

Halle didn't arrive at the farm until late in the evening. She was wearing an oversize T-shirt, a pair of yellow corduroy shorts, and she looked exhausted. She motioned for Ben to follow her outside.

"Let's take your car," she said. "Yoel's at Orion."

As they walked to the truck, she began to recount everything that had just happened. She said she'd gone to pick up

Paul and Jeremy and several others at the county jail that morning. She'd been one of the masked protestors who had split off into the orchard before the cops came. The idea was to have a few people avoid arrest, to remain on the outside, and also to make it harder to track Yoel as he ran through the orchard. Before the protest, they'd planted a car on the other side of the property, on a frontage road. They'd all rendezvoused at the car and drove east on Bennett Road.

The other protestors, she explained, had been taken to the county jail. There were so many of them that the cops apparently had to get a bus to transport them all. At the jail, they'd been searched one by one, facing a wall, and then loaded into group cells by gender. There were metal bunks, no blankets or mattresses, and the cells were cold.

"Jeremy said the cops were saying all sorts of stuff to them when they put them in there," she said. "Shit like, 'This is gonna teach you a lesson.'"

Ben shook his head. The idea of Jeremy being pushed around by guards infuriated him. His mind wandered back to the first time he was imprisoned, held on bail. The moment when the cell was closed and locked, when he realized that there was no way he could get out. The terrible trapped feeling. He knew how frightening that was.

They kept the protestors there overnight, Halle continued, fed them bologna sandwiches for dinner. In the morning, they were brought before a judge and all released with minor fines for obstructing a public place and public nuisance. That's when Halle drove over to pick them up. But after she'd collected them, her car got a flat outside the Save Mart. She didn't have a spare so they had to sit around eating candy bars and waiting for another friend to pick them up. Then Halle got her car towed to the mechanic, got a new tire, and drove over to the farm.

"It was a whole disaster," she said.

Ben pulled out onto Mountainview, drove them up over Rose Mountain and onto Sherwood Road. The same drive they'd done a hundred times that summer. Off to the right, the quiet ravine, with its big black oaks. Off to the left, the valley, with its open grasslands and serpentine rock. And then, appearing in the distance, the rows of grapes at Orion, smooth parabolas of green. They drove under the stone gate, past the statues and the fruit trees. At the circular fountain, however, instead of going off to the right, Halle directed him to continue straight up the hill.

In all the time he'd come over to visit the Garcias he'd never been to this part of the property, and it was strange to see these structures up close. They passed the old tasting room, which was no longer in use, and one of the main residential buildings. Eventually, they came to a stop in front of the theater.

The building was one of the tallest on the property and surrounded by an iron fence and gate. Inside the fence, in front of the building, there was a small sculpture garden. Most of the sculptures were simple ovals or circles. At one time it seemed to have been more finely landscaped but now it was all brown and abandoned. In one corner of the garden, Ben noticed, with some horror, the carcasses of a few dead sheep. Coyotes perhaps? There was a creepy feeling to the place, but it also had an austere beauty. The front doors were made of redwood, the stone steps clearly cut from nearby granite.

Halle opened the doors with a key and motioned for him to follow. Inside there was an atrium with a ticket counter. Off to the right, some kind of abandoned concession stand, with an old popcorn machine. There were a couple of posters for shows on the walls. They looked like original prints. One of them was dated 1981: *Of Mice and Men*.

They walked by the concession stand, through a velvet-colored door, and entered the main theater. Slopes of seating descending downward, probably sixty chairs or so in total. Up above them, on the ceiling, a cracking fresco depicting some kind of saint floating through the sky. Halle led him down the aisle, past an old inlaid Steinway piano in the pit, and through a side door. The side door opened onto a hallway, along which there were several other doors. She nodded to the third door on the right.

"He's in there," Halle said. "I'll let you two talk. I need to go to the winery for a second."

She walked away, leaving Ben alone in the hallway. He knocked on the door. No answer. Was he even in here? Maybe she'd pointed to the wrong door? He looked in Halle's direction but she was gone already. He knocked again.

"Yoel," he said.

He heard a rustling and, moments later, the door cracked open.

"Come on in," he said.

Inside there were two large mirrors, two seats with swivels. Maybe where the makeup had been done? In the corner of the room, Ben saw a bedroll and a sleeping bag and a big jug of water.

"Before you say anything," Yoel said, "let me explain myself."

Yoel stood next to one of the chairs. He was wearing a green-and-tan baseball cap pulled low over his eyes, and he too looked like he had been up all night.

"This was not without intention," he continued. "I know it seems extreme, but what is a little property damage compared to the damage we're all about to feel? What we've already felt. You need to open a wider flank of attack. You need to open up a wider flank so that they come to the table."

"Yoel—" he started.

"The San Andreans are good people. I promise you. This wasn't just a thoughtless act."

"Yoel, I'm on your side. I understand what you're trying to do."

His son paused. He lifted his cap, combed his bangs, and put the cap back on.

"Cause the way I see it," he said. "We need to be doing more. That's how I see it."

"I agree," Ben said. "Should we sit?"

They settled into the chairs and Ben looked around the room again. He noticed a couple books by Yoel's bedroll, a box of granola bars, a toiletry bag.

"I just want you to be safe," he said, turning back to Yoel. "Are you OK? Why are you staying here?"

"They thought it was smart for me to lay low for a week. Not go anywhere I'd normally be. In case something happens. Are they looking for me?"

"They're looking for someone. They don't know it's you."

"Good."

"What are you doing for food here?"

"The guys who look after the property, Adam and Bogdan, they brought me a meal this afternoon."

"They're going to bring you food every day?"

"No Seba's going to bring me some too, I think, and Halle. I'm OK, Dad, you don't need to worry."

There was a fan above them, spinning languidly. Yoel stood up, pulled the cord, and the fan's speed accelerated. It also began to make a loud, rhythmic buzzing noise. He watched it for a moment, then pulled the cord a few more times.

"This thing is so fucking loud," he said.

"Are you OK on supplies here?" Ben said. "Do you need anything from the house?"

"No, no, I've got what I need."

Yoel was still staring up at the fan, trying to figure out if it was slowing down or speeding up.

"I could bring over anything you need," Ben said.

"No, you should stay away," Yoel said, looking down from the fan and back at his father. "Just in case. Does Mom know?"

"She knows. She's coming home."

"For me?"

"She was coming home soon anyway," Ben said. It wasn't totally true but that didn't matter. "What about work?" he asked.

"Work is . . . if they haven't fired me already, they will in the next few days. I don't care. I was going to quit anyway. And I'm not going back to LA. I'm staying here."

"You are?"

"Yeah. What am I going to do down there?"

He walked over to the water bottle, picked it up with both hands and took a long drink. Then he set it down, wiped his mouth with the back of his hand, and sat down on the bedroll.

"No," he said, looking up at Ben. "No, I want to be here."

"What are you planning to do?"

"I don't know," he said. "But we've got to do something."

Ben nodded.

"Well, just promise me one thing," he said. "Be careful about it. Be smart. Use your smarts."

"I will."

"I can't lose you, OK? Promise me that."

"I promise. It'll be all right. Hopefully, this blows over soon. Only been here a day and I'm tired of being cooped up."

"Of course you are." Ben watched his son. "Look at you," he said. "An outlaw just like your old man."

Yoel smiled. "I guess so," he said.

12

THE WEATHER HAD started to cool off, but still there was no rain. In town, they dreamed of that first downpour. It was so easy to picture it: the dark clouds rolling in, the storm breaking open. In the morning, the golden grasses would be soaked in rainwater, insects humming about their wet stalks. The buried seeds would be drenched, ready to germinate. Then the strong winds would roll in, the Junction winds. In other parts of the state they were called other things but in Rose County, they called them the Junction winds. It had always happened this way, the start of the rains, and then the winds, but the rains would not come. Sunny day after interminably sunny day. The land growing ever drier. Even the least reactive among them had begun to admit concern. It did not feel right.

The dry conditions alone were enough to create a volatile environment, but the fallout of the protest made things even more extreme. For the past few days, the town had been buzzing about the events on Highway 99. Who were these protestors? What was happening to the community? On social media, some voiced support, but the majority of the voices were critical. Ben tried not to get too deep in the comment threads, though he did look occasionally. He wanted to keep an eye out for any possible suggestions that Yoel was behind the window-smashing. The only alleged suspect Ben had seen someone name was one of the Strange brothers, Aaron, who still lived out by Dutch Flat. This was, of course, ridiculous. Aaron was in his sixties, like Ben. Anyone who had seen what happened that day, or had even read the profile of the suspect, knew this was an absurd claim.

When Ada got home from Amargo, she was tan and covered with insect bites from the hot springs. She immediately went to see Yoel at Orion. It was his third day there now. She reported back that he seemed to be in good spirits. As far as they knew, there were no leads in the case. They had learned this from a follow-up article in the local paper. The article was brief, and mainly focused on the fines the protestors had received. There were also several angry letters to the editor in the paper, which attacked the protestors. One letter, however, from a man named Bud Meakin, seemed to understand the philosophy of the action. He said he came from the Catholic worker tradition.

"Righteous property destruction," he wrote, "in my opinion, falls within the bounds of nonviolence."

That night, Ben and Ada cooked dinner together. Shakshuka in the cast iron, a recipe of Seba's. They ate outside, on the back patio, and opened a bottle of the house wine. It was one of the last bottles they had.

"I can't believe he's staying," Ada said. "You think it's good?"

"He seems happy about it," Ben said.

"But what's he going to do when all this dies down?"

"I don't know."

She reached out and put her hand on his.

"He's going to be OK, right?" she said. "I can't deal with another trial in this lifetime."

"He's going to be fine," he said. "They don't have anything. If someone had a video to turn in, they would've turned it in by now. And even if they did, he was masked."

"I hope you're right," she said. "I'm just going to believe that's true and you're right."

Ada reached into her wine glass, fished out a gnat.

"OK, let's talk about something else for a moment," she said.

"There's another one in there," he said.

She reached in and fished out the second gnat.

"One thing," she said, "is that I think we need to get rid of the Toyota."

"Maybe."

The truck had broken down on the way back from Amargo, when she stopped in Beatty. Fortunately, there was a mechanic right down the block who was able to come over and get it running again.

"Sort of a cursed vehicle," Ben said.

"I know you're partial to it."

"It's fine."

The conversation moved on. They talked about Ada's cousin, who had started building living roofs in Fresno. They talked about a residency Ada wanted to apply to. After they finished their food, they sat around drinking wine. The sun had yet to go down and the mosquitoes were being strangely merciful. Ada had lit a citronella candle so maybe that was helping.

"What do you think he's doing right now?" she asked.

"I don't know, probably reading."

"He said he was bored as hell when I was there earlier. I wish we could go over more, but I guess that's a bad idea."

"I've been playing chess with him on my phone," Ben said.

"Really?"

"He kills me every time. Just a way to keep him company. I texted him the app and said, 'download this.'"

"Let's do it right now," Ada said. "Let's play him."

"OK, here," he said. He took out his phone, opened the app, and passed it to Ada. Then he slid his chair over next to her, showed her how to invite him to a game. Yoel accepted the invite within seconds. Ada clicked on the in-game chat function.

"R u ready to lose?" she typed. "This is your mother."

THE NEXT DAY, in hopeful preparation for the rains, and in part to distract himself from Yoel's situation, Ben set about building check dams on the hill behind the house. Wick came over to help him. They drove six-foot T-posts into the slope, stacked fire debris and rocks between them. Ben had read more about check dams since Ronaldo had recommended them. The goal, he'd learned, was not to stop the flow of water and debris, but to slow it down from fifty miles per hour to five miles per hour, so the sediment could drop out of the current and stay on the slope.

When they were done for the day, Ben suggested they open beers and jump in the pool to cool off. The mornings and nights had gotten colder lately, dropping into the low forties, but the afternoons were still warm. Out in the backyard, white butterflies floated through the evening light and dragonflies buzzed over the water. Off in the distance, a pair of ospreys perched in their nest at the top of a blackened snag.

They changed into bathing suits and dove into the water. The pool had not been cleaned in a while, and it was not looking great. There were so many leaves floating in it that, when you paddled around, you felt a bit like you were swimming in a pond. Ben was exhausted from the day's work so he mostly just stood up against the side of the pool, leaning his head back on its edge. Wick swam a couple of laps and then joined him on the far side of the pool.

"Everything OK with the wine?" he asked.

"Yeah, it's all still on track," Ben said.

"Good, because I'm waiting for my work trade, you know. You better not stiff me."

"Don't worry, it's coming," he said. "Supposedly this woman from the *Chronicle* wants some of the bottles, might review them."

"Wow, that's exciting."

"Yeah, Halle said she got an email from her the other day. I guess they're connected through a friend of a friend. Shit, I need to follow up with her on that actually."

"Yeah, well everything's been a little crazy, I guess."

Wick looked around, then lowered his voice.

"Tell me," he said. "Is he doing OK?"

"He's fine, yeah."

Wick nodded. He put his arm against the side of the pool, propped himself up.

"I know now's not the time," he said. "But there's a woman, actually, who wants to meet him."

"What do you mean?" Ben said.

"I met her at my brother's place, she was over for dinner. Younger gal. She was asking about the protests."

A jolt of fear seized him, and he turned to face Wick.

"You didn't mention Yoel, did you?"

"No, no, I didn't say anything about Yoel or anyone else."

"Because she could be undercover or something."

"She's not," Wick said. "She's not. My brother knows her. She just wants to get involved with the San Andreans. She's a good friend of his wife's. But I didn't tell her anything. I figured I'd ask you and if it made sense we could connect her somehow. She said all her friends are talking about it."

"Really?"

Ben relaxed again, leaned his head back against the edge of the pool.

"Yeah, and they all want to help," Wick said. "I was glad to hear that, because I saw some of those op-eds in the paper. That was disheartening."

Wick looked out across the pool, toward the old blue plastic slide. Then he turned back to Ben. His voice grew serious.

"You know, when I was trying to get out last time, and I was gathering everything, it was taking me so fucking long. Because of all the dogs, you know, and also because I had just moved in so I didn't have anything ready. My shit was all over the place in boxes. And I could hear the sirens going, I could hear the other cars leaving. And of course you could smell the smoke. I was never one of those people who thought a fire couldn't hit the town. I wondered about it, the way things were going, and the course of this one seemed dangerous. So I was trying to get out, and get up to Alfonso's. But there was all this stuff I couldn't leave. I mean, the files for the business, for example.

It was all on my laptop, which was tucked away somewhere in all the moving stuff. And I couldn't fucking find it."

He paused, massaged his jaw, then sniffed. There was an unfamiliar and sorrowful look in his eyes.

"Anyhow, I'm starting to take stuff to the car. The dogs were already in there at that point, but I still haven't found my laptop. And I couldn't leave it. I had nothing backed up. The business would have been in shambles if I left it. So I'm putting stuff in the car and racking my brain at the same time, trying to think where I might have put this laptop. And when I turn around to head back inside, I see this cop. And it's just him and me on the street now. Almost everyone else is gone. It's like a ghost town. And he looks at me and tells me I need to get the hell out of there, and I tell him I'm trying, but I need to get a few more things. And he says, 'OK,' and he pulls out a notebook. And then asks me for my name, my phone number. He takes my picture. And he asks me if I have any piercings, tattoos, scars, or implants, so they could identify my charred body. That feeling . . ."

He nodded a few times, slow nods. Then he shook his head and continued.

"Anyway, I found the laptop," he said. "I got out, you know the rest. And I sort of just put it all behind me, after it happened. I joked about it. That was my way of dealing with it, I guess. But that moment stays with you, it changes you. You know what I mean? Like when my dad, rest his soul, when he had his first heart thing, and they put in a stent, and he came back from the hospital, and his face was just slightly different, slightly turned down at the mouth. That's how I felt. And I hate that, man, and so to me . . . to me, I love the San Andreans. To me, they're heroes, plain and simple."

"I agree," Ben said. "One hundred percent."

He paused for a second.

"And I'm so sorry to hear you went through that," he said.

Thinking about Wick like that—filled with fear, rushing out of the house—it broke his heart.

"It's all right, buddy," Wick said. "It's OK."

The sun was starting to go down now. They got out of the pool and toweled off. Wick took a seat on one of the lounge chairs. He had a towel wrapped around himself. It was covered in pink seahorses. When Ben turned to face him, he noticed that he was looking over at the ducks. They were all gathering on the slope of the hill, next to the coop.

"I've never been much for ducks," he said. "But they look nice over there. They just gather like that at sunset?

"At the end of the day, yeah."

"I like that," Wick said. "That's nice. Very peaceful of them."

They sat there and watched the ducks for a few moments. Then Wick began putting his clothes back on. As he buttoned up his shirt, he looked over at Ben.

"Damn, this thing's soaked," he said. "That was a real workout."

"Like life in the placer mines," Ben said.

"No kidding."

"I owe you one."

After Wick left, Ben opened a second beer and walked out to the porch. He felt tired and worked but intensely clear. The night air was cold and refreshing, the first stars emerging. He thought about how good Wick was. He'd needed every bit of his help this summer and he'd shown up every time, never asking questions. His un-fair-weather friend. That was a lucky thing to have.

When he was finished with his beer, he walked back inside to cook dinner for himself and Ada. Pasta with sausage and olives and kale. He put on Wick's backgammon podcast as he cooked. The episode was about a Russian prince who popularized the game in the United States in the sixties. It was one of the better episodes. Ben was still cooking when it finished so he walked over to his phone to put on the next one. But there wasn't another episode. He tried refreshing the feed a couple of times but still nothing. That was it. That was the end of the series.

ON FRIDAY Ben awoke to what was, up to that point, the coldest morning of the year. When he walked into the kitchen, his nose was cold and his toes were cold and he could even see his breath. He set the kettle to boil and stood in front of the kitchen window, rubbing his hands together for warmth. The sky had been cloudless for the past week but today it was muted, gray. Out in the vineyard, the vines were now entering the dormant phase. Their leaves had started to turn yellow and orange and soon, with the first frost of the year, they would begin to crisp up and drop to the ground. The plants were now focused on conserving energy, storing the carbohydrates and other nutrients that they would need in the spring.

Once he had made his coffee, Ben walked back to the living room, and sat down to read the paper. No news of the protests or the search. Ada was already out of the house. She'd left that morning to visit Yoel at Orion, bring him some coffee and groceries. He was still going to hole up for a few more days, but they figured he was pretty much in the clear at this point. Ben would have joined her, but he needed to move the ewes down into the Primitivo lot this morning, to begin to sanitize the vineyard. They would clean up the remaining fruit that was not harvested and any other vegetative detritus. For the next month or so, he would cycle them throughout the different blocks until they had cleaned the entire property. Eventually, when the weather started to get even colder, he would move them back up on the hill, so they had access to the shelter of their pen for the winter months.

After he had finished his coffee, he put on his boots and walked over to the irrigated pasture. He had set up all the electric fencing yesterday so all he had to do today was guide the sheep from the irrigated pasture into the vineyard. Outside the dry cold really hit him, a strong wind blowing down from the mountains. He was wearing his green suspenders, carrying a tin pail of cracked corn. When he arrived at the pasture, he found Eddie sitting under the fig tree. The guard dog blinked twice when Ben entered the gate, a sign of welcome.

"Come on girls," Ben called, rattling the pail. "Come on."

None of the sheep moved.

"Come on girls," he repeated.

Rule number one when moving sheep was keeping them comfortable. No yelling, no haranguing. Just calm, pleasant tones and warm encouragement. Slowly, they began to pad toward him. He fed them a bit of the cracked corn and then continued walking toward the edge of the paddock, the sheep following a bit more closely now. Eddie followed too. At a certain point, Ben noticed one of the sheep had not come with them. She was still sitting at the far end of the paddock. He turned around and walked toward the lone sheep and, as he did so, the group that had been following him also turned around and went back the other way.

"Wrong direction here, team," he said.

When he got closer to the other sheep, he realized that she'd been sleeping. She hopped up when she heard him approaching, slightly dazed.

"Come on, dear," he said. "Time to go."

Now, the whole group united, he led Eddie and the sheep back across the irrigated pasture and out the gate. He drove them down the hill, walking on their left side and using the forest as a barrier on the right. When they got down to the Primitivo block, they encountered the movable metal fencing he'd set out, which guided them to the left, and into the vineyard. Once they had entered the new electric perimeter, he shut the gate behind them, and poured out the rest of the cracked corn onto the ground. The sheep ate it up and then proceeded to wander off into the vineyard.

Ben looked around at the Primitivo. Its green shoots, which had supported the growth of fruit, would soon be thin woody canes. In February, he would prune away these canes, leaving renewal spurs for the following year. As he was standing there, looking out at the vineyard, he saw Halle's car in the distance, driving along Mountainview. He watched her turn right and head up the drive toward the house. He felt his pocket for his phone, to see if she'd texted him about something, only to realize he'd left it inside. He began to walk up the hill. When he got to the house, he saw Yoel and Ada looking around, calling his name. Halle was nowhere to be seen. And why had Yoel left his hiding spot?

"Jesus, there you are," Ada said, when he got closer. "Why weren't you picking up your phone?"

"I didn't have it on me."

"Dad—" Yoel said. "Whatever, forget it. We have to go."

For some reason, the smoke hadn't reached this part of Mountainview yet, Yoel explained, but Sherwood Road was thick with it. The fire was already in the canyon. It had started northeast of them, near Dover, and was now moving southwest, toward 51. Everyone at Orion had evacuated and evacuation orders had just been issued for town too.

"Where's Halle?" Ben said, nodding at the station wagon at the bottom of the driveway.

"The Toyota wouldn't start so she gave us her station wagon. She drove out with Yami and Seba."

"Shit."

Ben felt a wave of panic, starting in his stomach and moving up into his chest. They were going to need to get all of the animals in one trailer. For a moment, he thought he was going to be sick but he steadied himself.

"OK, let's go," he said. "Let's do this quickly."

He grabbed the crates for the birds and handed them to Yoel, who then turned and headed over to the coop. As he began to wrangle the birds, Ben and Ada jogged over to the house. There wasn't any room in the station wagon—it was already full with Yoel's stuff from Orion, and duffel bags of Halle's stuff—so they would have to pack all of their belongings into the cab of the truck. First, Ben leashed Harriet and

George and put them in the backseat. Ada grabbed her red backpack, double-checked that she had her novel notebooks, and brought those to the truck too. Then it was back inside to gather their other things: the binder of paperwork, the bugout bag, their computers, his phone. When he picked up the phone, he saw that there were many texts and missed calls from Ada and Yoel.

Once they'd gotten what they needed from the house, Ada went over to help Yoel with the birds, and Ben began hooking up the truck to their trailer. After he got it hitched, he backed the trailer up against the open garage. Inside the garage there were two small pens: one for holding the sheep when they came in from the outside, and the other for guiding the sheep into the back of the trailer. In between the two pens was a door, much like the door on their pen at the top of the hill. Ben would drive the sheep up to the back of the garage and then direct them through the two pens and into the back of the trailer. Once he had the whole loading area ready, he ran back down the hill, toward the Primitivo lot. He was starting to smell smoke now. He was trying to think of what else he might need.

"Come on girls," he called, straining to keep his voice calm. "This way."

Eddie looked at him, perplexed. *We're moving again?* He seemed to be saying. *We just got here.*

The sheep responded well, trotting out of the electrical fencing and back up the hill, along the edge of the forest. Ben guided them into the open back door of the garage, and closed it behind them. Once they were in the first holding pen, he opened the door that connected the two pens. The key was to open the door and let them go through themselves. They were curious and likely to walk through any open door available to them. But if you tried to force them, they would revolt.

One by one, the sheep slipped through the opening of the door. Now that he had them all in the second pen, Ben closed the door, and hopped over the fence. To his right was a piece of metal fencing that was designed to divide the trailer in two. He picked it up and started walking toward the sheep. With nowhere else to go, the sheep began to hop onto the trailer. Eddie followed after them. Ben stepped onto the trailer and locked the metal fence into place, breaking the trailer in half. Then he shut the door behind him and ran off toward the coop.

Yoel and Ada had gotten all of the birds crated up except for the emus and the two feral chickens. Ben quickly rounded up both of the emus, grabbing them from behind, so they couldn't kick him. This left only the two feral chickens. Yoel said he'd tried to grab them but hadn't been able to. Ben made a couple of attempts and also failed. Whenever he got close, the birds flapped away a short distance.

"Guess we just have to leave them," he said. He was gasping for air.

The smoke had grown much thicker in the past several minutes. All around them, flecks of ash were floating on the wind.

"You've got all your notebooks?" Ben asked.

"Got those," she said.

"Is that it then?"

At that moment, a horse emerged from the forest, running in their direction. They all turned to face it and watched as it ran right past them, toward the road. Ben was pretty sure it was one of his neighbor's horses, the man who owned the walnut farm, though he wasn't positive. On its side, someone had spray painted a phone number.

YOEL AND ADA got into the station wagon and Ben followed behind them in the truck. He found he was tearing up, the image of the horse still in his mind. But what could he do? They had no room. From the road he called Halle, said they were just leaving the farm, that they'd gotten all the animals. She said they were almost in Bidwell now, but that they'd hit a lot of traffic on the way out.

"Thank god you guys are on the road," she said. "See you soon."

They headed down Mountainview, toward 51, which they were planning to take west out of town. He patted the dashboard of the Ford. He was towing more weight with it than he usually did, but at least it wasn't the Toyota. Off to his right now, he could see an orange glow. The ash falling from the sky had become thicker and there were now also large, blackened embers raining down. Minute by minute, the daylight seemed to be receding, the world growing darker. The smell of smoke had grown more intense. He pulled out his N95 from the glove compartment and put it on. He turned on the radio but there wasn't much useful information: all the broadcast could say was that there was a fire outside Dover, that evacuation orders had been issued for Natoma and all of Rose County.

About halfway down the hill, they passed an older woman standing outside on the street. Ada pulled over and Ben did too. He vaguely recognized the woman but he didn't know her name. She was wearing a sweatshirt and sweatpants and she had a small bugout bag next to her. She told them she was waiting for her son, that her son was coming up to get her.

"Why don't we take you down the hill and you can call your son?" Yoel said.

"No, no, because he's coming here. He'll get confused."

"We can call him once we get service."

"I don't know," she said. "He's going to get worried. I'll just wait here. He's going to come."

"I really don't think you should wait," Ben said. "Do you see how dark and smoky it's getting?"

"He's on his way," she said.

As they were standing there, a Cal Fire pickup truck pulled up behind them. It had been coming down from the top of the hill. The driver leaned out her window and told them they all needed to get down the hill. The old woman explained that she was waiting for her son.

"No," the driver said. "You have to go. Do you not have a car? You can come with me."

"But he's going to get confused."

"Ma'am, he won't be able to get up here. There are lots of roads closed."

The old woman looked at Ben, and then back at the driver, who was wearing a yellow shirt with Cal Fire patches on the shoulders.

"OK," she said.

She picked up her bag, walked over to the truck, and got in. As the driver pulled out onto the road, Ben saw that there were others in the back seat.

· · · · ·

CONTINUING ON DOWNHILL, he heard the sound of propane tanks exploding in the distance, each one like a small bomb. The wind was blowing forcefully across the canyon, shooting down through the ravines and out toward the valley. He kept checking his phone, to see if his service had come back but it was still out. There was little traffic on Mountainview, all of it going downhill, with the exception of one fire truck, which drove past them in the opposite direction. As he approached the entrance to 51, however, the road began to grow more congested. By the time they got to the bottom of Mountainview, they were in bumper-to-bumper traffic. Yoel rolled down his window and turned around to yell back at him.

"You OK?" he said.

Ben gave him a thumbs up and he gave one back.

Briefly, as they were inching toward 51, the service on his phone came back. He called Wick and was able to get through to him. His voice sounded hoarse but calm. He said he was heading over to his brother's house in Ponderosa.

"Were you able to get everything out?" he asked Ben.

"Most everything."

"Do you want me to go up there after I'm done in Ponderosa? I've got a trailer with me."

"No, no, don't go up there."

"OK, did you see—"

But then the call dropped. Ben looked at his phone, which now read "No Service" again. He tossed it onto the passenger seat, slammed his fist on the dashboard.

"Fucking piece of shit," he said to himself.

They eventually merged onto 51, but traffic was still crawling forward. This part of 51 had two westbound lanes and only one eastbound lane. It twisted along the ridge, through a forested area, and then dropped down toward Smith Flat Road. If it got really bad, he figured, they could pull into the eastbound lane to move more quickly. Outside, it was now pretty much completely dark and most cars had their lights on. Along the side of the road, he could make out the dim shapes of the surrounding pine trees, and beyond that, the black heaps of the mountains.

They passed a couple of people who had pulled off to the side of the road to rearrange their possessions. Most of the faces he saw looked scared. Ben drove by one woman who, along with another man, was tightening down a ratchet strap over two duffel bags. As Ben approached, the woman looked over at him. There were tears in her eyes. They glanced at each other for a brief moment and then the woman turned back around to finish dealing with the duffel bags. Ben continued on past them. In the rearview mirror, he watched the woman and the man get back into the car and turn on their left-hand signal. To his relief, another car let them get back into traffic.

Based on the amount of ash that was falling, and the amount of smoke, he could tell this fire was much bigger than the last one. They knew it had entered the canyon, which meant it was certainly heading for town, and might have already swept past the farm and Orion. It could all be gone—the house, the winery, everything. Some of the embers that were falling now were just massive, the size of bicycle tires. He turned around and looked back at the dogs, who were alert but composed.

"OK," he told them, "we're just going to keep driving here."

.   .   .

OVER THE NEXT few minutes, the situation began to worsen. To his right, above the orange glow, he could see dark clouds blowing toward him. People were still not moving and they had begun to honk at one another. They remained stuck on this same section of 51, had not even advanced as far as the feed store, let alone the old hotel. The clouds to his right appeared to be roiling and he could see fire falling from the sky. It was surreal but there was no other way to describe it: in the distance, splashes of fire were falling from the sky.

He looked back toward the traffic in front of him. Why were they not moving? They needed to get moving here. What was going on? Along the sides of the road, spot fires had begun to burn. Flames lapped at the bottom of telephone poles. Ben could feel the temperature inside the truck rising. He touched the window and felt its warmth. Some cars were pulling into the opposite lane to get ahead. He tried to signal to Ada to see if she wanted to do this, but she wasn't looking back at him. Ben rolled down the window briefly to yell at her but that didn't work either, and also let a billow of smoke and heat into the cab. Moments later, to his horror, the station wagon began to smoke.

Ada veered off to the side of the road and Ben pulled over after them. When he stepped out of the truck, the heat nearly overwhelmed him. Burning pine needles whipped through the wind. The sound of the fire was everywhere now, a great humming roar. He ran over to the station wagon and Ada quickly handed him a duffel bag. She and Yoel grabbed bags themselves and, wordlessly, the three of them sprinted back to the truck. Yoel wanted to return for a second load but Ada said no.

"Halle's other bags are still in there," he said.

"We just have to leave them," she said.

Once they were all in the truck, Ben tried to edge out into traffic. Two vehicles drove by without letting him in but the third car, a maroon sedan, allowed him to pull out. Ben tried to wave at the person behind him to thank them for this, but he knew they couldn't see him. The smoke was so thick now, you could barely make out the car in front of you. He needed to stay alert, he told himself. Getting in an accident would be very easy in these conditions.

"Hopefully the car survives," Ada said.

"You have the key, right?" Yoel said.

"Yeah," she said.

Ben looked over at his wife and then back at the road. The opposite lane had now ground to a standstill, packed up with cars trying to exit. He felt panic rising in his chest, but he tried to settle himself down. Up ahead, some people were getting out of their cars, running down the road or off into the woods. Yoel noticed them too.

"Jesus," he said.

"We're going to be OK," Ada said.

"Should we run?" Yoel asked.

"I don't think so," Ben said. "It's too hot out there. Those people are going to have to get back in cars soon."

Ben took out his phone to call his brother, to tell him what was happening and where they were, but he still had no service. And then, all of the sudden, the fire was fully upon them. It was like water, eddying and flowing, filling the space before it. It was everywhere. Within a few moments, they had been surrounded.

Should they consider running now? He looked off toward the forest, tried to identify the direction they should go, if they did leave the car. *Stay alert*, he thought. *Stay alert*, he kept thinking. *Stay alert, stay alert, stay alert.* Everything was bright and roaring with light. A tree to their left burst into flame. Sparks skittered across the hood of the truck. Smells of burning metal, burning rubber. At one point, he thought he saw a fire truck coming up the road toward them but no, nothing was there. Nothing was coming to save them.

"Someone help!" Yoel screamed. "Please!"

When he stopped screaming, they fell silent for a moment. And then, almost as if he had spoken it into being, the cars in front of them began to move. Slow at first, but then picking up a bit more speed. Within a few minutes, they were cruising at thirty miles per hour, following behind a black truck. The air in the car was cooling. Ben felt something akin to normal consciousness returning. They passed the feed store and the massage and wellness clinic and Ada was cheering: "Go, go, go!"

Then they were flying down the hill, toward Smith Flat Road, and god it was beautiful to move. The smoke in front of them was starting to clear a bit. He didn't want to speak too soon but it seemed like the sky was growing a bit lighter. They passed a couple burned cars that had been pushed off to the side of the road. Perhaps these vehicles had been the cause of the traffic jam. He wasn't sure.

"Slow down, slow down," Yoel said, looking off to the right.

He turned and followed his gaze: there was a man walking along the side of the road. Ben pulled off onto the shoulder and motioned to him. The man ran over and hopped into the back seat of the cab. Almost as soon as he got in the back of the truck, he started talking. It was a kind of a stream of consciousness, how he had been walking back to his car over by the hotel, but for some reason he couldn't get there. He proceeded to talk about everything around them, everything that had just happened to him. Some of it was intelligible and some of it wasn't. After several minutes of this, it started to become somewhat irritating, but they could tell it was a kind of self-soothing he was doing, so they just listened.

At the Smith Flat juncture, there were two utility trucks parked on the side of the road. They both had huge, well-lit booms, which had been extended over the road to illuminate the intersection. Two first responders were in the middle of the intersection, directing cars to turn off 51 and take Smith Flat Road around to 99. Ben followed their direction, driving on past the brewery and the taqueria and a few other businesses. Everything was abandoned and seemingly without power. His phone was still not working and the radio was out now too.

He looked down and noticed he had less than a quarter of a tank of gas left. Probably enough to get him to Bidwell, or he hoped so. He looked off to his right, through the passenger window. In the distance, he could see a huge amount of smoke near Natoma. A lot of it was burning. You could just tell. There was too much smoke for it not to be burning. Ada was looking at the plume of smoke too. She turned around and the two of them shared a glance. Ben knew she was thinking the same thing he was.

In the background, Ben could hear the man still talking ninety miles per hour. He took a few deep breaths and looked over, one more time, at the plume of smoke. He thought of Wick and Alfonso, said a prayer for them. Thought of Paul and

Jeremy, of Rudy, of Lisa and George Vermont. Even the sheriff. He could find it in his heart to pray for him too, he found. *Let them all make it out*, he thought to himself. *Let them make it out.* He tried to fix the town in his mind, the whole county. He thought about the quiet of the farm. The wide encompassing solitude of the mountains. This had always been a place he could rely on. Its streams and its hills and its grasses. He thought about what it felt like to walk outside in the winter and smell the smell of wet plants on the wind. He thought about the river, with its scoops of scalloped granite. He held onto the beauty of it all, and then he let it go, and turned to what was next.

ONCE THEY GOT onto 99, they could see the sky again. They began to discuss a plan. They needed to get gas, for one thing. Dennis—this was the man's name, they had now learned—was saying that he had a sister in Bidwell. He said she lived over by Carlson Park and he asked if they would drop him at her house. They said they could do this. They also agreed to go a little farther before stopping at a gas station. They wanted to put more distance between them and the fire before they stopped.

Thirty minutes later, when they pulled into the AM PM off 99, Ben could tell most of the other people there had also been fleeing the fire. They had plastic storage bins strapped to roofs, had trailers hitched, had cars stuffed full of possessions. And then there were the RVs, many people in RVs and campers, planning to go who knew where. Ben looked down at his phone to see if he had service but still there was nothing. He walked over to the back of the trailer, opened it, and looked inside. Protests from everyone involved but no one seemingly wounded.

Each of the bird crates had a small hanging waterer attached to one of its walls. From his bugout bag, Ben took one of the gallon jugs, and began refilling the waterers. He made his way to the back of the trailer and did the same thing for the sheep, who had their own waterer. As he poured from the jug, he noticed that his hands were shaking. He did his best to steady them.

Once he was sure everyone had water, he closed the gate and walked back to the truck to begin pumping gas. A couple minutes later, as he was standing there, waiting at the pump, Dennis stepped out of the truck. He was on a phone call with someone.

"Yeah, they picked me up," he said. "They're taking me to you. Yeah, yeah."

Dennis wandered away toward the air and water station. Ben looked down at his phone and, this time, saw that it had service. His phone had never buzzed but it was now registering a flood of voicemails and a text from Wick.

"We're out," it said. "You OK?"

"We're OK," Ben texted back. Then he immediately called his brother.

"We're OK," he repeated. "We're out. We're OK."

They spoke for just a few minutes. Andrew said he'd get the guest bedrooms ready for them, that he'd see them in a few hours. Ben thanked him, told him he loved him, and hung up.

More texts flooded in, including a few from Halle. They were at a motel in Bidwell. Did they want to join them there? He couldn't respond yet. He was still so overwhelmed by what had just happened. Yoel had hopped out of the truck and was on the phone with someone, presumably Halle. Ben watched him for a few moments. His mind felt blank, his brain swollen.

When he got back into the truck, seconds later, he had started to cry. Ada was in the cab, looking down at her phone, texting someone. When she saw him, she put the phone away, and leaned across the cab to hold him. She started to cry too. They stayed like that for some time, holding one another. Over Ada's shoulder, he could see the traffic continuing to move along 99. It was all rushing west, rushing steadily, rushing on, on, on.

Acknowledgments

Huge thanks to David Harde and Toby Landis, whose guidance and generosity were crucial.

I'm very grateful to Martha Wydysh, who supported and shaped this novel in countless ways. She is a wonder.

It was a true privilege to work with Ben Schrank and Signe Swanson at Astra House. Their edits were thorough, exacting, and deeply perceptive.

I also want to thank Rachael Small, Tiffany Gonzalez, and everyone else at Astra who helped with the book.

Thank you to Dave Eggers, who continues to be an inspiration.

To Claire Vaye Watkins and Tommy Orange, two exuberant talents: thank you.

Much love to my colleagues at *The Believer*: Rita Bullwinkel, Justin Carder, Annie Dills, Ginger Greene, Heidi Julavits, Kim Hew-Low, Ed Park, Sunra Thompson, Amanda Uhle, Vendela Vida, and Dan Weiss.

Thank you to the brilliant king of light, Mark Davis.

These good people all helped:

Hayden Bennett, Mark Boyle, Will Brewer, Hayley Chill, Evan Daniel, Bob Darr, Kitania Folk, Barbara Fremont, Lisa Fremont, Nick James, Joey Kahn, Amy Kurzweil, Elan Landis, Noah Landis, Emily Lang, Julia Leonard, Rebecca Marcyes, Tommy McDermott, Niela Orr, Wiley Rogers, Dani Rozman, Katya Schoenberg, Andrew Standeven, Stephanie Ullmann, Carlo Urmy, Michael Ursell, and James Yeh.

The Hermitage Artist Retreat provided me with time and space to write and revise. I'm very thankful for that place and its whole staff, especially Larry MacKenney.

As always, love to my family: Jesse, David, Ellen, and Richard Gumbiner.

Finally, the two people to whom this book is dedicated deserve special thanks:

John Mulroy, who has lived through many fires and was an indispensable resource, and who will always be my dear and indispensable friend.

And Claire Boyle, who is the best of aces to hold in your hand, a true emotional genius, who willed this book to life, and who enriches my every day with her love.

ABOUT THE AUTHOR

Daniel Gumbiner's first book, *The Boatbuilder*, was nominated for the National Book Award and a finalist for the California Book Awards. He is the editor of *The Believer* and a 2022–23 Hermitage Fellow. He lives in Oakland, California.